dirty tricks

Also by Kiki Swinson and Saundra
Schemes

Also by Kiki Swinson
Playing Dirty
Notorious
Wifey
I'm Still Wifey
Life After Wifey
Still Wifey Material
The Candy Shop
Still Candy Shopping
A Sticky Situation
Wife Extraordinaire
Wife Extraordinaire Returns
Cheaper to Keep Her series
The Score
The Mark

Anthologies
Sleeping with the Enemy (with Wahida Clark)
Heist and *Heist 2* (with De'nesha Diamond)
Lifestyles of the Rich and Shameless (with Noire)
A Gangster and a Gentleman (with De'nesha Diamond)
Most Wanted (with Nikki Turner)
Still Candy Shopping (with Amaleka McCall)
Fistful of Benjamins (with De'nesha Diamond)

Also by Saundra
Her Sweetest Revenge Series
Her Sweetest Revenge 1, 2, 3

Published by Kensington Publishing Corp.

KIKI SWINSON

dirty tricks

SAUNDRA

KENSINGTON PUBLISHING CORP.
www.kensingtonbooks.com

DAFINA BOOKS are published by

Kensington Publishing Corp.
119 West 40th Street
New York, NY 10018

All Kensington titles, imprints, and distributed lines are available at special quantity discounts for bulk purchases for sales promotion, premiums, fund-raising, and educational or institutional use.

Special book excerpts or customized printings can also be created to fit specific needs. For details, write or phone the office of the Kensington Sales Manager: Kensington Publishing Corp., 119 West 40th Street, New York, NY 10018. Attn. Sales Department. Phone: 1-800-221-2647.

Dafina and the Dafina logo Reg. U.S. Pat. & TM Off.

ISBN-13: 978-1-61773-945-3
ISBN-10: 1-61773-945-6
First Kensington Trade Paperback Printing: September 2017

eISBN-13: 978-1-61773-946-0
eISBN-10: 1-61773-946-4
First Kensington Electronic Edition: September 2017

10 9 8 7 6 5 4 3 2 1

Printed in the United States of America

STAY SCHEMING

Kiki Swinson

PROLOGUE

"*S*hit. *Not again,*" *I mumbled under my breath as sweat beads as big as raindrops ran a race down my forehead and dripped into my eyes. I tried to blink them away as quickly as possible to keep my burning eyes from being closed too long. No second could be spared. I couldn't afford to take my eyes off the piece-of-shit traitor in front of me. I am not sure if it was the anger or the shock or both that had my knees knocking together, but whatever it was, my entire body trembled like a leaf in a wild storm. My heart thrummed so hard I felt like it was sitting outside my chest. I sucked in my breath and squinted. My nostrils flared on their own.*

Be tough, Karlie. You've been through worse, *I told myself. I had certainly been through some shit over the past six months. My life had always been full of challenges, though. Nothing ever came easy for Karlie Houston. Not even childhood, when shit is supposed to be care-free and fun. I can't remember a time in my life that was free of cares, worries, drama, and just plain old bullshit.*

I sometimes wondered why God was punishing me all the time. Abuse, poverty, death, and destruction were the words that summed up my existence.

"I'm not playing with you." I had finally found my voice. But I was immediately mad at myself because my voice was trembling like a scared child, and I couldn't make it stop. I could see the amusement light up his ugly face.

"Oh, you think it's funny? You must think I'm some punk bitch. But I'm telling you now, I will do it. I swear to everything I have left and everything I ever loved . . . I will do it. I don't have shit else to lose," I said through my teeth. *That was the truth as plain as I could say it. I had nothing left to lose.*

The muscles in my arms burned as I kept them extended in front of me, elbows locked, grip tight. The bastard shook his head dismissively and smirked at me like he didn't take me seriously at all.

"What? What you gon' do?" He chuckled evilly. *All that was left was for him to stick his tongue out at me, stick his thumbs in his ears, and twist his hands like kids do when they tease each other. Fire flashed in my chest. I had never taken too kindly to being teased.*

"Watch and see," I said, shifting on my feet.

"You ain't gon' do shit, that's what. You all talk. You always did think you were smarter than everyone else around you . . . family and friends. Somebody must've lied to your ass, little girl. I'm not one of those simple-minded niggas you can game into doing your dirty work or get over on. You might have had some of those lames by the balls, but me, I'm one step ahead of your ass. You think I don't know how you tried to set me up? Huh?" he spat, with his face curling into the most evil snarl I'd ever seen. *If I didn't know better, I would've thought I was standing face-to-face with Lucifer himself.*

"I never liked you, Karlie. All these years, there was always something grimy about you, your trashy-ass mother, and that little bitch sister of yours that I didn't like."

He was still speaking, but suddenly I couldn't hear him anymore. Did he just mention my sister? Did he just go there? *He knew that was a sore topic for me.*

My nostrils flared and I swallowed hard. How fucking dare he say something about Miley? I had always been fiercely protective of my sister, but now, I felt more of a need to defend her name and her honor.

"Shut the fuck up about her," I growled almost breathlessly. *"Don't you ever say anything out of your rotten-ass mouth about my sister. You bitch-ass nigga. I swear I will blow your ass away. I don't care who you are."*

I could feel my chest heaving. My jaw rocked feverishly as I tried to hold on to my composure. I didn't want any more bloodshed. I really didn't. That was the only reason he was still alive. I was tired of death and destruction around me. But that didn't mean that I wouldn't do what I had to do. Especially if it meant the difference between me coming out of this alive or him leaving in a body bag.

"Oh, does the truth hurt?" he snarled. "You don't like anyone to tell you the truth? You don't like to hear that you and your sister were two scandalous bitches that got everything y'all deserved? From the time y'all were kids doing sneaky shit to get over, stealing money, stealing food, I knew y'all would grow up to be just like your mother . . . a piece of shit."

"Shut up," I said in an eerily calm voice. My voice completely contradicted the raging inferno burning inside me. I don't know why I was so calm, and that scared me more than he did.

Unlike mine, his extended arm didn't waver or shake. His aim was steady. Sure. Purposeful.

"Nah, I'm going to tell it. You don't think y'all got what was coming after years of scandal?"

I swallowed hard again, but the lump in my throat just wouldn't go away. I shifted my weight from one foot to the other. I was going to have to kill this nigga. I could feel it all down in my bones. It was going to be him or me.

"All I want is for you to leave. We can call it fair. You did some shit and I did some shit. It's a draw. You walk away, I walk away. End this. Nobody has to get hurt. Ain't nothing else to prove." I still spoke calmly, another last-ditch effort to end this shit without death. My insides were going so crazy—churning stomach, racing heart. I felt like I'd throw up any minute. This wasn't my first time facing down death, but that didn't make it easy to deal with. I had watched everything and everyone around me get destroyed. Suddenly my sister Miley's face flashed through my mind. Her sweet smile. Her laughter. Even her annoying nagging when she was being spoiled.

I could also hear my boyfriend Sidney's voice in my ear . . . I love you, baby. Just be careful. Let me take care of you. *He used to say that all of the time.*

I felt my knees buckle a little bit. If I could have just lain down and curled into a ball and cried for hours, I would have. Some people would say what was happening at the moment was karma for some of the things I'd done in my lifetime, but I say fuck karma—everything that happened and what was happening now was because of evil motherfuckers like the one I was standing in front of at the moment. I had learned the hard way that evil exists in human form, and I was surrounded by it. I was confronted by it. It was a part of my own family. And I was going to either destroy it or be destroyed by it.

"So what's it gonna be, Karlie? Giving up?" *he asked, his gun pointing right at my forehead.*

"Hmph," *I scoffed and bit down hard into my bottom lip. I adjusted my grip on my gun, which was now pointing directly at his heart.* "Nigga, please. You better give up. You better try and end this if you know what's good for you."

He shook his head.

It was a standoff. A duel. A draw. One thing was for sure, at least one of us was not going to walk away from this.

"End this? Nah, baby girl. You can't start some shit and then think you can just end it. See, in the streets and in life, when you start something, you ain't got no choice but to see it through," *he replied. Then he cocked the hammer on his gun.*

"A'ight. Suit yourself, motherfucker," *I spat, sliding my right pointer finger into the trigger guard of my Glock. He laughed again, an evil cackling laugh that caused tight goose bumps to crop up on my body.*

"I'll see you in hell, bi—" *he started to say. That was enough . . .*

BOOM. BOOM. BOOM.

I fell backward. My ears were ringing. Neither one of us uttered another word. The smell of the gunpowder immediately settled at the back of my throat. I coughed. I gurgled. I was suddenly freezing cold and then hot again. I couldn't breathe.

How did it all come to this? Why? Why me?

That was the last thing I remember thinking before the darkness engulfed me.

CHAPTER 1

LUCKY TO BE ALIVE

Three Months Earlier

"No! Please!" I begged, gagging from the mixture of snot and blood running over my lips and into my mouth. The salt from my tears stung the open wounds on my bottom lip. But that was the least of my pain. Another slap across the face almost snapped my neck from my shoulders. The hit landed with so much force, blood and spit shot from between my lips and splattered on my assailant's crisp white shirt. I wasn't going to escape this assault. That much was clear.

"Just let her go. It's my fault," I groaned through my swollen lips. "Please. She didn't do anything wrong. It was all me. I swear," I rasped, barely able to get enough air into my lungs to get the words out.

"Oh yeah? It was your fault? Well, look at what you've done," he growled evilly. "Just look!" He grabbed my face and forced me to watch again.

"Agggh!"

Miley let out another pain-filled scream. I could hear another crackling round of electric shocks rocking through her body. It sounded like the sizzle, crackle, and pop of the mosquito light *in my uncle's backyard cooking the little nuisance bugs when we were kids. I couldn't even stand to look over at my baby sister's naked body, dangling like a captured animal. They had Miley's arms extended over her head and her wrists bound to a thick silver pipe that ran across the warehouse ceiling. Her face was covered in a mix of tears, snot, and blood. Her hair was soaked with sweat and matted to her head. I could see tracks of electricity burn marks running up and down her stomach and extending down her thighs. I knew then that even if by some miracle we made it out of this shit, Miley would never be the same again. I sobbed at the sight and at the thought. It was my greed that had landed us here. It was my need to prove a point to the world. A world that didn't give two fucks about me or what I had anyway. More skin-searing sizzles interrupted my thoughts. More screams from my sister sent my emotions over the top.*

"Miley!" I screeched until my throat burned. I strained against the restraints that held me to the cold metal chair. "Miley! I'm sorry! I'm so sorry! I'm sorry! Miley!"

"Karlie. Karlie, wake up!"

"I'm sorry, Miley!" I screamed as I jumped out of my sleep and whipped my head around frantically. My chest pumped up and down so fast I had to cough to catch my breath. My eyes slowly began to focus and I took in my sister's face. The scars on her left cheek and the healing gash over her right eye brought me back to reality. Miley had been through a terrible ordeal, but she had survived.

"Hey. Hey. You were dreaming," Miley said softly, concern creasing her face.

"Oh my God," I gasped, placing my hand on my chest. I looked around my hospital room again to make sure I was really dreaming. The nightmares of our experience were relentless. They came every night. I couldn't close my eyes without think-ing about what had happened to us. It was the reason we were holed up in the hospital now. A near-death experience was an understatement.

"I'm right here. What are you saying sorry about?" Miley said, touching my hand gently. "We are here together. I thought you would be excited that they moved me to your room. That means I'm much better. No more ICU, no more close monitoring. I am on the mend, big sis. That's good news," she continued.

I finally relaxed against the pillows on my bed. She was right. It was good news. I looked at the remnants of the cuts and bruises on my sister's face and the sling that still held her arm and sighed loudly. Of course the guilt came crashing back down on me. It was a miracle Miley was alive after the torture she'd endured. I'd always known my sister was strong, but now I knew for sure she was a fighter . . . a damn warrior.

"I'm happy you're here, Miley. We are lucky to be alive, and I'm actually overjoyed you're right here with me," I assured her, parting a weak smile.

"Good, because I came to get on your nerves as usual. I will be right up your butt until they let us out of here," she joked, limping over to the other bed. I let out a halfhearted chuckle, but deep down inside I was still dealing with my guilt over what had happened to her. It had been my idea to set up the EZ Cash payday loan store I worked at to be robbed. At the time, with our bills mounting, no prospects of getting any real money, and exposure to all of that cash on a daily basis, it seemed like a foolproof, solid plan that would net us enough cash to pay off some of our debts and get us straight for at least a little while.

At first, the robbery planning and execution had seemed to go smoothly. Miley and I had insider information about the stores, the operation times, the safes, the surveillance cameras; all of the necessary things a stickup crew would need to know. I also thought then that my boyfriend Sidney and his crew were the right dudes for the job. Boy, was I wrong.

Too bad I didn't find out until much later. With my help, Sidney and his friends had actually pulled off the perfect heist. We had stolen enough cash to do everybody involved a world of good. But you know what they say, right? What can go wrong, will go wrong. Oh yeah, the part that I planned—the robbery—went down smoothly. Well, I mean as smoothly as a robbery could go. It was the aftermath that went awry.

The whole crew counted up the money afterward and decided as a group we would fall back from spending it until the police heat after the heist died down. We decided to stash the money in different places. Smart, right?

I thought so until things slowly began to fall apart. "No honor amongst thieves" is an understatement. First, each one of Sidney's friends started popping up dead. Somehow, their identities were made known. I thought it was their stupid bragging, but then again, nothing was as it seemed at that time. I do know their murders scared the living shit out of me and Miley.

Next, Miley and I were kidnapped and beaten almost to death. Then my sister and I were miraculously saved by a detective who we had thought of as the bane of our existence during the whole time we were hiding the money, but who turned out in the end to be our savior. Truthfully, I am shocked that we are both alive. When I arrived at the hospital, I was told they didn't think my sister would make it. I was in bad shape myself, but I prayed and prayed to God that my sister's life be spared. My prayers had been answered. Weeks later and here we are . . . alive. Still a little beat up, but alive nonetheless.

"What are they saying about the use of your hands?" I asked Miley, trying to change the subject and get my mind off the past.

"The physical therapy is helping, and I'm praying soon I will get some of the feeling back," she replied as the nurse helped her settle her things into the space across from mine.

"At least I don't have to be stuck on that critical unit anymore. The doctors said the electric shocks could've done irreparable damage to my heart and other vital organs, but thankfully, they didn't," Miley said. "I'm lucky as hell."

I closed my eyes and turned my face away from her. I knew in my heart my sister would really never be the same. If I was having nightmares about our ordeal, I was sure Miley needed drugs just to get to sleep.

Within a few seconds, I felt Miley climbing into my bed next to me. I moved over slightly. Miley hugged me tight. I felt warm inside. Not warm enough to erase the guilt I felt, but a warm comfort that only my sister and I shared since being left by our mother as kids. I was responsible for Miley then, and I always took that role seriously. Even now.

"Karlie, please stop blaming yourself. I was down with everything too. I knew exactly what I was getting into, and I didn't back down. None of this is your fault. Besides, you were just as beat up as I was, and I'm just glad we are alive. Alive and together. That's all that matters to me," Miley said softly, giving me another squeeze. I smiled a little bit. We lay there for a few long minutes. I know her mind was racing with thoughts just like mine. We would definitely have to rebuild our lives. And I had a gut feeling that it wasn't going to be easy either. Nothing in our lives had ever been easy. And to my dismay, I would soon find out that nothing had changed.

CHAPTER 2

SECOND CHANCES

Miley and I had been in the hospital for two more days when Dr. Dubois, our main attending doctor, walked into our room and interrupted our ratchet TV watching.

"Ms. Houston." Dr. Dubois nodded at me first, then turned slightly to face Miley. "Ms. Houston." Miley and I both stared at him expectantly and said "yes," almost in unison.

"I think it is safe to say you are both well on your way to full recoveries. I think it is time to break you both out dis joint," he said using awkward Ebonics as a dry joke at the end of his statement.

"Yes. About time," Miley chimed in a few seconds later, raising her good arm in the air. "We've been ready to get up out of here," she said.

She wasn't lying. Miley and I had been talking about how our life was going to be after we left the hospital. We definitely couldn't go back to our old apartment. Detective Castle had already told us it was way too dangerous. We didn't have the money from the robberies, so it wasn't like we could just go cop a new spot to live. After the cops saved our lives, we of course had to give up the cash. It was all part of the cooperation that helped us stay out of legal trouble. It wasn't lost on the detectives that we had set up the robberies, but the murders had overshadowed our responsibility in it. Our cooperation sealed the deal.

I got an instant headache just thinking about it all. Shit, our circumstances were worse now than they were before the heist. Forget about a job. Our faces had been plastered all over the news, so there was no way any business in the Tidewater area—or *any* area, for that matter—was going to hire us. Hustling was out of the question. We had tried that once when we were teenagers. It hadn't gone so well. We had made too many enemies way too fast in that business. Besides, Miley was way too flashy and I was way too impatient and leery for all of that looking-over-your-shoulders and figuring out who had your back versus who was going to stab you in it.

"I guess that's good news," I said, trying to fake my excitement about getting released from the hospital.

"You guess? No, it *is* good news," Miley followed up.

I sighed. I was worried as shit about everything, especially about where we would go from there.

"Great. Well, once the nurse comes back with your prescriptions and gives you instructions on how to take care of your healing wounds, you are free to go," Dr. Dubois said. "Good luck out there. You girls are truly lucky. It was good getting to know you both. Stay out of trouble," he said, shaking first Miley's hand and then mine.

"Thank you for taking care of us," I said.

"Yeah, thank you, Doc," Miley said.

"You're very welcome. Now you ladies take care of yourselves."

"We will," Miley and I said simultaneously.

Immediately after the doctor left the room I looked at Miley and said, "Now it's back to reality. What the hell we gonna do now? This hospital was a false sense of security, chick. We are literally starting from scratch."

Miley let out a long sigh. Something glinted in her eyes that told me she hadn't thought about our next steps. "Tell me about it. We ain't even got no damn clothes. Starting from scratch is a damn understatement, Karlie."

I shook my head and rubbed my chin. I had to think. I was always the one who had to think. I was always the one who had to get us out of every single situation. I couldn't help but feel a little annoyed. Guilty or not, it was exhausting looking out for myself and Miley for so long.

"What you thinking?" Miley asked. I shot her a look. As soon as I looked over at her and saw her scars, I quickly softened my face. I couldn't be mad at her. I had done this to her.

"I'm thinking we gonna need help. I guess I will call Sidney and tell him we're ready to go. And being released," I said. Sidney had also survived a good ass-whooping behind the robbery. Unlike us, he had walked away with a busted knee and just some minor cuts and bruises and a black eye. Not even enough to keep him in the hospital for one week. Lucky him.

Just as I was about to dial Sidney's cell phone number, our room door swung open and Sidney limped in with his cane in hand. My eyes lit up.

"Damn, boy. You're always on time. I was just about to call you," I sang and smiled brightly.

"Oh yeah? Why? What's up? They letting y'all go or something?" Sidney asked. I had to admit that the cane and the limp gave him a sexy swag that I liked. He was already gorgeous, with the most beautiful hazel eyes and a body to die for. A quick tingle came over me. Damn. I couldn't help but think about Sidney finally being able to touch me again like I like to be touched. Sidney and I had been through a lot. We had been together almost three years and we'd had our fair share of side chick incidents, prison stints, and now, we could add a near-death experience to the drama. It didn't matter how much he might irk my nerves . . . I loved that man. I already knew that I wanted to be with him for life.

Sidney was six feet, two inches of caramel gorgeousness, and his dick game was the best I'd ever had in my life. And trust me, with the rough way I had to grow up after my selfish mother killed herself with drugs and abandoned us, I had had my fair share of dick—wanted and unwanted. So I knew Sidney was top notch.

"Yeah, the doctor just came in here and told us we could go home. Which means, you're our ride and possibly our spot to lay our heads too," Miley said from her side of the room.

Sidney chuckled and looked back at me. "Ain't nothing change about this one, did it?" he said, jerking his head in Miley's direction. "Still the spoiled and bossy little sister. She telling me what to do already and ain't even out yet."

"That's right," Miley sang, sticking out her tongue playfully.

"Still a pain in the ass, you mean." I laughed. "But she's *my* pain in the ass, and at this point, I wouldn't trade her for anything in the world."

"A'ight good. So let's go. Shit, we wasting time. A nigga always got moves to make." Sidney motioned for me to get out of the bed.

"Calm down. We gotta get our meds first. Dr. Dubois said the nurse would be in here in a few minutes," I explained.

Sidney looked a tiny bit disappointed.

"Oooh. The nigga can't wait to get you home," Miley joked, rubbing her two pointer fingers on top of each other—the playground way of saying hanky-panky.

"You damn right. I miss my baby," Sidney said, moving in and kissing me on the neck. My entire body got hot and my cheeks flamed over. I couldn't wait either. I was suddenly hot and bothered but had to play it off.

"Stop, crazy," I said coquettishly, pushing him but not hard enough to move him.

"A'ight, well, I'm gonna go and get the car from the parking garage and pull it up to the front entrance so you don't have to walk far. And by then y'all should be ready."

"Yeah, we will. Make sure you got that Meek Mill or Drake on blast. I need to hear some good music. Oh, and don't forget we have to stop at someplace boss to eat. I'm dying for some good food. Being trapped in here got me fucked up," Miley said.

Sidney just shook his head and laughed. "This girl," he mumbled as he headed for the door.

"Sidney," I called after him. He looked over his shoulder.

"I love you," I said.

He flashed that gorgeous smile. "You already know what it is, bae," he replied.

I am not sure what came over me at that moment, but for some reason, I felt like I had to tell him that I loved him. It wasn't something we said often throughout our relationship. It wasn't something I said often in my life, period. I guess now it was the time to do so.

CHAPTER 3

UNLUCKY START

You would have thought I was the one in worse condition. I was moving slow, and Miley was speeding ahead of me through the hospital corridors toward the exit.

"Damn. Slow down," I huffed, trying to keep up. My back ached and so did my legs. I guess that was muscle fatigue after being cooped up in the hospital for weeks. Miley didn't seem to be suffering at all.

"I want out of here," Miley called over her shoulder. "You better c'mon. I already told you I'm starving."

I had to laugh at my sister. Once the nurse had come back with the doctor's handwritten prescriptions and instructions on how to properly take the medications and care for our healing wounds, Miley damn near pushed the lady out of the way. Miley was hyped to leave the hospital. She hated the food, and so she'd promised to treat herself to an order of Bang-Bang Shrimp from the Cheesecake Factory the moment she got out.

"I want out of here too, but damn, slow the hell down," I grumbled, winded.

Miley was thinking about simple shit like food and what damn rapper she was going to listen to on the way home. I, on the other hand, had more important things on my mind. Important things like where the hell we would live and work. How we would eat, not just today but every day. I swear, I dreaded the thought of it all. I knew one thing, though; we were going to have to come up with another damn plan. The thought scared me. The last plan had nearly gotten us killed.

Just like he promised, Sidney was sitting outside in a brand-spanking-new black Tahoe with the shiniest oversized silver rims I had ever seen. I smiled so wide I felt the air on my teeth. *This dude. Gotta love him. Always on the come up.*

This was another thing about my man that I always admired. Sidney was a true hustler. He may have had bouts of being broke, but he never stayed that way. He always seemed to land square on his feet, even after he would get knocked all the way down.

Sidney rolled down the windows when he noticed me. He and I looked directly into each other's eyes and started cheesing. A thin layer of sweat cropped up on my body. I simply could not wait to be alone with Sidney again. Thinking about him touching me made my insides warm up a little bit. The way Sidney would touch me and trail his long, hot, wet tongue down to my titties would make me so damn weak. I could just imagine getting to a safe place to stay and being alone with him so I could ride his thick pole until my pussy pulsed with a rip-roaring orgasm. Mmmm. Even now, just thinking about it made me tingle all over.

For the moment, Sidney had me optimistic that things were going to be all right, because he was going to take care of everything. The tension in my shoulders eased a little bit.

"If you don't get your happy ass out of that car and help us," Miley yelled at Sidney jokingly. Oh my goodness. She was definitely recovered. My loud-mouthed, fast-talking, greedy-for-food, broke-but-fabulous little sister was definitely alive and well.

Sidney laughed and shook his head at Miley's demands. But he surely got out of the truck, came around, and started toward us.

"You and that mou . . ." Sidney started, but his words seem to choke back down his throat. All of a sudden his eyes bulged unnaturally and his lips hung open. The look on his face caused me to pause. My face folded into a confused frown. Immediately, I heard the thunderous sound of feet pounding the pavement coming from my left. Miley must have noticed the look of terror on Sidney's face and heard the thunderous footfalls too because she whipped her head around. I opened my mouth but no sound came out. It was shock, I'm sure. Suddenly, Sidney seemed to be moving toward me in slow motion with his left arm extended out in front of him.

"K-a-r-l-i-e!"

I heard my name but it sounded drawn out, like a slow-motion scene from a movie.

"R-u-n!"

Before I could grasp what was going on, something slammed into my chest with the force of a wrecking ball. I stumbled back. Instinctively, my arms flew up.

"Agh!" I screamed. My sister was against me. She had fallen backward into my arms. Confusion and chaos clouded my mind, my judgment. There was noise. Loud noise. The air was thick with smoke clouds the color of cement.

Then my brain finally registered the loud, rapid explosions around me. Someone was shooting at us. Another powerful jolt slammed into me. I couldn't withstand it this time. The back of my head hit the ground with so much force my jaw clicked and my teeth slammed down into my tongue. My mouth filled with blood, and the sharp, tinny taste threatened to gag me. I sucked in my breath, yet I still felt like I was suffocating. Miley was on top of me, her back to my chest. When she'd fallen, I couldn't hold her weight, so we both fell down onto the ground. She was making a terrible noise, like she was struggling to catch her breath. I felt warm piss running down my legs. Fear had caused my bladder to involuntarily release.

"Those bitches are dead! Let's get out of here!" I heard a man's booming voice. I could feel the presence of someone next to me. It was like a black cloud of death was hovering above me. I kept my eyes closed and my head sideways. Miley's head hung just past my shoulder. I could still hear her struggling to breathe.

"Nah, this one still alive," another man said. I held my breath. I was praying.

God, please. Please don't do this. Please spare us. Please forgive me. Then . . .

BOOM. BOOM.

Our bodies rocked. My heart jerked almost out of my chest. I felt fire light up my shoulder. Suddenly the hissing sound coming from Miley stopped. There was no more movement or sound. If her head wasn't slightly to the side the bullet might've gone straight through and hit me in the head too, but it didn't. I was hit in my shoulder, but Miley was hit in the head this time. I played dead, but really, something inside me died at that moment.

Like a fucking coward, I hid under my sister's body and played like I was dead. I felt her blood running down my arm, seeping into my skin. The smell was so putrid that it settled at the back of my throat. I prayed that death would come snatch me. I felt the heat searing through my side too and I knew I had taken another bullet. Why didn't I die? Why was God sparing my life?

"Call the police! Get three stretchers! Three victims! Multiple gunshot wounds!"

I could hear screaming and chaos going on around me. Within minutes I was being hoisted up from the ground and slammed down on a stretcher. I finally opened my eyes, just in time to see Miley on a stretcher across from me. Her eyes were open, but they were blank. The front of her clothes was painted with her blood. Panic rushed through my entire body. I wanted to scream for her but I couldn't get the sound out.

"Hurry up! She seems to be the only one alive! Three victims. Two fatalities."

The stretcher I was on was being pushed in a fury. I turned my head sideways just in time to see Sidney. They had him on a stretcher at the back of the car, but there didn't seem to be any rush to get him treatment. I lifted my weak left arm and reached it out.

"Si . . . Sid," I gasped, the blood in my mouth choking me.

"Don't try to speak. You need to save all of your strength," said one of the doctors running next to my stretcher. "We are going to save you. We have to save you."

I closed my eyes. Tears drained out of the sides and pooled in my ears. We had been ambushed. But why? I thought life would be easy, knowing that the real owner of the EZ Cash had been locked up after he tortured us.

Who could've wanted us dead? Everyone who logically would have wanted us dead was locked up, right? So what the fuck was going on? I guess that was going to be all up to me to figure out now. The weight of it all finally came down on me.

"No! No! Get off me!" I screeched, flailing my arms and kicking my legs. "You're trying to kill me! I want my sister! Where is my sister!"

"Get her a sedative!" a nurse screamed, right after she took a slap to the face from my wild flying hands. About ten nurses and doctors converged on me. Someone held my head, a few lay across my legs, and there were some on either side of me controlling my arms. I felt a needle being jammed into my thigh.

"No," I groaned. "Miley," I said weakly just as the drugs started taking hold of me.

Oh my God! How am I going to get out of this? What am I going to do? was the last thing I remember thinking before my entire world slipped into darkness.

CHAPTER 4
ON THE MOVE

"Ms. Houston?"

I moaned, a low, vibrating moan that rocked my throat, but I didn't open my eyes. I could feel my head throbbing.

"Ms. Houston . . . it's me, Detective Castle," he whispered, like he was my lover waking me up for a quick nightcap.

Still I couldn't open my eyes. Thinking about the effort it would take hurt, let alone actually doing it.

"Just squeeze my hand and let me know you can hear me and understand me," Detective Castle said, with slightly more bass in his voice. I moaned again and gave his hand a weak squeeze.

"We have to move you, okay?" he said. "It's not safe here. The attack on you, your sister, and boyfriend was planned. That much we know."

With that, I ignored the pain stabbing through my skull and opened my eyes into slits. The air stung my eyeballs and tears drained from the sides. Detective Castle's image was blurry at best, but I needed to look at him for this.

"Who . . . who wa . . . was it?" I croaked through my dry, cracked lips.

He hung his head. "Unfortunately, we have figured out that it was a planned attack, but we don't know who did it. They called me because of my connection to you from the robbery case. I have my people digging down into it now. But my best guess is that whoever it was is very familiar with you all. This attack was deliberate and intentional," Detective Castle said.

I closed my eyes and let out a painful breath.

"So, we know that you're still in pretty grave danger, Ms. Houston. We're going to move you to another location. Someplace we can be sure you'll be safe until we figure this all out," he said.

"Where?" I asked, my forehead creasing with worry. I had heard about witness protection from some of my homeboys from the hood. Most of them didn't last because they were cut off from their families and friends and made to live in places they just didn't fit in.

"Well, the department has a program where we can place you. But that's what I came to talk to you about. Before we drum up a location in the middle of nowhere, I'd like to give you the option of telling me if there is a place you can think of: one, no one would readily associate with you; two, far enough from here that it wouldn't be obvious; three, a place you might feel comfortable; and most importantly, a place you trust with your life."

Again, I closed my eyes. The throbbing in my head quickly intensified. I turned my head to the side. This was a hard one. In my entire life I hadn't ever had a place I felt totally comfortable and trusted with my life. We were always moving and fighting and sleeping with one eye open. In that moment, I realized my sister and I had never lived comfortably.

"Any place . . . a distant relative . . . friends," Detective Castle said, pushing my thoughts along.

The only place that came to mind and that came close enough to a place I thought no one would associate with me and that I might be half safe was the *House*. That is what we had always called my grandmother's farmhouse back in the day. *I'm dropping y'all off at the House and I don't want to hear no damn crying. Y'all better behave too*, my mother would say to Miley and me. I shuddered thinking about our childhood experiences out there in the middle of nowhere.

"Well?" Detective Castle pressed. "If you can't come up with a place, I'm sure my office can. But I'll warn you. The last place we got for someone was in Hilldale, Utah."

My eyes shot open. Fuck the pain. I shook my head.

"Hell no. Utah? Ain't nothing but crazy Mormon white folks out there," I said.

"Exactly," he replied.

"I have a place," I said reluctantly. "My grandmother owns a big house and farm out in Suffolk County," I said barely above a whisper.

"Great. Then Grandma's house it is," Detective Castle said excitedly. "We will be moving you in a few hours. Then we will work together to figure out who is responsible for this."

I nodded and closed my eyes again. My mind was racing with thoughts of returning to the House.

CHAPTER 5

IT WAS 1999

"*C'mon, Miley. Just let go of me and walk,*" I said, annoyed at my sister holding on to me like she would never see me again.

"*Don't leave me,*" Miley whined. "*I don't like it here. I don't want to go in there.*"

"*I'm not leaving you. Mommy said we have to go inside and stay here until she gets back,*" I said, trying again to free my waist from Miley's clutches. Even though I was only twelve, I was already like Miley's mother. I made sure she ate, bathed, combed her hair, read at least one book a month, and took her asthma medicine when she needed it. Our mother was too busy on a mission to get high every single day to bother. Some days our mother took care of us first—she'd cook or buy us food, make us take a bath, and lock us in whatever new place we lived in at the time. Other days, she left us hungry and dirty like we didn't exist, and then there were the days like that day . . . when she'd make us stay with our grandmother, who we despised and who equally despised us.

"*But she's mean. She always blames us for stuff,*" Miley had said, nearly in tears. I sighed.

"*But Mommy said—*" I started when I was interrupted.

"Get y'all behinds in this house!"

Miley and I both almost jumped out of our skin. We stood at the bottom of the steps to the House with our eyes stretched wide with terror. I could literally feel Miley's heart beating against me.

"Your mother ain't have the decency to tell me she was leaving y'all no-good asses out here in my damn yard, and now I'll have to feed you little greedy dogs. All I get is a little Social Security check and food stamps, yet somehow, I always got two raggedy, nappy-headed little scavengers left at my house begging for food," Granny Houston shouted from the top of the steps where she stood hunched in her faded paisley housecoat, head full of pink sponge rollers and wearing skin-colored knee-high stockings. I remember thinking how much our mother must've hated us for subjecting us to this woman.

We weren't at Granny Houston's house for two hours before she blamed Miley for taking one of what seemed like two hundred dusty, sun-faded porcelain figurines.

"I'm gonna ask you again, what happened to my shaggy dog that was here?" Granny Houston growled, her long, yellow pointer fingernail stabbing at Miley's forehead.

Miley and I stood in front of Granny Houston's antique glass-front cherrywood corner curio. The six glass shelves inside housed all of Granny Houston's ugly porcelain and glass animal figurines. Miley was shaking her head no.

"I . . . I . . . didn't take it," Miley cried, moving on her legs like she had to pee. I was biting my bottom lip as my insides began to boil. I knew damn well that Granny Houston wasn't missing that figurine. It was a setup. I knew that in the hours that we had been there, Granny Houston couldn't find anything else to get on us about. We had been almost pin-drop quiet, even using hand gestures to communicate so we would stay out of sight, out of mind. We hadn't asked for food or drink. We hadn't asked to watch TV. But still, Granny

Houston lied. She wanted a reason to discipline us. She always wanted a reason.

"I didn't take it," Miley said, her voice quivering.

"Gotdamn liar!" Granny Houston roared. "Just like your no-good mama. A nasty liar and thief! Get over here!" Granny Houston pulled her thick, black leather belt from its usual place.

"She ain't take it," I said, my eyes squinted into dashes.

"Oh, you bold now, huh? You think you grown? One thief and one grown-ass little girl is what I got here, huh?" Granny Houston spat. With that, she wrapped the top of the cow skin belt around her left fist and let the other end hang long so she could get a good swing on it. Miley and I both knew how adept Granny Houston was with swinging that belt.

"I got something for no-good kids like y'all," she hissed.

"Please don't. I didn't take it. Search me," Miley pleaded through tears, fanning the bottom of her shirt and dog-earing her pants pockets for emphasis. She was only ten, but I was twelve. I could take it. I stepped in front of Miley.

"She said she ain't take it," I gritted again, sticking my chest out defiantly. "And you ain't gonna hit her with that belt."

"Oh yeah? We gon' see about that," Granny Houston said through her teeth. Without further warning she swung her belt, and it caught me right across my face.

"Ah!" I shrieked, stumbling backward.

"Don't hit my sister!" Miley screamed. And without warning she rushed into Granny Houston with the force of a tiny wrecking ball. Caught off guard, Granny Houston fell and landed with a thud on her back. Miley and I both heard the crack at the same time. Miley jumped back like her strength had even surprised her. My eyes popped open. I knew the situation had just gone from bad to worse.

"Help me! They're attacking me! Help me! These devils are trying to kill me!" Granny Houston hollered.

"Nuh-uh. You were trying to kill us," Miley cried. "You did it!"

I don't know how long the shock lasted, but it seemed to me that Granny Houston's neighbor, Mr. Samuel, came crashing into the house almost immediately after she fell.

"Sam! Help me! These devils are trying to kill me. Oh Lord! Help me! My own flesh and blood trying to kill me!" Granny Houston cried out, her body splayed on the floor.

Miley and I looked at one another, shaking our heads. Miley was crying, but I didn't shed a tear. Even with the thick purple welt that had cropped up on my cheek from the belt, no one seemed to believe that Miley and I had been the ones under attack when Granny Houston took that fall. We couldn't believe how our grandmother was playing the victim role. Mr. Samuel called the ambulance and the police at the same time.

"I'd like to report an attack," Mr. Samuel said into the phone.

I shook my head, trying to get rid of the memories. I swiped at the angry tears falling from my eyes. "That bitch," I grumbled, licking the salty tears from my lips. Needless to say, after the run-in with Granny Houston, Miley and I weren't welcome back to the House for a long time. Even after my mother died, our grandmother refused to have us stay with her. That was how we ended up with our crooked-ass uncle, our mean-ass aunt, and our slave-driving-ass great-aunt before we ended up just settling on the foster care system.

"Damn," I hissed, slamming my fists on the bed. If I wasn't in this desperate position, there was no way I'd be going back to that woman's house. I didn't even know how she would receive me after all these years. I would just have to pray and take my chances. I had no choice. It was definitely a matter of life or death. And it was *my* life that was hanging in the balance.

CHAPTER 6

WITNESS PROTECTION

I let out a soft moan and a puff of hot breath. Sidney had taken in a mouthful of my right nipple and ran his tongue over it with gentle passion. My stomach fluttered and my pussy pulsed. I was waiting for him to enter me. Longing to feel him deep inside me. My thighs and entire body trembled with anticipation.

"You ready for me, baby?" Sidney whispered in my ear. I sucked in my breath and let out a breathy "yes, baby."

Sidney leaned up and slid my black lace panties down over my thighs, past my knees, and off. He put them up to his face and sniffed deeply.

"Mmm, that pussy smells so good," he said.

My body was on fire. The heat of lust coursing through me made me want to scream. I put my hands up and urged Sidney closer.

"I want you," I gasped. "Please. I need you. I need you now."

"You want me? You sure? Tell me exactly what you want," he teased, flashing his gorgeous smile.

My facial expression became serious. I didn't want to be

teased in that moment. The longing was too strong. The desire filling my loins had me feeling like I would bust. I could feel my clitoris throbbing . . . waiting for some relief.

"Don't do this to me. Don't tease me. I want to feel you so bad," I groaned.

"Okay, baby. I won't make you wait any longer. Here I am," Sidney said, falling down between my legs.

He used his knee to part my legs so he could get in. Then he eased himself into my warm, gushy center. Feeling his long, thick dick filling up my insides made me scream out. As soon as the meaty girth of his love muscle filled me up, I let out a satisfied squeal. I lifted my waist from the bed and returned Sidney's thrusts, one for one. It was awkward at first, but soon we were matching each other thrust for thrust.

"Oh, you fucking me back? I like that," Sidney grunted. I twisted my hips in circular motions and picked up speed until I was the one in command of our lovemaking session.

"Oh shit," he gasped, bucking his waist. "I don't know if I can take that shit right there."

I giggled. I love making him lose control.

"Shit!" he said gruffly. He buried his face in my neck as he pumped and I swirled until the sensations were too much to take. The feeling was right there. It was so intense my thighs trembled hard and every muscle in my body tensed.

"I'm there. I'm right there. Oh God," I yelled out. That gave Sidney more motivation. He slammed into me hard. But that shit hurt so good.

"Aggh," I belted out. "I'm co-ming!" I screamed.

"Me too! Argh!" Sidney growled, crushing his mouth over mine just as he bust his nut. Suddenly his body eased and so did mine. He lay between my legs, both of us out of breath.

"I love you, girl," Sidney panted.

"I love you too, baby," I gasped. "Don't ever leave me. Don't ever leave me. Don't ever leave."

"Don't ever leave me, Sidney. Don't ever leave me."

"Karlie. Karlie," Detective Castle called me as he shook my shoulders hard. I jumped like I had been hit with a jolt of lightning.

"Wha . . . what happened?" I stammered, looking around, bewildered. I touched my face, my chest, and then slid my hand between my legs.

Detective Castle chuckled. "You must've been dreaming. Seriously dreaming," he said, nodding toward my hand between my legs. My face immediately turned red. I quickly lifted my hand and put both in my lap. I exhaled and cleared my throat.

"I was . . . um . . . dreaming, I guess." I lowered my head and could feel the tears welling up in my eyes. I missed Sidney so much already. I realized I had been dreaming, but it was so real that my panties were soaking wet. I swallowed hard and quickly dabbed at my tears. Just knowing I'd never feel Sidney touch me or fill me up with his love again was almost too much to take. I touched myself one more time to make sure it had all been a dream. Yup, I felt the sting of my own pinch and knew Sidney wasn't there. Which reminded me that my sister wasn't there either. My stomach sank.

"I didn't mean to alarm you out of your sleep like that. But we're here," Detective Castle said, interrupting my moment of sadness. "At the address you gave us."

I craned my neck to see out of the window of the SUV that had transported me. I sighed. Yup. We were there.

The familiar surroundings caused a lump to form in my throat. I didn't have any good memories of this place, but I also knew it was the only place I had left to go. Suddenly, bat-sized butterflies slammed around in my stomach. I felt like I did the first time Miley and I were dropped off at a strange foster home—empty. It was an unexplainable hollow feeling of abandonment, fear, and anger all rolled up into a hard ball that lodged itself in the center of my soul. I didn't think I could

ever shake that feeling, and I was right because here it was
again, causing me to want to bend over and throw up.

"Yeah, this is it," I said, barely above a mumble. The House
wasn't just the 1,700-square-foot crooked shingled-roof clap-
board living quarters in front of us. The House was also the surrounding large expanse of empty, unattended, weed-choked,
sandy-dust-colored land surrounding it, the old, chipped red
paint shed and tall, leaning, rust-stained silo behind it. The
House consisted of where Granny Houston used to torture us
as kids and everything around it. And it was just as I remembered it, only now it appeared much older and much more de-
crepit than it did when I was twelve years old.

I inhaled the smell of wet wood and moldy soil and exhaled with a cough. It even smelled the same—like what I
imagined sadness mixed with evilness and misery to smell like.

I wouldn't say I was religious, but I said a quick, silent
prayer. I would need more than a higher power and all of my
mental strength to deal with my grandmother.

I walked a few steps closer, careful not to aggravate my old
and new injuries. Detective Castle and his partner immediately
moved to either side of me like they knew I'd need some for-
tifying before I could face Granny Houston.

"I'm good," I said, holding up my hand to halt their efforts.
I was a grown woman now who'd been through enough to
feel like this . . . this facing my past . . . was going to be a cakewalk by comparison.

I stepped to the left and stared around the side of the
House. The long, wooden porch seemed to slope on the left
side more than I remembered. The old-fashioned rocking
chair Granny Houston had out there was now so covered with
a thick tangle of overgrown ivy and weeds that I couldn't tell if
the wooden slats were still white. The windows on the front of
the House had a thick gray coat of dirt that served as nature's
window tint. I couldn't see a thing through those windows.
The front steps, although visible enough to climb, had tall

stalks of green snaking through them. It actually looked like some abandoned, haunted house that no one had inhabited in a hundred years. A pang of panic flashed through my chest.

What if Granny Houston is gone?

Detective Castle looked at me through wide eyes. "Um . . . you . . . um, sure . . ."

He was at a loss for words.

"Yeah. I'm sure. This is it. Now you see what I meant when I said not one damn soul will be coming all the way out here to look for me," I told him. "Not one damn soul."

I started toward the House's steps and was suddenly halted when the raggedy front door creaked open.

"Who that?"

I recognized that grating, stupid voice before I even saw his ugly face. I sucked my teeth and rolled my eyes.

"It's me, Darwin. Karlie . . . your niece," I shouted. I hadn't expected to find him there.

"Karlie?" Darwin questioned, stepping all the way out of the house to the edge of the steps. He squinted and put his hand over his eyes as a visor against the sun. His high-yellow skin gleaming against the sun made him appear like a ball of light.

"Damn, girl. I ain't seen you in years. Ain't think I would ever see y'all again," he said with a nervous grin.

"Yeah, me either," I grumbled as I ambled forward reluctantly. I couldn't stand my uncle. He was my grandmother's youngest child, and he was a no-good piece of shit. Miley and I had lived with his trifling ass after my mother died. That is, until I found out Darwin was collecting our Social Security check but we'd be starving and had old, too-small clothes and raggedy, tight shoes. Living with him was no better than being on the damn street. He hardly ever bought food for the house, and he *never* bought us clothes. Darwin would be fly—dressed in name-brand jeans and expensive sneakers—and had a bunch of hood jewelry, while Miley and I walked around with clothes so raggedy we looked like two homeless people. Our stay with him didn't last long. I seriously preferred foster care over my own family.

"I came to see Granny Houston," I chimed, trying my best to sound cheerful. Trust me, it was a hard act.

"Oh yeah? Who you got there with you?" Darwin asked suspiciously.

I shifted my weight from one foot to the other. I knew what my criminal-minded uncle thought about the police.

"They're just dropping me off," I said. "They're not thinking about you, that's for sure."

I moved closer to the House. I figured I'd better get up on Darwin as fast as I could so he couldn't run inside and lock me out. That's the type of shit he was capable of . . . straight grimy.

"You in some kind of trouble?" Darwin pressed, darting his eyes between me and the detectives. "Because I can't have no trouble around here."

"I just came to see my granny, Darwin," I snapped. Now I was annoyed. I mean, who the hell was he? The damn guard dog?

"Ms. Houston, we just need you to sign off on this paperwork saying we relocated you to a safe place," Detective Castle said.

"Oh, y'all want to abdicate the responsibility, huh? Well, what about what you promised me about making sure my sister and Sidney get a proper burial and me being able to say goodbye to them?" I said, my tone going from slightly annoyed to weepy within seconds.

"As promised, I will arrange for you to say your last goodbyes to your sister and boyfriend. But understand, Ms. Houston, your safety comes first," Detective Castle said seriously.

"Safe or not, I need to say goodbye to my sister."

An ominous feeling crept over me as I walked into the house. I don't know if it was the smell of mothballs and antiseptic that made it worse, but I wanted to lean over and retch up my last meal.

"Granny?" I said softly, pushing on her bedroom door gently. I heard my grandmother grunt from inside.

"Granny Houston? It's me, Karlie. I came to see about you."

"Who is it?" Granny Houston barked, her voice more feeble than I ever remembered it.

"Who is that coming in here, Darwin?" she shouted, sounding more panicked but also more forceful.

I jumped and stumbled back a few steps. Her loud, angry tone took me back to my childhood for a few seconds. My heart started pounding like I was a little kid in trouble again.

"It's one of your ungrateful granddaughters," Darwin announced from behind me.

I whirled around, off balance, and almost fell.

"Seems like she needs a place to stay. From what I can tell, she in some type of trouble. Had the police bring her here."

I finally got my bearings and glared at him. My jaw rocked and my fists curled at my sides. I owed Darwin an ass kicking anyway. I swallowed hard and turned toward my grandmother.

"No, Granny Houston. I'm not in any trouble. I just wanted to come see about you. You know . . . let bygones be bygones once and for all," I said in an innocent, soft baby voice. I stuck my tongue out at Darwin.

"Come on around here and let me see you, Karlie," Granny Houston demanded in a tone that for her was friendly and soft. I stepped all the way in her room and finally got a good look at her. I almost fainted from shock.

The bottom half of my jaw went slack and caused my mouth to hang open. My grandmother—who was always a round woman with full, chubby cheeks, huge full breasts, and wide hips—was now reduced to a tiny, hunched-over old lady with barely any meat on her bones. Her right hand was curled in and the right side of her face was sagging, including her right eye.

A stroke, I thought. I had seen that same thing happen to my friend Tamra's grandmother.

"Hi . . . hi, Granny Houston," I managed, the shock probably still evident on my face.

"Girl, where have you and your sister been?" Granny Houston asked. It was the first time I had picked up on the slur in her words. I surely hadn't heard that slur when she first screamed at me. I tilted my head sympathetically and fought back tears. I don't care how mean she was to me as a child; nothing could've prepared me for seeing her reduced to this.

"Um . . . we . . . um . . . I been around," I struggled to say. My eyes darted around Granny Houston's junk-cramped room. I never remembered her being a pack rat like that. In fact, growing up, she was pretty meticulous about the House. Although her possessions were old and worthless even back then, everything had its place. Not now. Her bedroom was a mess, to say the least. It had to be a fire hazard to have that much trash, old newspaper, old magazines, old clothes, and just a bunch of useless bullshit strewn all over the room. I could barely see my grandmother's bed. And forget her nightstand. There was a gang of foam-paper cups half-filled with moldy drinks, what looked like a hundred different-sized tan pharmacy bottles of medicines, and dirty tissues all over the chipped wood of her nightstand.

"Where's that Miley?" Granny Houston asked, her sagging, medicine-dilated, jaundiced eyes roving over my shoulder as if she expected Miley to step from behind me. My heart sank and my knees buckled. I had to brace myself against the door to keep from crumpling to the floor. There would be no hiding the tears this time.

"She . . . she's . . . Miley is . . ." I choked on the words. "She died, Granny."

"Oh Lord. No, Jesus. What happened to that baby?"

I was surprised to hear Granny Houston sound so concerned about Miley, but it also made me sad that Miley and I had never come back and set things straight with our grand-mother. My shoulders rocked with grief. I couldn't keep it to-gether. I ran out of my grandmother's room and straight out of the House. I ran out into the empty fields and kept running until my legs finally gave out. I collapsed onto my knees in a thicket of tall reeds and sobbed until exhaustion overtook me. Finally, I sprawled out on the ground on my back and stared up at the sparkling dots twinkling in the sky like a weaved-together blanket of Christmas lights.

"God, only you know how this is all going to play out," I whispered. "Only you know."

It was the truth. I had no more answers or expectations for my life. I didn't know what was coming next, and I damn sure didn't know how I was going to survive it all without Miley.

CHAPTER 7

SECRETS WILL BE REVEALED

That first night, I had crept back into the house from the fields drenched in sweat and tears, longing for a hot shower and a clean bed. As soon as I came through the front door, Darwin stepped in my path and startled me.

"Shit," I huffed, my eyebrows immediately dipping between my eyes. "Why the hell are you creeping around like a damn ghost or some shit?" I snapped, my hand still flattened over my chest.

Darwin parted a wicked smile. "A better question is, why are you so scary?" he replied sarcastically.

I sucked my teeth and shook my head. "Look. I don't want to argue or fight with you. I want to see about Granny Houston and help out where I can. It damned sure looks like y'all need it around here," I said. I figured when it came to my grease-ball uncle, I'd get more with sugar than I'd get with shit. Maybe if he figured he wouldn't have to take all of the responsibility for my ailing grandmother, he'd get off my back.

"Oh yeah?" He moved a few inches to the side, dug in his pocket, pulled out a cigarette and lighter, and lit it. He leaned against the wall. "You? You came to help me wipe Mama's shitty

ass, deal with her outbursts, and have her throw food at you?"
He chuckled.

Damn. I didn't know he was dealing with all of that. I
folded my arms across my chest and looked down at his feet.

"Yeah. Whatever needs to be done for her. I came to help."
I lied so easily the words felt like melted butter on my tongue.

Now Darwin laughed hard. A low, guttural laugh that felt
so out of place it made the hairs on my arm prickle.

"Nah. Matter of fact, hell nah," he said, his eyes hooding
over before he blew a ring of pale gray smoke in my face. "I
believe you came around for more than that, and I'll find out
why soon enough. There's just something about the stink of
that lie that reeks all over you," Darwin said, another puff of
smoke billowing from his mouth like the tip of a hot pistol
after it's been shot.

I squinted at him. I truly couldn't stand his ass. "When you
find out something different, you let me know," I snapped and
stomped away.

"Them other two rooms are mine," he called after me.
"And I ain't giving them up for the likes of you."

That first night in the House was miserable. I didn't know
being back there without Milcy was going to make me so de-
pressed.

The makeshift bedroom Darwin forced me to stay in was
all the way up in the tiny, cramped attic. To get up there, I'd
have to climb up a slim set of stairs that dropped down from
the ceiling in the front room where Granny Houston kept all
of her plants that I remembered she'd given all male names—
Bobby, Johnny S., and Tommy. She'd said giving a plant a female name made them jealous of each other and they'd never
grow. She also kept an old, threadbare recliner in that room,
propped in front of the big bay window so she could always sit
and watch anyone coming up the main road. The front room
was exactly how I'd remembered it back then. It was also the
place I remembered getting several beatings with that cow skin

belt. I shuddered and tugged on the string to pull the attic stairs down.

As kids, Miley and I were always scared to go up in the attic. It was where Granny Houston would send us as punishment because she knew we were afraid, which meant we spent a whole bunch of time up there.

We had made up this whole story that a ghost lived up in Granny Houston's attic, and the ghost ate kids. Now as I stepped on each of the tiny steps gingerly, an eerie feeling crept down my spine.

"You think the ghost lives in those boxes?" Miley had asked, clutching onto my arm as tight as a vise.

"Shh. If you talk, the ghost will come out," I had whispered back, my heart thrumming against my chest wall.

Miley started to cry. I held her tight and told her to close her eyes and I would keep mine open to watch for the ghost. We fell asleep huddled together until Granny Houston stuck her head up through the floor and started screaming at us to wake up.

"Stop it, Karlie. There are no ghosts, and that is the past," I whispered and shook my shoulders a little bit.

I wasn't a kid anymore, but that didn't change the fact that I was still scared as hell to go up in that attic. It took several starts and stops before I finally made it up the steps. I wanted to scream when I got up there. The air was heavy and smelled like mildew, leftover cigarette smoke, and old potpourri. I put my wrist up to my nose and coughed. There was a thick layer of dust on the floor that kicked up into little fuzzy balls as I tried to move around the cramped space. I could barely stand up straight. I inched over and tugged on the tiny string that hung from a shade-less lamp sitting in the corner on the floor. The light bulb was dull, but it illuminated the space enough for me to see. I exhaled and shook my head. I couldn't believe that this was where my life had ended up—back at the very place I had always been trying to escape.

"How the fuck am I going to survive this?" I said out loud to myself. My little hood apartment would've been like a mansion compared to that attic. The ceiling was damn near touching the flat, shapeless feather bed that was on the floor in the center of the room. When I lay down I had to close my eyes to keep from feeling like I would suffocate because there was barely enough space between the ceiling and my head to sit upright.

Let's not talk about how uncomfortable the temperature was in that mousetrap. It was sweltering hot up there, with only a tiny window a few inches from the bed for a breeze. Trust me, there was no breeze coming in either. I don't remember falling asleep, but I knew under those horrendous conditions, it had to be sheer exhaustion that finally carried me off into a fitful sleep.

The force of the blow to my chest instantly took my breath. I made a loud sucking noise as I tried to keep air in my lungs. My eyes and mouth popped open in shock in response to the pain crashing into my chest. I felt like a ton of bricks had been dropped on me from the ceiling.

"Mmm," I moaned. My mouth and nose were covered. "Mmmmm." I kicked and flailed, feverishly protesting. I tried to move my head from side to side in an attempt to loosen the grip that was holding me captive. I could smell and taste the leather from the glove suffocating me. Suddenly it registered in my brain that I was being attacked. I started kicking my legs even more wildly, but another blow to my midsection abruptly stopped that. I felt vomit leap up from my stomach into my throat. I was choking. I was dying. The next vicious punch to my gut gave me pause. It landed with so much force that it made a small bit of urine escape my bladder.

"Stop fucking fighting or I'll blow your sister's fucking brains out right in front of you," the assailant hissed. I went

stock-still at the mention of Miley. My heart was squeezing so hard it hurt. Tears leaked out of the corners of my eyes.

I felt my body moving. I extended my arms, trying to find something to hold on to. The next thing I felt was my legs hitting the floor with a thud. My heels crashing to the floor sent small shock waves of pain up my legs, causing my thighs to tremble. The carpet burned the heels of my feet as I was dragged. I tried to twist my head in protest, but that caused pain too. It wasn't until I finally was positioned in such a way that I could see my sister with a black cloth bag over her head that I started to fight with everything I had in me.

"Miley! Miley! I'm going to save you!"

"Miley. Miley." I groaned. I tried to sit up abruptly and hit my head on the sloped walls hovering above me. The sharp pain in my head made me realize I had been dreaming. Nighttime was the worst for me. Every day I'd relive bits and pieces of my ordeal behind the EZ Cash robbery. It was starting to drive me crazy.

I flopped back down on the uncomfortable bed and looked around. This space was worse than those stupid little houses I'd seen on that television show *Tiny House Hunters*.

"Oh my God," I gasped, touching my chest. I turned my head and looked over to the tiny attic window. Even through the thick layers of dirt on the small, square windowpanes, I could see the sun starting to rise. Thank goodness I had survived it. One day gone, only God knew how many more to go.

As soon as the sun came all the way up, I slid out of the bed and inched down that skinny-ass staircase. I needed to get the hell out of there. My oversized sleep T-shirt stuck to me from sweating all night, and my hair was plastered to my scalp like I'd been doused with water. Although it was early in the morning, my mind was already racing with thoughts on how I would make a change to this living arrangement.

I made my way down the long, dark hallway that led to the

kitchen, when I paused at the sound of voices. I flattened my back again the hallway wall so I could listen without being seen. I tried to slow my breathing so I could hear better, but for some reason my heart was racing and I was breathing hard. After a few seconds, I could finally make out what was being said.

"Please, Darwin. You can't keep doing this to me. I need my money for my medicine and things," Granny Houston cried.

"Shut up. I know what I'm doing. I'm the one here wiping your shitty ass every day. Nobody else even cares about you. If I take all the money, so what," Darwin said cruelly.

"Them people said this money is for my care. They pay you already as the caregiver, so why you taking my little bit of money too," Granny Houston whined.

"I said shut up. I'm telling you, Mama, I'm going to leave your ass here to rot one of these days if you keep on coming at me like this," Darwin threatened. My grandmother was silent after that. That wasn't the Granny Houston I remembered. In all of my life that lady had never been a pushover, not even for her kids.

I stood still listening with my insides boiling at how Darwin was talking to Granny Houston. But I was also feeling a bit conflicted. Was this karma coming back on her for how she'd treated my mother and Miley and me over the years?

Hearing Granny Houston being reduced to a sobbing, weak old lady kind of gave me a quick flash of satisfaction inside for how evil she had been toward us all of our lives; but hearing what Darwin was doing to her also made my insides churn with anger. Who does that to their own mother? I didn't think he could get any lower than what he'd done to us when we lived with him, but treating his own mother like this had to be the lowest of the low. Darwin was one of those people that God could've skipped breathing life into and the world would've been better off without him.

A door slamming caused me to jump. Before I could react, Darwin was moving toward my hiding place. I tried to make it seem like I had just gotten there, but I think my arched eyebrows and slightly opened mouth told him that I was caught out there. He knew I'd been listening. His eyes went dark and his nostrils widened.

"Fuck you doing creeping around? Nobody ain't ever tell you snooping is rude?" he snarled, standing in my way like he wanted to slap me or push me or better yet, drag me to the front door and toss me outside.

I was a little shaken by his look but I played it off. I rolled my eyes and pushed past him and headed to the kitchen. "If you weren't doing grimy shit, you wouldn't be worried about me creeping or listening, now would you?" I retorted. He was hot on my heels. I could feel him behind me like a strong gust of wind. He grabbed my arm and forced me to turn around.

"Ow. Get off me," I gritted, trying to wrestle my arm free from his tight grip. Pain pulsed in the area he was holding. I bit down into my jaw and spoke through my teeth. "I said get the fuck off me."

His breath was hot on my face, the stale smell of cigarettes and dirty teeth threatening to singe the hairs in my nose.

"Don't come in here making trouble. I got a good thing going here and I'm finally free from y'all, your stupid-ass mother, and anybody else standing in the way of me and my relationship with my goddamn mother. What goes on between me and my mother is *our* business. If you don't want to be on the streets, I suggest you mind yours," he said through releasing me with a shove.

"Oh, I'm definitely going to mind my business, and she *is* my business now," I gritted. "Don't think I forgot everything you did to me and my sister when we lived with you. Don't think I ever forgave you for forcing us to have to go into the system when you were my mother's blood. I never forget shit."

Darwin laughed and shook his head. "You think I give a

rat's ass what you remember? Naw, I don't." He moved closer to me. "Oh, I found out some stuff about you, Miss Karlie."

"Yeah, and?" I retorted defensively. My stomach was already in knots before he could even say a word.

"And I know all about that robbery, the money, and that you were the cause of this," Darwin said, slamming an old newspaper down in front of me.

My eyes roved down to the paper and I quickly snapped them shut. I swallowed hard.

"What? You didn't know your sister and your man's murders had made front-page news?" Darwin taunted. "Looka here . . . there's a reward for any information about the killers. So what do you think that means?"

I shrugged, trying my best to act like he wasn't getting to me when really I wanted to just turn into a pile of salt on the spot and blow away with the wind.

"C'mon, Karlie, you're a smart girl," he pressed, chuckling evilly. "Okay, well, I'll tell you what it means. It means that if there is a police reward for the killers, there is a street reward for the one person who didn't die . . . and that would be you," Darwin said, placing his hand on my shoulder.

His touch made me feel like I was standing barefoot on a patch of ice.

"Fuck you," I spat.

He let out a raucous, evil laugh. "Naw, you might be the one getting fucked," Darwin said.

I could literally see fire flashing in his eyes. The last time I had seen that kind of hatred in someone's eyes, that person had tried to kill me.

CHAPTER 8

FAMILY TIES

The next day, I awoke and went down to the kitchen. I tried to get down there early, before my creepy-ass uncle awoke. I bumped into someone.

"Oh, goodness. You scared me." I clutched my chest.

"I'm sorry. I'm just gathering a few things before I go," the short, stout black home health aide said.

"You're leaving already? I thought my grandmother is supposed to have help until at least eight at night," I questioned her with my eyebrows raised.

"Oh, you didn't know? Someone in the family requested that the service be discontinued."

"What?" My eyebrows shot up into arches. "You must have it wrong. Nobody here would cancel the service. My grandmother can't walk and can barely get her words out."

The home health aide slid her pocketbook off her shoulder and dug into it. "Here is the order," she said, extending the pink paper toward me.

I snatched it and read over it. I bit down on my bottom lip and exhaled.

"Between me and you," the home health aide whispered,

looked over her shoulder and then back at me, "I know it was canceled so that more of the monthly money is freed up. When these older people have these services, there is a certain amount taken from their checks. If they don't have any services, more money comes in the check. More money in the check sometimes means more for family members to pocket." She looked around again to make sure we were alone.

"I fully understand," I said. "I will take care of this right away," I assured her.

When she was gone, I went to check in on Granny Houston. As soon as I walked into her room, my nostrils were assailed by the smell. I immediately cupped my hand over my nose and mouth. I could hear my grandmother sobbing. My insides melted. Here she was, the woman I'd known all of my life as tough as steel, lying in her own feces, crying like a helpless baby. I grabbed a mask from the tall dresser near the door of her room and stretched it over my nose and mouth. I also grabbed a pair of latex gloves from the home health aide supplies on the dresser.

"Granny, don't worry. I'm going to make sure you get the care you're supposed to have. I'm going to help you now," I told her.

I can't lie, I was struggling with my own emotions as I went about getting my grandmother out of her soiled clothes. As I went to pull off her housecoat, she grabbed my arm with force. It caused me to freeze. It reminded me of how she would grab us roughly as kids. I crinkled my brows and looked at her with widened eyes.

"Karlie, I always loved you girls," Granny Houston slurred.

I felt something inside my core tug like little people were pulling on the veins and arteries in my heart. I turned my face away because I couldn't control the tears I knew were about to fall.

"Your mother was my heart when she came along. I . . . I . . . just loved her so much."

The tears were running down my face now. My grandmother was struggling to get the words out, which already
made it hard, but what she was saying made it even harder to
listen.

"Granny," I croaked, putting my hand up.

"No. I don't want to leave this earth until you know the
truth."

I couldn't move. Even with the stench in the room, I was
rooted to the floor. I had waited all of my life to hear the story;
to try and understand why my grandmother resented us and
why my mother couldn't kick her drug habit.

I nodded.

Granny Houston continued. "When your mother told me
my brother had been touching her, I didn't believe her."
Granny Houston hiccupped a sob. "I was too worried about
being accepted by my own family to believe my own child.
That changed things inside your mother. She grew angry and
withdrawn. She would stay out all times of the night. She
would fight me, fight Darwin, and fight your aunt Verona. I
knew she was on the drugs, but I ain't want to believe it. When
she came home pregnant with you, I treated her bad. I barely
let her eat. I reminded her every day she was a whore." Granny
Houston sobbed out her words.

I was crying so hard my shoulders rocked and my chest
quivered. I pulled off the mask because I could barely catch my
breath.

"That's the past," I whispered, tears running over my lips.

"I was wrong, Karlie. I didn't know no better. I treated my
own child like dirt and my grandkids too. I just want you to
know I'm sorry. Now your mother and Miley ain't here for me
to tell them, but I'm telling you. Whatever trouble you're in . . .
you gotta fix it. You have to save yourself. I don't want to see
you end up dead."

I choked back my tears. "Granny, I won't end up dead. I
promise it will be me and you in this house together until the

Lord sees fit," I said, trying my best to crack a smile to lighten the mood.

"That's right. Until the Lord sees fit," Granny Houston agreed.

"Or over somebody's dead body," Darwin's deep voice boomed from behind me.

I whirled around so fast I almost lost my balance and fell on the dirty pile of clothes.

"So you trying to get close to your grandmother all of a sudden," Darwin snarled. "Well, we don't need any help around here."

"Clearly you do. She's been sitting in her own waste, and the home health aide has been let go for some strange reason," I retorted. "But maybe it's not a strange reason at all. Maybe it's because someone wanted more money to steal. And maybe there's some government official that might be interested in knowing that." I folded my arms across my chest and cocked my head to the side for emphasis.

Darwin's face grew dark and his nostrils flared. "I've already warned you to mind your fucking business. This is my last warning. If you don't want to end up like your sister, you better fall back."

"And if you don't want to end up like *your* sister, you better stop fucking with my grandmother." With that, I snatched off the dirty gloves, shoved them into his chest, and stormed out of the room.

Darwin was a problem that I needed to get rid of sooner rather than later.

CHAPTER 9

IT'S EITHER MOTIVATION OR DESPERATION

My entire body grew cold until I shivered so hard my teeth chattered.

I balled my fists tight and stared down at Miley's stiff form. I shook my head side to side. *No. No. No.*

This wasn't right. This wasn't how things were supposed to be. My baby sister wasn't supposed to be lying dead in front of me while I was still breathing.

"Miley, I'm so sorry," I whispered, my voice cracking with grief. I couldn't bear to look at her like this. It wasn't her, I tried to tell myself. Just a body. No soul. My sister was gone. Even any resemblance of how she used to be was gone. Her beauty had faded with the time between the shooting and this private viewing.

The funeral home had dressed her in an all-white old-lady dress that was provided by them. It was definitely something Miley would've never been caught alive or dead in if she'd had her way. The sheer material overlay on the dress fluttered from the air conditioner, making it appear like Miley was still breathing. I blinked a few times to make sure. They had covered her hands in shiny white satin church gloves. Miley would've had a fit about that too. She had been too much of a fashion-ista to be dressed like some old-school church usher.

I placed my hand over my aching heart. Tears ran down my face in streams.

"Oh, Miley. If only I could rewind time," I sobbed. I wasn't supposed to outlive her. I was the oldest, and these roles were supposed to be reversed. We were supposed to be old ladies to-gether and I was going to die first.

I wiped my eyes so I could look at her one good time again. All I could do was shake my head and sob some more. Miley definitely didn't even look like my beautiful little sister anymore. The undertakers had slathered her skin with a thick layer of caked-up makeup, and she seemed to have a perma-nent grimace on her face. I guess she had died in pain and there was no fixing the terror that had become etched on her face for good, even with that studio makeup. I couldn't stand to see her like this. I finally doubled over at the waist, too weak to stand up straight any longer. Detective Castle grabbed me just before I hit the floor.

"Sit down, Karlie," he said, leading me to a row of chairs lined up neatly in front of the casket. I had to admit, Detective Castle had come through just like he'd said he would. Since I couldn't be in our hometown to handle Miley's funeral ar-rangements, he had taken care of it for me. I understood that he'd gone above and beyond what most cops would do for some random black girl like me. Detective Castle had arranged a small, private last viewing and goodbye for Miley at a secret location in a small town right outside of Virginia Beach. Just like he'd promised.

"I can't believe she's really gone," I croaked as I hugged myself and rocked back and forth in the chair. Detective Cas-tle patted my shoulder but remained silent. I guess there was nothing he could say to that.

"What about Sidney?" I asked, sniffing back the snot rim-ming my nostrils. "Is there going to be a service for him? Did his family claim his body? Will I be able to see him before they put him in the ground?"

Detective Castle stopped patting my shoulder, leaned his forearms on his knees, and hung his head. "Well, that's complicated, Karlie," he mumbled.

I furrowed my eyebrows and shifted in my seat. "How complicated can it be? His mother or sister would claim his body and they'd plan a funeral, and you'd take me there with protection so I can say my goodbyes . . . just like you promised. Right?" I replied, urgency lacing my words.

Detective Castle sat back up straight and pinched the bridge of his nose. "Well, Karlie. Sidney's um . . . family . . . I mean his . . . um . . . his . . ." Detective Castle stammered. I turned slightly in my seat and glared at him. What the hell was his problem? He tugged at the collar of his shirt like it had suddenly gotten too tight for his neck. I had never seen Detective Castle seem so nervous and evasive.

"What the hell are you trying to say? I'm confused. Just tell me," I demanded.

"Sidney had a woman . . . well . . . another woman," Detective Castle finally blurted.

My stomach immediately clenched. I started breathing hard.

"A woman? What? What are you talking about?" I pressed, shaking my head no. "You're wrong. I am . . . was. I mean . . . I am his woman," I snapped, getting to my feet, my strength quickly restored.

"I'm sorry, Karlie. I know how hard this news must be to hear. I didn't want to be the bearer of bad news, but I wanted you to know what was going on," Detective Castle lamented.

I laughed, which contradicted the way I was really feeling at that moment.

"I don't fucking believe you. You're lying. Sidney was with me and only me. You just don't want to be bothered with taking me to the funeral," I accused, jutting my finger in the detective's face.

"I wouldn't lie to you. I know how much you've been through, Karlie," Detective Castle replied. I buried my face in my hands and more tears came. Deep down inside I knew that he wouldn't lie to me. I just didn't want to believe it.

"How? Why?" I cried.

"When it was time to claim his body, I was surprised to learn that a woman had come forward along with Sidney's mother and two sisters. She said she was his . . ." Detective Castle paused. I guess he was trying to gauge how much more this information would destroy me. I knew Sidney had had moments of cheating, but having someone else who felt comfortable enough to claim his body was insane.

"Wife," I filled in the word in an almost inaudible whisper. Detective Castle nodded. "Yes. She said she was his wife."

I shot up from my chair and ran out of the chapel. Outside, I wrapped my arms around my waist and paced as my shoulders shook with sobs. This news just made everything worse. If Sidney was alive and I'd found out he had a wife all of this time, I would've wanted to kill him all over again. It just didn't make sense. All of those nights he'd spent with me. All of the plans we had made together. I had been to his so-called house and met his mother and sisters. It just didn't make any sense that he had been living a double life.

Within a few minutes Detective Castle was at my side.

"Karlie, I'm sorry for all of this," he said, shoving his hands deep into his pants pockets. "This is all so unfortunate. I wish I could make it all change."

"What else haven't you told me?" I asked, pausing for a few minutes with my eyes squinted at him. "What other secrets do you have to reveal, because I want to know everything I am up against. So no more surprises. I've had enough of that," I said with feeling.

"Well," Detective Castle said, dragging out the last *L*.

I let out a windstorm of breath. I had to silently ask myself how much more shit could I take.

"I was going to wait until you had your time with your sister and had a chance to properly say goodbye before I brought this up, but if you want to know . . ."

"Tell me!" I snapped, causing Detective Castle's eyebrows to shoot up on his face. "I can't deal with these fucking secrets. Everybody has all of these fucking secrets," I shouted.

"We think we have a lead on who might've made the hit on you, Miley, and Sidney," Detective Castle said. His words were slow and deliberate, like he wanted to drive home the point. "It's such a strong lead that I have more than two guys from my squad running it down. We are doing what we can to verify the information."

I dropped my hands at my sides and tilted my head expectantly. I didn't even realize right away that my foot was tapping.

"Get to the point," I grumbled.

"Guy named Jay King," Detective Castle said, hesitating a little bit. "Pretty long rap sheet. Lives in the Tidewater area. Used to be a petty thug, but moved up over the years. Dangerous."

"Yeah, and what does he have to do with me and my sister? Why would this random guy, Jay King, want to harm us? I've never heard his name a day in my life."

"I'm getting to that," Detective Castle said, holding his hands up in front of his chest as if to tell me to calm down. "I hear he is the cousin of Ashton King."

"Who? Who the fuck is Ashton King?" I was getting really freaking confused and my patience was growing short.

"Ashton King is the man you came to know as El Jefe. The one that had you and Miley when we busted in and saved you both."

The words *El Jefe* caused my heart to slam so hard it stabbed against my chest bone.

"You mean to tell me this nightmare is not over?" I said, my words coming out on short, exasperated puffs of breath.

"Unfortunately not, Karlie. Ashton King is one of the biggest drug lords in the world. He came over from Jamaica fifteen years ago and made millions in a short time. He tried to keep his money clean by opening a series of legitimate businesses . . . like the EZ Cash payday loan storefronts. That was the money he used to keep all of his government officials paid off, to buy legitimate houses and cars. It was his clean way of handling millions of dollars in illicit cash. But you messed that all up," Detective Castle said. His words exploded like small bombs in my ears. I had no idea I had stepped into the path of not just a dangerous man, but from what I was hearing, a dangerous family.

"From what I've learned, the entire King family is notorious. Their lineage is made up of dangerous drug kingpins who have no mercy when it comes to their enemies. Jay King is next in line since his cousin, Ashton, is locked up. They all know you're responsible, and that whole incident with the EZ Cash robberies shed a lot of light on the Kings' empire. Light that dangerous men like that don't take too kindly to having shone on them. That is why it's so important that you lay low . . . for good. Never to return to the city. Start a new life with your grandmother and just fade away. From what I hear, this guy is young, carefree, with no cares and probably much more ruthless than his big cousin, El Jefe. Trust me, these are men who have nothing to lose, and they're more interested in revenge than money. But they also have a lot of people they're on the hook to, so even if it stops with them, if you don't disappear for good . . . it may not be over for good."

I swallowed hard and closed my eyes for a few seconds. "So you heard all of this from other police? That seems like a lot of information coming from cops. What? Y'all got an insider? An informant or something?" I pressed.

"We have our sources. That's not important right now. What's important is that you stay safe. You have to trust me on this one. Just move on. I know Miley was important to you and you may be thinking about revenge, but you have to understand what you're dealing with here."

"What's the talk in the streets?" I asked. I knew for damn sure that the streets were always talking. I knew that if any place had the real scope, it would be the ghetto news. It was where the most valuable information came from. Hands down, the rumblings on the streets were much more accurate than anything stupid cops could develop on their own.

"Word is, Jay King has put an unofficial one-hundred-thousand-dollar bounty on your head. Some say he's offering more. Some say he's offering less. My guess is it is probably more. The King family has big money. Money is not an issue for them. They have enough money to pay a gang of hit men, which is why Miley and Sidney are dead. My sources say the word hasn't gotten as far as it could yet, but it's getting there. I'm sorry to say this, Karlie . . . but you're in a lot of danger if you don't stay away," Detective Castle said sorrowfully.

I contemplated what he was saying, and all sorts of things began swirling around in my mind—*a drug cartel family is after me now; there's a bounty on my head; Sidney was married and I'll never even get to say a final goodbye to him; I'm living in terrible conditions with my grimy family members; and, worst of all, this is all happening while I'm all alone, without my sister.*

"It is what it is, Detective," I said, throwing my hands up in surrender. "What else can they do to me? I'm alone, with no life anyway. Trust me, the way I feel right now, looking at my sister in that pine box, stiff and lifeless, this person may be in more danger than me," I gritted, stomping away from Detective Castle. I meant every word of it too. Fear was an emotion I had become so used to it didn't even have the same effect on me anymore.

I heard the gravel crunching under Detective Castle's feet and knew he had turned around to follow me with his eyes. He probably wanted to know what the hell I was thinking about. He probably thought I had finally snapped apart and lost my mind.

I would've told him if he'd asked. Seeing my sister in that casket and hearing that the love of my life had a secret life that didn't include me had changed something inside me. My fear had morphed into a huge, white-hot ball of anger and desire for revenge all wrapped into one. At that moment, I had decided that this person Jay King that Detective Castle seemed to think was so big and bad would have to find me before I devised a plan to find him first. God was going to be the only one who could save him once Karlie Houston put her mind to destroying him. From that moment forward I was not only running for my life, I was on a mission to end someone else's life.

CHAPTER 10

SETTING THINGS UP ONCE
AND FOR ALL

For two days after my sister's private service and my conversation with Detective Castle, I couldn't eat or sleep. I finally decided to take action.

The third night, I had lain awake for hours waiting for the House to finally be silent. The constant arguing between Granny Houston and Darwin was driving me crazy, especially because I was still feeling crazy over the information I had gotten from Detective Castle.

It was three o'clock in the morning before that bastard Darwin finally went to bed. I climbed down from the attic and crept through the House being as careful as possible not to make any noise. That was a big feat in itself. I wasn't a skinny chick, so walking on those old wooden floors was like walking on a tightrope. The floors were so creaky and noisy that I had to stop at least three times to make sure no one heard me.

I held my breath as I tiptoed past Darwin's room. His door was cracked and I could hear him snoring like a bear. He had probably gotten drunk like usual and crashed. I usually hated when he got drunk and started acting belligerent, but at that moment his drunken state was working in my favor.

Granny Houston's door was closed, so I knew she wouldn't see or hear me. Everything was diminishing for my grandmother—her sight, her hearing, and even her good sense. She had also been doing a lot of crying lately, a major vulnerability in her that I had never witnessed as a child. It was really weird for me to see her like that. I never thought she would be so weak in her old age. I was grateful she and I had had our soft moment.

I finally made it to the back room where the washroom and back door were located. Darwin kept his car keys on a peg by the back door. I spotted them, and something inside me jerked. My nerves were on a wire's edge, but I had to forge forward. It was now or never for this power move I was making.

With my chest heaving, I finally made it to the peg and gently eased the keys from it. I clutched them in my hand like I had just found a hidden treasure. I waited a few seconds and listened for any noises. Each step of this mission was important. I already had a story formulated in my head if Darwin happened to bust me out there with his keys in my hand.

After a few long minutes of listening, I realized the House was still silent. Darwin wasn't creeping up behind me, and I was almost there. I let out a puff of breath and slowly twisted the back door's knob slowly. The door made a loud squeaky noise. The sound almost gave me a damn heart attack.

"Shit," I huffed under my breath, stopping again to make sure Darwin didn't come running after me. When nothing happened, I continued out the door. I pulled the door in behind me but didn't lock it.

Once I was in the yard and felt the night air cool on my face, I inhaled, held my breath, and darted to Darwin's car. I opened the door and hastily slid behind the steering wheel. Every muscle in my body was tense with fear and anxiety. My chest was pumping up and down so hard I could barely catch my breath. My hands trembled so badly I could barely get the key in the ignition, but I finally did after three tries.

A warm feeling of relief washed over me when I cranked the car and threw it into drive. It didn't matter if Darwin had heard the engine revving at that point, because by then I was already driving away. Free and clear.

I can't lie, though. As I drove away from the House, all I heard was Detective Castle's voice playing in my mind like a broken record: *This is why you need to stay out of town, Karlie. You need to stay away from the city where anyone might spot you, recognize you, and ultimately find you. It's too dangerous for you to ever return to where you're from. The protection program can only help you if you follow the rules. If you break the rules, you only put yourself in harm's way with no chance of us protecting you. We are not liable if you don't stick to the program.*

I waved my hand near my head to rid it of all of those intrusive thoughts. Forget all of that. I had made up my mind. I wasn't about to sit in my grandmother's house and be caught out there like a lame duck waiting for this Jay King character to find me. I wanted to find his ass first. I had always been the confront-my-problems-head-on type of chick. If I could get to my enemies first, that's how I liked to play the game. I guess you could say I was proactive whereas most chicks—and dudes, for that matter—were reactive.

It took an hour for me to get to my girl Aisha's house. She had gotten a car accident settlement check a couple of years back and moved out of our old hood where we used to live in the state-funded apartments. Now she lived on a tree-lined block of medium-sized houses that all looked the same except for the different color shutters on the fronts. Those houses looked so much alike, I had to roll through the block twice before I spotted Aisha's car, which told me I had found her house.

Shit, if Aisha wasn't such a hood queen and didn't have tags that said *Bad Bee* (meaning bad bitch) I might've missed the house altogether. Yes, Aisha Campbell, reformed hood rat, had moved up in the world. But you know what they say . . . you can take the girl out of the hood, but you can't take the hood out of the girl. I looked at those personalized plates and smiled.

I hadn't seen Aisha in over a year. I can't even remember what happened that had kept us apart so long this time. It was so commonplace for Aisha and me to fall out and make up that half the time neither one of us remembered what we had been fighting about the next time we saw one another. I was sure it would be like that this time too. I had a deep love for Aisha that no matter what would never really fade.

Aisha and I had been friends since we were eight or nine years old, but we had the kind of relationship that had so many ups and downs that sometimes we would be the best of friends and other times we behaved like enemies toward each other. A few of the times Aisha and I had fallen out was over he said/she said, but for the most part, there was never a complete loss of love between us. She had proven herself to be a ride-or-die type of friend more than a few times. And no matter how old we got and how far we might've grown apart, I could never forget how we met in the first place.

It was the first day of third grade and my first day at a brand-new school. My mother had decided to move for the tenth time that year. But the neighborhood she'd chosen that time had to be the worst we'd ever lived in.

Recess time had come, and I walked out onto the raggedy playground, alone.

"Look at her. She's a bum," a big, fat girl named Cora pointed at me and taunted. The little group she was with all started to laugh. I heard them and saw them, but for some reason I still looked over my shoulder as if I thought they were referring to someone else. I mean, I wasn't bothering anybody. I had been quiet the entire first day in my new school, so why would I think these girls would pick on me? I was wrong. Before long, Cora and her little group of loyal followers had me

surrounded. I felt my head yank back. Someone in their group had pulled my hair.

"She probably stinks too. Look at those run't over shoes and that nappy hair," Cora said, causing more kids to gather around and look at me like I was a circus spectacle.

My cheeks were burning and my stomach did flips. I had my fists balled just in case any of them tried to touch me again, but I was really scared.

Before long, kids from all three third-grade classes had me surrounded. I didn't know whether to run, scream, or just stand there and take their jeers and taunts. I felt so small I wanted to ball up like a slug after salt was poured on it. I was frozen with fear, but I was also low-key angry inside. My heart was pounding painfully against my sternum and I didn't even realize I was spinning around and around like an animal about to be caught for slaughter. I looked from one ugly, scowling face to another. These kids were evil.

"Bum."

"Dirt bomb."

"Welfare rat."

"Crack baby."

"Food stamp queen," were all the nasty things they were yelling at me.

"Let's put her in the dirt where she belongs," someone in the crowd yelled. I jumped and put my hands up in a fighting stance. The kids started moving in closer. I could feel sweat soaking the back of my shirt. In all of that, not one teacher had come to my rescue.

"Just leave me alone!" I shouted. The next thing I heard was someone scream out.

"Ouch!"

I turned just in time to see Cora fall to the ground holding her face. Her head was bleeding and she was screaming and rolling side to side like she was in a lot of pain. I had no idea what had happened, but the crowd started to disperse like roaches when the lights came on.

"All of y'all get away from the new girl," a voice boomed. Everyone's eyes grew wide when they saw Aisha standing there with her hands on her ample hips like somebody's Big Mama.

Even in third grade, Aisha was a big girl. She was round with big breasts like an adult. There was no way she looked like a third grader, but her size had saved me that day. None of those kids wanted any problems with Aisha.

"I hate bullies!" Aisha barked. "This one here don't got nothing better to do than bother a little skinny new girl. Now look at her," Aisha said, kicking her foot so that a puff of dirt and a tiny rainstorm of pebbles hit Cora.

"Nobody mess with her from now on. She is my friend, and if I hear about anybody saying anything about her or her clothes, they will have a problem with me. Understand?" Aisha barked, going around in a circle and pointing in random faces. I don't think I had ever seen kids with so much fear dancing in their eyes from another kid before that day.

I stood there in wide-eyed shock.

"Th . . . thank . . . you," I stammered as Aisha put her arm around my shoulders and walked me past the crowd of shocked kids.

"Hold up." Aisha stopped and let go of me. She walked over to one of the mean girls and punched her in the arm.

"Ow!" the girl screamed, holding her arm.

"Now, see? How you like somebody messing with you just because you're new?" Aisha growled. "And you better not tell on me.

"Anybody else?" Aisha asked, and put her hands up like a boxer. The group of bullies split up so fast their departure resembled the Red Sea parting. "Your name is Karlie, right?" Aisha asked when she returned to my side.

"Ye . . . yes," I stuttered. I was still in shock at how Aisha had commanded the whole crowd.

"Well, you're down with me now, so ain't nobody going to mess with you again," Aisha told me. I just kind of stared at her. I was in awe and didn't understand why she had decided to help me.

Even then, in third grade, there was something more grown up about Aisha. She spoke like an adult and was more powerful than some grown people I knew. I had an instant respect for Aisha, and I was damn glad to be called her best friend after that.

I snapped out of my reverie and realized I had probably been daydreaming for a few minutes too long. I parked Darwin's car on the corner and watched Aisha's house for a few minutes more before I felt comfortable pulling up in front. Leaving the safety of my grandmother's house and traveling to Aisha's was a risky move, but so necessary. I was going to have to get my resources, together and this was the first one on my list. If Aisha was anything, she was very resourceful.

Aisha was a real around-the-way type of chick that knew more about the streets than most niggas in the hood. I came straight to her because if there was going to be anyone who could help me find out where Jay King hung out, who worked for him in the streets, who all his bitches were, it was going to be her. Aisha always had her ear to the streets and her finger on a trigger ready to buck if she needed to buck. I had always loved that about her too.

When I was finally comfortable with the surroundings, I pulled Darwin's Honda in front of Aisha's house and got out. I looked around, head whipping frantically, making sure there was no one outside watching. I wasn't too worried because like I said, Aisha had moved from the hood where niggas hung out all times of the night. Where she lived now she had real neighbors, the kind of people that went to work and went to bed at a decent hour. Four o'clock in the morning that neighborhood was so quiet you could probably hear a rat pissing on cotton.

I rushed up to Aisha's door and laid on the doorbell. I had no choice. I knew I would have to make my approach urgent or Aisha might ignore it.

I already knew what to expect once I started ringing that bell like I ain't have no sense. My girl Aisha was no joke. I saw when her upstairs light came on. I got excited. But I also got a little nervous when I imagined her face drawn tight into an angry mean mug and the cuss words she was mumbling under her breath. My shoulders still slumped with relief when that light came on.

"Thank God she's home and not out with some nigga or up in the club," I murmured. I looked around again, paranoid. But there still wasn't a soul stirring on that block.

"Come on, Isha . . . open the door," I mumbled, saying her nickname.

"Who the fuck is it?" Aisha barked from the other side of the door.

"Isha, it's me . . . Karlie," I said, trying to be loud enough for her to hear but not loud enough for the whole neighborhood to hear. Good neighborhood or not, you never knew who knew who out there.

"Who?" she shouted, but this time she yanked the door open. "Who the hell is it?" Aisha wore a scowl that would have scared ten men away. She was also holding a baseball bat. I didn't laugh at that moment, but it was damn funny how tough this girl was.

"Fuck is it? You better say something," she squinted and growled before she opened her locked screen door.

"Isha, open the door. It's Karlie. I gotta get inside," I said with urgency. "Karlie. Your BFF."

"Karlie? Oh shit, girl," Aisha gasped, her facial expression going from scowling and angry to surprised and sympathetic. She quickly moved aside, a silent welcome.

"Girl, I can't believe it's you. I heard you was dead. Then I heard only Miley was dead. Then I heard Miley and Sidney was dead. I ain't know what to think," Aisha rambled as I stepped inside. "I am damn glad to see you alive."

"Lock up quick," I said, still looking over my shoulder. It had become like a habit now.

"Yeah. Yeah. I always lock up this bitch," Aisha said as she went about locking up her doors. "Make yourself at home, girl. Oh my goodness, I am so happy to see that you're okay. I was like, who the hell is at my door ringing the damn bell like the police and shit." Aisha was looking me up and down like she didn't believe I was really standing there. I guess it was a weird moment for both of us.

"I know. Sorry for waking you up in the middle of the night like this, but I couldn't take a chance coming out here in broad daylight," I said. "There is so much going on, Isha." I shook my head pitifully. I felt my bottom lip trembling, but I refused to cry.

"It's all good, chick," Aisha said, reaching out and giving me a hug. "I'm just real glad to see that you're good. When you hear stories, you just don't know what the hell to believe."

"Thanks, girl. I know that's right. It has been some shit. I have been through some shit for sure. I never thought my life would end up on this path. I'm all alone out here now, Isha. My sister is gone." I exhaled. This time the tears fell.

"Sit down," Aisha said softly and pointed to her couch. She sat on the edge of the couch right next to me. Her eyes sagged at the edges with sympathy. "I heard so many different stories. I'm glad you're here to tell me the truth of what happened."

"It's just so much." I hesitated and shook my head. I secretly wished I could shake my head and it all be one big nightmare. I wrapped my arms around my waist and hugged myself tight. I actually hated talking about my ordeal, but I knew in order to get Aisha to help me, I would have to tell her what had happened.

"Well, I ain't got nothing but time because I need to compare whatever you got to tell me to the shit I heard in the streets," Aisha said, her tone serious.

Damn, I was hoping she wouldn't ask me to relive the bullshit all over again. I closed my eyes and leaned my head back on her couch.

"It all started . . ." I closed my eyes and began reliving it.

"Agh!" Amy Gaines, the youngest loan clerk at EZ Cash, let out an ear-shattering scream. I was standing right next to her, but my back was turned toward the store's door. Amy had been the first one to notice them. Her screams startled me. I whirled around on the balls of my feet just in time to come face-to-face with the barrel of a shiny, silver, long-nose Desert Eagle.

"Don't move, bitch!"

My heart sank and my stomach curled into a tight knot. I gasped and clutched my chest. Amy would not stop screaming.

"Shut the fuck up!" the masked man snarled at her. She quickly clamped both of her hands over her mouth to stifle her screams. I swallowed a hard lump that had formed in my throat.

"Y'all bitches better get down right now before I put one of these slugs in your fucking heads!" the masked, gun-waving assailant barked. He was so tall I had to crane my neck to look up at him. I didn't have any trouble seeing his gun, though. It was leveled in my face.

I was the manager at the EZ Cash, so I felt like I was responsible for everyone's safety.

"Just do what he says," I instructed. Immediately, the two loan clerks I was in charge of got down on the floor like they had been told. Both started begging and pleading for their lives.

"Bitch, did you hear me! This ain't the movies. I will lay all y'all asses down with no problem!"

My hands were shaking. I swallowed hard as my eyes

darted around wildly. There were two gunmen in my immediate sight. All sorts of things ran through my head, but my thoughts were quickly interrupted when I noticed the third gunman barreling toward us, his gun waving out in front of him like he was nervous.

"Please don't kill me," Amy begged, tears streaming her face.

"Yes, please let us live. I have kids. You can have it all. My kids ain't got nobody else. I can't die." Trina Long, the other clerk, rambled pitifully. I could hear the fear rattling through her words.

With sweat beads dancing down the sides of my face, I moved forward apprehensively. "Listen, leave them out of this. Please don't hurt them. I . . . I am the supervisor here, and no one is going to call the police if you just take what you want and leave us be," I said, raising my hands in surrender to let the masked gunmen know I wasn't going to resist. "There is a safe. I'm the only one who can get you inside," I offered, nodding toward the back of the store.

"I want every fuckin' thing you got in here! Every dollar, bitch!" the second assailant growled through the black material of his mask. A strange feeling flitted through my chest. I swore I saw the devil dancing in his eyes. A shot of heat engulfed my body, and for the first time since they had burst through the doors, I felt a dizzying mixture of anger and fear grip me tight around the throat.

"Look, all we got right here is fifteen hundred dollars. It's in my top right drawer. That's all we keep in the immediate vicinity. The safe is in the back. So just take it all and leave," I said, my tone a little testy. It was a bold move, and I instantly regretted it.

"Oh my God, Karlie, please don't make them angry," Amy whispered from the floor, her fingers laced behind her head like a hostage in some movie. "Take them to the safe. Give them everything," she whimpered.

"Oh yeah?" The biggest of the robbers took three steps toward me and pointed his pistol toward my head. "Bitch, you don't run shit in here right now! I do. Now, get the fuck over here before I kill you in this motherfucker!" he boomed. His words reverberated through my chest like the booming bass of a party speaker. I swayed on my feet a little. I hadn't been expecting that.

"I'm only trying to—" I began, but before I knew it, the monstrous, gorilla-sized assailant lunged forward, snatched me from behind the counter, and shoved his gun into the small of my back.

"Shut the fuck up and show me where the safe is!" he barked, pushing me forward. I stumbled toward the back office with my hands over my head. My insides were churning so fast I just knew I'd throw up.

Once we were in the back office, I quickly went to the safe, which was wedged between two tall, old-school gray filing cabinets. I got to my knees. My hands were shaking so badly that I didn't get the combination on the first try.

"Don't fuck around! Open that safe or else," the gunman ordered, swiping his gun across the back of my neck. I let out an exasperated breath as I fumbled with the ancient combination dial again. This was one of the times I resented how cheap my bosses were. What thriving business didn't have an electronic keypad safe these days? What thriving business kept its old-school safe just sitting on the dusty, torn-up tile floor too? I went to work on the combination lock again with my hands trembling. Left. Right. Left.

Click.

Finally.

I breathed out a long, unsteady breath of relief. It had taken me six fuckups to finally get it right.

"Move," the gunman demanded, pushing me aside so hard I scraped my knee on the raggedy, ripped-up linoleum tile.

"Jack-fucking-pot! Yo, bring that duffel bag," he called out to the others.

The other two assailants herded Amy and Trina into the back office, where I was just easing myself up off the floor. Amy was shaking like a leaf in a wild storm. Trina moved clumsily, her nerves clearly muddling her movements.

"Sit the fuck down," the tallest and meanest of the gunman commanded. Both girls flopped to the floor without hesitation.

"Okay, I gave y'all everything we have in the store. Just please go," I said sassily.

"What, bitch?" the mean one snarled. *"You don't tell us what to do, we tell you,"* he growled, getting close to my face. He was so close I could smell his cologne.

"I'm just trying to—" I started. I never got a chance to finish. Before I could react, I felt metal connect with my skull. My teeth clicked, and my eyes snapped shut on their own.

Crack. Crunch.

The gunman had swung the butt of the pistol at me and cracked it over my head. Flashes of light sparked behind my eyes like someone had set off a round of fireworks in my brain. I smelled the blood before I tasted the metallic, tinny flavor on my tongue. The scent and the taste only lasted a few seconds. My ears went deaf. I remember emitting a mousy squeak right before the impact from his strength and the blow of the gun knocked me out like a light. After I hit the floor, everything in my world went black.

I shivered as I snapped out of reliving the whole EZ Cash robbery scene. Aisha's mouth was slightly open, and I could tell she was definitely hanging on my every word. I recalled everything, except the fact that I had set the whole robbery up. It didn't take long for her to bring that up, though.

"But wait, Karlie. I heard that you set up that whole robbery and that's why the shit is hot on your name in the streets,"

Aisha said bluntly. She wasn't hiding behind no fake smiles and pretending. That's why I respected her, and that's why I was at her house at that moment.

"That's what the word is, but it ain't all true. It is true that I got blamed for setting it up and that a lot of people died behind the shit. But there was more to the story," I lied.

Aisha twisted her lips and raised one eyebrow and looked at me. "C'mon, chick. I know you. I've known you since we were knee-high to a fly. We used to get money together back in the day, Karlie, so I know how smart you are and how calculating your mind is," Aisha said flatly. "We can't get far if we don't keep it real with each other, boo. The one person you ain't got to front for is me."

I hung my head. "You're right. But all I did was let the dudes know what was going on inside the businesses. It wasn't my idea from the gate. I didn't know exactly how they were going to do it. I ain't do all the rest that went into it. And I damned sure didn't know all of this death and destruction would follow behind a simple snatch-and-grab robbery," I said.

"That's better. Starting at the truth and admitting shit is the first step," Aisha said, easing back on her couch. "Well, here is what I heard . . ."

I moved to the edge of my seat so I could hear everything she had to say loud and clear. Aisha was the hood's Lisa Ling; she had all the undercover reporting on lock.

"Niggas is saying some dude that calls himself King was the owner of them stores. He's like the plug for all these corner dudes. They said he knew right away it was you and Miley that was on the setup because King's bitch worked in the stores. They said y'all got away with over five hundred thousand in cash that was drug money that this dude was hiding in them spots. Like, it's no joke, Karlie. He's some big-time Jamaican cartel dude or something. Anyway, they said he got arrested because of you, so he got his people out there searching. Niggas saying this dude is hell-bent on revenge, and he got all these bum bitches and bitch-ass niggas out here like fiends looking for you for that reward money. I'm talking about what he's offering is a shitload of money if you a hungry nigga," Aisha said, her eyes widening for emphasis.

The more she spoke, the harder my heart pumped. I sighed loudly.

"I knew you would know the scoop," I said, shaking my head. "Isha . . . I need your help girl. I'm not going to be able to hide for the rest of my life. I just need to find a way to nip this shit in the bud and quick." I finally just laid it out there. "Ain't no way I'm going to survive being in the protection program, and in order for me to get out here and get to this nigga's peoples first, I need a real good plan. I know if anybody can help me, it's you."

Aisha leaned back and rubbed her chin. I could tell she was contemplating what I was saying. I could also tell she was probably thinking what's in it for her.

"Yeah, Karlie. I can probably help you. But then I would be putting me and my son at risk. Not that I don't want to help you, girlie, but I don't know if it will be worth it," Aisha said, being honest. I knew that was coming next.

"What if we can figure out a way to collect on that money this dude is offering, but also get me out of this situation?" I said, my mind racing in a million directions.

Aisha sat up straight when I said that. "I'm listening," she said.

I knew I had her on board as soon as I mentioned the street reward money. Even I knew that Aisha wouldn't pass up the chance at collecting a hundred thousand stacks. I just had to make sure that the idea of all of that money didn't turn my friend into the next devil in sheep's clothing.

CHAPTER 11

GETTING RID OF THE DEAD WEIGHT

I was back in the House before Darwin awoke later that day. I knew my bum-ass uncle didn't get up until after one o'clock in the afternoon most days. I used to wonder how someone who didn't work got tired enough to sleep all damn day like he did. It was so bad I had become Granny Houston's caretaker now, while he was the one collecting all of her money.

I crept back to my tiny attic space and changed back into my sleep clothes to make it seem like I'd been there all night. After I hid the gun Aisha had given me in a safe place under one of the attic floorboards, I rustled my hair up, rubbed my eyes to make them look a little red, and checked the mirror to make sure I looked like I'd just woken up. When I was satisfied, I came back down from the attic. I had made it downstairs just in the nick of time.

"Oh Lord! Help me! Help me! He's trying to kill me!" I heard Granny Houston crying out. The words were familiar and sent a chill down my spine, but the urgency behind her pitiful cries still spurned me into action. I broke out running down the hallway toward her room.

"Shut up! Ain't nobody going to hear you! Stupid old

lady! I'm the only one that cares about your ass!" I heard Darwin yelling at her. Then, right before I reached the door, I heard the sound of skin connecting with skin, followed by a yelp from my grandmother. I knew immediately what that meant.

"That bastard slapped her? Oh hell no," I growled under my breath. That was it. I had tolerated Darwin canceling her services and I had listened to him abuse her over and over since I'd gotten there. I had finally had enough. The past didn't matter to me anymore. Right was right and wrong was wrong. He had crossed the line a long time ago. And I had made my peace with my grandmother.

I busted into Granny Houston's room like the police with a warrant. I rushed into Darwin like a wrecking ball trying to knock down a brick building. That is how mad I was.

"Get your fucking hands off her, you piece of shit!" I screamed so hard I could feel the veins in my neck cording against my skin. "I'm sick of this shit! You're a fucking punk for putting your hands on a helpless old lady!"

Darwin was too shocked to react and the impact of my sudden attack caused him to stumble sideways. He fell into the commode at the side of the bed, and the bucket that catches the waste slid out from the bottom and spilled all over him.

"You little bitch!" he spat, slipping around in the piss and shit, trying to get up so he could come after me. I was too angry to laugh, but it was funny. Darwin was a literal shit head at that moment.

"You're a damn bully, Darwin. There is a special place in hell for people like you that fuck with kids and old people. Nothing good is ever going to happen for a piece of shit like you so long as you do dirt." I squared up and barked at him, "You ain't tough. Your ass wouldn't do shit like this to a nigga in the streets, but you here abusing your own sickly mother? How fucked up are you, Darwin? All this for a lousy little disability check? Just like you left me and Miley hungry and damn near naked for a little check. It ain't nothing you won't do for some money. Just disgusting."

Granny Houston was sobbing pitifully. It was hard to watch her reduced to this. The stroke had taken all of the brute strength she used to have. She could barely sit up at the side of her bed without assistance from pillows.

"He . . . he's been taking all of my money. I don't have all my medicines or nothing," she managed through her sobs. "I was always good to my kids. I don't know what happened to them. I always tried my best. I wasn't perfect, but I tried my best."

"Shut up! You shut the hell up! You wasn't no perfect mother for sure. We had to learn from somewhere!" Darwin screamed at her. The tension swirling in that room was enough to suffocate all of us.

I had tears in my eyes now. There was so much generational pain between my grandmother and her kids. My mother had hated Granny Houston, and I had to wonder if my mother was alive, would she be the one treating Granny Houston this way instead of Darwin. I moved a few steps closer to my uncle with my jaw set.

"Don't say shit to her. You're so low you could suck an earthworm's dick, I swear. You're so lucky she's right here or else. But I'm going to get on that phone and call those elder abuse people, and they're going to take care of your ass. They lock motherfuckers like you up and throw away the key, and you will owe all that money back. Niggas in jail don't take to kindly to punks who abuse their own mothers," I threatened. I could truly feel that my blood pressure was sky high. My face filled with blood and my temples throbbed.

Darwin squared up on me, the front of his shirt covered in piss and smears of brown from the feces. "You fucked with the wrong nigga, Karlie. I tried to be nice and let you lay low here and all of that, but now you crossed the line. You ain't going to fuck up my life. Not before I fuck up yours. I got something for your ass," Darwin hissed, his eyes hooded. I felt his threat at the core of my soul. I knew at that moment I had just made another enemy, except this time, I'd be sleeping in the same house with one. I had to hurry up and put my plan in motion, because with the way things were now, it was going to be me or Darwin. One of us had to go. And it certainly wasn't going to be me.

"Hi, I'm Karlie Houston." I introduced myself when the two white ladies showed up at the House two days later.

"I'm Mrs. Baker and this is the visiting nurse, Ms. Cromwell," the shorter of the two ladies replied, sticking her hand out for a shake.

"Come in." I welcomed them inside. I had given them a time to come when I knew Darwin had to go visit his parole officer. He thought I was playing, but I wasn't. I needed to get rid of his ass so I could live in peace once and for all.

The two women stepped inside and I walked them to the small living room. It was weird sitting down in the living room because as a kid Granny Houston never allowed anyone in there. In fact, the couches were still covered in their thick, hard, yellowing plastic slipcovers. The plastic cracked and cackled as the two ladies took a seat.

"I called you in because I've found out that my uncle who is living here has been abusing my grandmother. He's taking her money, barely buying her food or her medicine, and two days ago I caught him slapping her," I snitched. It was against every street code I had ever learned, but I can't front, it felt real good telling on Darwin.

Mrs. Baker had a look of disgust scrawled across her face. Ms. Cromwell's mouth sagged at the edges like she wanted to cry. I nodded at her.

"That's how I feel too . . . disgusted and sad," I said.

"How long have you been living here?" Mrs. Baker asked me.

I hadn't anticipated answering any questions about me. I shifted in my seat.

"I wouldn't exactly say I live here, but when I heard my grandmother was sick I decided to stay a few nights," I lied. "Once I saw the conditions and what was going on, I just couldn't bring myself to leave her here alone. I don't live here full time per se, but I'm truly afraid for her life."

Mrs. Baker seemed to contemplate my answer. We exchanged a telling glance. She knew right away that I was smart enough to figure out that if they thought I was living there, once Darwin was out of the house, I would be the primary caregiver on record, and Granny Houston wouldn't get her full services back, and I surely didn't want that. I wanted Granny Houston to get all the help she could from the state.

"Can we see her?" Nurse Cromwell asked, interrupting my thoughts.

"Oh . . . yeah, sure," I said, bouncing up from my seat. I led the women to my grandmother's room.

"Granny?" I called to her. "I have some nice ladies that want to see you. They came to make sure you're okay," I said softly.

Granny Houston was groggy. All she could do was lift her hand and wave it lazily.

"She's just tired," I said, making excuses, although it was kind of strange. She didn't seem like herself, but I waved it off. I told myself that she was just extra tired.

The nurse did a quick exam on Granny Houston and then turned toward me and Mrs. Baker with a strangled look on her face.

"She's got horrible bedsores. Some bruises around the ribs and on the legs. I don't know if I can recommend that she stay here unless the alleged abuser is removed from the home at once. I think we should make a police report," she said.

I smiled wickedly. "Will my uncle be arrested?" I asked.

"There's a strong possibility. I mean, your grandmother has clearly been abused," Nurse Cromwell replied, shaking her head like it was shameful.

"I'll make the report right away. If you'll guarantee me you can stay overnight, I can have someone out here in the morning with an order to get him out of the home. It will be a crime for him to return," Mrs. Baker said.

"I promise to be here," I said, raising my right hand.

"Good. Then this should be an easy fix. I'm really glad you contacted us, Ms. Houston. We see hundreds of elderly patients a year that lose their lives because of frustrated caregivers. This could've been much worse if you hadn't come over," she said.

"And that is a shame," I said, breathing out heavily.

"Your uncle will be held accountable and he will be excluded from this home. This nightmare should be over soon," Ms. Baker assured.

"Perfect," I replied, smiling. "Absolutely perfect."

CHAPTER 12
THE BEST LAID PLANS

I was standing there smiling so wide every single one of my teeth was showing when the police came into the House, woke Darwin's sorry ass up with a flashlight shining in his face, and told him he was under arrest for assault and battery and larceny. I think the feeling of warmth that exploded inside me seeing Darwin's shock was better than an orgasm. I hadn't ever seen my uncle's eyes stretched so wide, and his trembling bottom lip made me want to laugh in his face.

"You ain't going to get away with this, you little bitch," Darwin spat as he was led past me in handcuffs.

I shrugged. "Whatever," I said, blowing on my nails to signal that I was unbothered by his threat.

"I got something for your ass. They can't keep me but for so long. This ain't no serious crime. I'll be out in a few days. Trust me, you better be gone," he continued.

This time I laughed at him. There would be an order excluding him from Granny Houston's home. For good.

"Ay. Ay. Shut the fuck up making threats," a tall, dark skinned police officer barked at Darwin, tugging on his handcuffs roughly. The cop smiled at me, though. I winked at him.

Darwin seemed to swallow the rest of his words, and it looked like it pained him to do it.

I let out a raucous belly laugh. "Yeah, shut the fuck up," I taunted.

With that, Darwin was gone.

I stretched my arms up over my head and danced through the House for a few minutes. It felt damned good to have him out of my way. I walked down to Granny Houston's room to make sure she was asleep. I twisted the doorknob slowly. I could hear the low hum of her snore. I smiled, stepped back, and quietly closed the door. She had no clue that the cops had just taken her problem off her hands. I set about making her some breakfast. I figured I'd leave it at the side of the bed with her morning medicines and when she was ready, she could just get it. My plan was to take care of Granny Houston, wait until evening when I knew she'd sleep through the night, and make my way to Aisha's.

When I was done taking care of my grandmother, I picked up the cell phone Aisha had given me and dialed her number.

"Hey, girl," Aisha answered.

"Hey, chica. Sorry it took a few days to call. But, I'm finally ready to get things popping," I said.

"Yeah, I thought you had got cold feet and shit," Aisha joked.

"Hell no. I need to do this. But are *you* ready for this setup?" I asked, making sure.

"You already know . . . shit, I was born ready for whatever," Aisha replied.

"So first things first . . . you got this dude's hangout down pat, right?"

We had a plan, but I wanted to make sure our shit was rock solid because it was risky and there was no room for mistakes. This was my last chance to be free.

★ ★ ★

I looked at myself one more time in the big standing mirror that sat behind the guest bedroom door in Aisha's house. Between the blond wig, dark shades, and big hoop earrings, I thought I looked way different than my normal, mostly conservative style.

"Yeah. You look like a regular old street ho. Definitely not like the Karlie they would be looking for," I said to my reflection. I turned to look over my shoulder and check my ass in the dress Aisha had given me. I would've preferred something else, but this would do.

"Girl, you got more booty than I remember," Aisha said from behind me.

I turned around, eyes wide. "Don't sneak up on a bitch. I am jittery as hell as it is."

Aisha laughed. "When haven't you been jittery? I always wondered how you were so jittery and gangsta at the same damn time."

We both laughed this time.

"A'ight, so listen. I was right about the information I gave you. Jay King hangs out at Club Broadway. Girl, they said he loves the hoes. So I got my team ready."

"I could just hug your ass forever and ever," I replied, grabbing my friend tight.

Kanye West's new joint, *Life of Pablo*, pounded through the club's speakers as I got lost in the crowd and played the corner that was not too far from the VIP that I couldn't see but wasn't close enough for anyone to notice me.

Aisha and her little crew of chicks were already out there and in action. I looked out into the club as the partygoers swayed their bodies and moved their hips and feet. I got a sick feeling in my stomach as I remembered the last time Miley, Sidney, and I had gone to the club together. Suddenly I felt weak. I grabbed onto the wall and spoke to myself silently.

Karlie, you have to be strong. This setup tonight is a matter of life and death. Stop it.

Within a few minutes, I felt a little better. I spotted Aisha looking too damn cute. She had let her hair weave loose, and it fell in long auburn coils down her back. The bright white form-fitting jersey dress she wore accentuated all of Aisha's hips and booty. She had on a banging pair of Loubs that made her look model-tall, and a full face of professionally applied makeup.

Aisha had found out that Jay King liked his chicks to look like video vixens, and trust and believe, Aisha and her crew were fitting the part.

I nursed a Hennessy straight as I kept my eyes peeled. Aisha had thought it was too dangerous for me to be out there, but I told her if we were going to make the nigga think she was turning me over to him, I needed to be nearby. I didn't want to drag this operation out.

I spotted Jay King easily. When he first entered the club, the dude seemed to be gliding on air as people moved out of his way like he President Barak Obama. From my view, everybody might as well have bowed down to his feet or something. Jay King was surrounded by at least twelve henchmen, and even from a distance, I could tell this dude had money.

My stomach clenched as I watched him. I balled up my toes in my shoes and clenched my fists so tightly my knuckles paled. This was the bastard that had killed my sister.

I was in a daze thinking about what all I wanted to do to Jay King when a small commotion erupted in the VIP. Jay King was being welcomed by the entire section. I swear this dude was sharper than a politician kissing babies. He was slapping hands and hugging his people. Then several women walked up and kissed him on the cheeks, some grabbed his hand and kissed his pinky ring. I was biting down on my bottom lip, taking it all in. Jay King and his crew were, of course, surrounded by throngs of women and a phalanx of his top men and security.

I watched from afar, but I was so thrown by my anger, I decided to ignore Aisha's plan, and I moved closer to the VIP section. I wanted to hear this dude's voice, watch his movements, learn his habits, and look into his eyes. I moved from my hiding place, and as soon as I did, I suddenly felt a tight grasp on my elbow. My body stiffened and I clutched my purse, where I had Aisha's gun hidden. She had paid a bouncer—that was the only way we could sneak it into the club. I rounded on the person touching me.

"Fuck off me," I growled, barely able to see him with the dark shades I'd kept on as part of my disguise.

"I was just going to ask if I could buy you a drink," the person said, quickly letting go when he saw the angry scowl on my face.

"I don't need a drink, and you don't touch me like that," I spat.

The man threw his hands up and backed away. The little encounter had me shook. I didn't want any attention focused on me.

I could feel the heat of the man's gaze on me as I made my way to an area closer to the VIP section. I was silently scolding myself for reacting so loudly.

I took a seat where I could hear Jay King partying raucously. Women surrounded him as he tossed handfuls of one hundred dollar bills in the air, laughing as the women scrambled around on the floor like hungry dogs trying to grab handfuls of the money.

"Call that one over here. The one with the big Amber Rose ass," Jay King slurred, pointing to Aisha.

Something inside me jumped as I grew excited to see our plan coming together perfectly. Aisha smiled and sauntered over to Jay King.

He grabbed her and pulled her down next to him. He was whispering in her ear and she was giggling. That meant she was going to get to leave with him. That's what we wanted.

I saw Aisha pointing to her crew of hit girls. Jay King's eyes went wide. I guess the possibility of having four beautiful video vixen chicks had made him excited.

"Yo, buy all these bitches their own bottle!" he yelled. Loud laughter followed.

I watched everything until Aisha signaled for me to go to the car. By the time the VIP section was almost cleared out, Jay King could hardly stand. He and Aisha were fondling and licking each other as his crew tried to urge him to leave.

That was my signal. I followed the mass exodus of club goers out the doors toward the parking lot. I made it to the rental we had gotten and climbed in, pulled out the cell phone, and waited for Aisha's text. My hands were shaking with anticipation so badly that when the phone finally vibrated with her text, I almost dropped the damn phone.

YOU CAN GO HOME. ABOUT TO TELL HIM I KNOW WHERE YOU ARE. BE READY FOR THE NEXT STEP TOMORROW AT THE HOTEL LIKE WE PLANNED.

I let out a long, nervous breath. "It's almost over, Karlie. It's almost over. You can do this."

CHAPTER 13

THE DOUBLE CROSS

I got back to the House and immediately knew something wasn't right. I noticed the broken glass on the floor as soon as I walked in. I immediately grabbed the gun out of the bag and held it tightly in my hand. I think I was holding my breath as I moved slowly down the hallways like a cop.

When I made it to my grandmother's door, it was cracked. "Granny?" I called out softly. She wasn't moving, nor did I hear any snoring.

"Granny?" My voice went up a few octaves as I made my way inside. I didn't have to even touch her to know.

"Granny! Granny!" I screamed. I held the gun in one hand and touched her neck with my other hand. I didn't feel any pulse.

"Granny!" I screeched. "No! No!"

"You did this to her. You killed her," a deep voice said from behind me.

I spun around, my gun out in front of me, my body trembling.

"Who?" I started, but then he moved out of the shadows until I was face-to-face with him. I started shaking my head.

He wasn't supposed to be here. I thought I had taken care of him once and for all.

"Surprised to see me? I guess your little plan didn't work," Darwin said, his eyes squinted into dashes.

"I . . . you . . . were gone," I stammered, unable to get my thoughts straight.

"Yeah, that's what you thought. But you see me standing right here like your worst fucking nightmare. Maybe having friends in high places that have bail money lying around ain't so bad," he said, chuckling evilly.

I was speechless. Suddenly my entire body was hot. Things were falling apart right before my eyes.

"Don't be shocked. Be afraid because I'm about to collect a whole bunch of money and then I'll be gone, and you . . . well, I don't know what they'll do with you," he said. He jerked his head toward Granny Houston. "She needed to be put out of her misery anyway. So for that, I want to thank you. If you had never come around here fucking with me and my little hustle, I would've just been here wiping her ass, stealing her measly checks with no prospects of collecting on that hundred-thousand-dollar reward I'm about to get for your ass," Darwin said with no remorse. He had his gun pointing at me.

"Shit. Not again," I mumbled under my breath as sweat beads as big as raindrops ran a race down my forehead and dripped into my eyes. I tried to blink them away as quickly as possible to keep my burning eyes from being closed too long. No second could be spared. I couldn't afford to take my eyes off the piece-of-shit traitor in front of me. I am not sure if it was the anger or the shock or both that had my knees knocking together, but whatever it was, my entire body trembled like a leaf in a wild storm. My heart thrummed so hard I felt like it was sitting outside my chest. I sucked in my breath and squinted. My nostrils flared on their own.

Be tough, Karlie. You've been through worse, I told myself. I had certainly been through some shit over the past six months. My life had always been full of challenges, though. Nothing ever came easy for Karlie Houston. Not even childhood, when shit is supposed to be carefree and fun. I can't remember a time in my life that was free of cares, worries, drama, and just plain old bullshit.

I sometimes wondered why God was punishing me all the time. Abuse, poverty, death, and destruction were the words that summed up my existence.

"I'm not playing with you." I had finally found my voice. But I was immediately mad at myself because my voice was trembling like a scared child, and I couldn't make it stop. I could see the amusement light his ugly face.

"Oh, you think it's funny? You must think I'm some punk bitch. But I'm telling you now, I will do it. I swear to everything I have left and everything I ever loved . . . I will do it. I don't have shit else to lose," I said through my teeth. That was the truth as plain as I could say it. I had nothing left to lose.

The muscles in my arms burned as I kept them extended in front of me, elbows locked, grip tight. The bastard shook his head dismissively and smirked at me like he didn't take me seriously at all.

"What? What you gon' do?" He chuckled evilly. All that was left was for him to stick his tongue out at me, stick his thumbs in his ears, and twist his hands like kids do when they tease each other. Fire flashed in my chest. I had never taken too kindly to being teased.

"Watch and see," I said, shifting on my feet.

"You ain't gon' do shit, that's what. You all talk. You always did think you were smarter than everyone else around you . . . family and friends. Somebody must've lied to your ass, little girl. I'm not one of those simple-minded niggas you can game into doing your dirty work or get over on. You might have had some of those lames by the balls, but me, I'm one step ahead of your ass. You think I don't know how you tried to set me up?

Huh?" he spat, with his face curling into the most evil snarl I'd ever seen. If I didn't know better, I would've thought I was standing face-to-face with Lucifer himself.

"I never liked you, Karlie. All these years, there was always something grimy about you, your trashy-ass mother, and that little bitch sister of yours that I didn't like."

He was still speaking but suddenly I couldn't hear him anymore. Did he just mention my sister? Did he just go there? He knew that was a sore topic for me.

My nostrils flared and I swallowed hard. How fucking dare he say something about Miley? I had always been fiercely protective of my sister, but now, I felt more of a need to defend her name and her honor.

"Shut the fuck up about her," I growled almost breathlessly. "Don't you ever say anything out of your rotten-ass mouth about my sister. You bitch-ass nigga. I swear I will blow your ass away. I don't care who you are."

I could feel my chest heaving. My jaw rocked feverishly as I tried to hold on to my composure. I didn't want any more bloodshed. I really didn't. That was the only reason he was still alive. I was tired of death and destruction around me. But, that didn't mean that I wouldn't do what I had to do. Especially if it meant the difference between me coming out of this alive or him leaving in a body bag.

"Oh, does the truth hurt?" he snarled. "You don't like anyone to tell you the truth? You don't like to hear that you and your sister were two scandalous bitches that got everything y'all deserved? From the time y'all were kids doing sneaky shit to get over, stealing money, stealing food, I knew y'all would grow up to be just like your mother . . . a piece of shit."

"Shut up," I said in an eerily calm voice. My voice completely contradicted the raging inferno burning inside me. I don't know why I was so calm and that scared me more than he did.

Unlike mine, his extended arm didn't waver or shake. His aim was steady. Sure. Purposeful.

"Nah, I'm going to tell it. You don't think y'all got what was coming after years of scandal?"

I swallowed hard again, but the lump in my throat just wouldn't go away. I shifted my weight from one foot to the other. I was going to have to kill this nigga. I could feel it all down in my bones. It was going to be him or me.

"All I want is for you to leave. We can call it fair. You did some shit and I did some shit. It's a draw. You walk away, I walk away. End this. Nobody has to get hurt. Ain't nothing else to prove." I still spoke calmly, another last-ditch effort to end this shit without death. My insides were going so crazy—churning stomach, racing heart. I felt like I'd throw up any minute. This wasn't my first time facing down death, but that didn't make it easy to deal with. I had watched everything and everyone around me get destroyed. Suddenly my sister Miley's face flashed through my mind. Her sweet smile. Her laughter. Even her annoying nagging when she was being spoiled.

I could also hear Sidney's voice in my ear . . . *I love you, baby. Just be careful. Let me take care of you.* He used to say that all the time.

I felt my knees buckle a little bit. If I could have just lain down and curled into a ball and cried for hours, I would have. Some people would say what was happening at the moment was karma for some of the things I'd done in my lifetime, but I say fuck karma—everything that happened and what was happening now was because of evil motherfuckers like the one I was standing in front of at the moment. I had learned the hard way that evil exists in human form, and I was surrounded by it. I was confronted by it. It was a part of my own family. And I was going to either destroy it or be destroyed by it.

"So what's it gonna be, Karlie? Giving up?" he asked, his gun pointing right at my forehead.

"Hmph," I scoffed and bit down hard into my bottom lip. I adjusted my grip on my gun, which was now pointing directly at his heart. "Nigga, please. You better give up. You better try and end this if you know what's good for you."

He shook his head.

It was a standoff. A duel. A draw. One thing was for sure, at least one of us was not going to walk away from this.

"End this? Nah, baby girl. You can't start some shit and then think you can just end it. See, in the streets and in life, when you start something, you ain't got no choice but to see it through," he replied. Then he cocked the hammer on his gun.

"A'ight. Suit yourself, motherfucker," I spat, sliding my right pointer finger into the trigger guard of my Glock. He laughed again, an evil cackling laugh that caused tight goose bumps to crop up on my body.

"I'll see you in hell, bi—" he started to say. That was enough . . .

BOOM. BOOM. BOOM.

I fell backward. My ears were ringing. Neither one of us uttered another word. The smell of the gunpowder immediately settled at the back of my throat. I coughed. I gurgled. I was suddenly freezing cold and then hot again. I couldn't breathe.

How did it all come to this? Why? Why me?

That was the last thing I remember thinking before the darkness engulfed me.

I don't know how long I was out of it before I heard a voice calling out to me, "Karlie. Karlie, wake up."

I groaned but realized I was still alive. I was dazed and confused, and everything around me was blurry.

"Karlie, we have to go. It's time."

"Isha?"

"Yes, girl. I had to use the damn Find My iPhone service to find you. We have to get out of here. That man is dead," Aisha urged.

She helped me up from the floor. I saw Darwin lying there bleeding from his chest, and I wanted to throw up.

"Oh my God." I cupped my hand over my mouth.

"That's what I said when I got here. But we have to go. Jay King is going to give me the money as soon as he can verify that you're at the hotel we set up. He's probably going to send his guys, that's why I got the girls keeping him busy with lots of pussy and drinks. Soon as they get the text from me, that nigga going to be done off," Aisha informed me.

"You're a lifesaver girl," I said.

I paced around the hotel room waiting for Aisha's call. Her dudes were in the adjoining room next to mine waiting too and she had about six others outside posted up. This was going down ambush style, but not until after Aisha had her hands on the money.

I jumped when the cell phone vibrated on the table. I rushed over and picked it up.

EVERYTHING IS IN PLACE. HE'S SENDING SIX DUDES FOR YOU. BE READY.

I stood still and said a quick prayer. "Lord, I know that I have done some things in my life that weren't worthy of your mercy, but if you let me make it out of this one, I promise that I will live righteously from now on. Please show me your mercy! Amen."

CHAPTER 14

LET'S TALK ABOUT FREEDOM

"Agggh!" I belched out a scream in response to the hotel door being busted open. Although I was expecting them, it still rattled me and almost gave me a heart attack. With my mind fuzzy and confused, I was on my feet within seconds. With a quickness I slid my hand to my waist and locked it around my gun. I took a deep breath.

It was only a matter of seconds before Jay King's goons were flooding into the room.

"Grab that bitch!" one of the goons growled as the other men barged in. Aisha's boys were right on time. Like something out of a movie, all of her dudes came from the adjoining room.

"She got a gun!" one of Jay King's men screeched.

"Yo! It's a setup," another one of his men yelled. It was too late for all of that. The lead goon's eyes went wide and his jaw dropped.

"I told you we needed to have more guns," another one of the men said as Aisha's men rounded on them and put their guns to Jay King's goons' heads so fast there was no running, hiding, or reacting. They were caught off guard, just how Aisha and I had planned.

"The boss said it was one little chick. I guess he got caught fucking slipping," one of Jay King's goons said, his hands raised above his head.

I took a long-barrel gun with a silencer from one of Aisha's men and gave him my gun.

"Nah, tell your boss I'm not one little chick, I am a big woman," I said, smiling. Then, without hesitation, I let off one shot into the chest of the leader of the goons. He collapsed to the floor like a deflated balloon. I saw everyone in the room react, even Aisha's men. No one was expecting that, not even me. I don't know what it was that took over me, but it was dark and it seemed to be controlling my actions. I was no longer a scared, cowering chick who had lost her sister and boyfriend and was running and hiding. I was a bitch out for revenge.

I stood over my victim with my chest pumping up and down and the gun still gripped in my hand.

"What the fuck?" Several of the men in the room had the same reaction. All of them seemed to pause with shock.

"I recognize you from the shooting that killed my sister. I can never forget a voice or a face. Die slow, you bastard," I growled as the goon writhed on the floor. I could've let off another shot and ended him, but I wanted him to suffer in pain. Suddenly the sound of my sister gasping for air flooded to the front of my mind. I had to fight back tears. There would be no signs of weakness shown in front of all of those men. I set my jaw, turned, and leveled my gun at Jay King's other cowering flunkies.

"Now, anybody else want to take a chance and fucking play with me? Jay King sent y'all, so that's who y'all blame when your mothers and kids gotta slow sing and flower bring at your funerals. Just like y'all didn't show my family no mercy, I don't give a fuck about yours," I said through my teeth. None of the men said anything, but one of them released his bladder all over himself. I guess he was their weakest link. Seeing that type of fear in a man did something to me inside. I didn't recognize the ruthless person I was becoming. I knew then that I had nothing left inside me. I had lost my mother, my sister, and even my grandmother, who I never thought I'd care about. I was a changed woman, and not for the better.

"Take this one's cell phone and make him call Jay King and tell him they have me so that he will give the bounty money to Aisha," I demanded of one of Aisha's men. Even those dudes looked like they were leery of my unpredictable actions.

"And don't try no funny shit when you make the call, or you'll get what he got," I said to Jay King's guy, placing the gun with the silencer to his head.

"Yo, boss," Jay King's guy said into the phone.

I could hear a little bit of fear and cracking in his voice, so I bent close to his free ear. "Make it sound convincing," I whispered harshly.

"Yeah, we got the bitch. Nah, she ain't know we was coming. A'ight, I'll meet you at the warehouse. One."

I stood up and clapped as I circled the dude. "Very good. You deserve an Academy Award. I guess the plan was to take me back to where the Kings torture their enemies. Naw, been there, done that," I said.

After the call was made, I waited for Aisha's text telling me she had the money and her all-girl crew also had Jay King. Shit was really happening the way we planned. But still, I wasn't satisfied. I needed more. I wanted more.

"Check their pockets and take all of their shit. Then tie them up. We need to get out of here like now," I commanded Aisha's men. They were probably tired of me bossing them around, but they also knew they were getting paid at the end of this whole thing so they dutifully did as they were told. I was trying my best to keep control of my galloping heart and the fire raging inside me.

"A'ight . . . now you." I pointed the long barrel of the gun in the face of one of Jay King's men. This one looked like he was maybe second in command. His scowling face and pursed lips told me that if he had the chance, he would probably rip my head off and shit down my neck. I chose him just because I knew it would piss him off even more. I placed the gun to his temple. I was sure the cold kiss of the steel would unnerve him.

"Tell me where all of the stash houses are located, where he keeps his money and what days he does his cash drops."

The dude sucked his teeth and chuckled like I was a big joke.

"Fuck I look like, snitching like that," he gritted, his face still folded into a frown. "You ain't getting away with this shit. You don't know who you fucking with. You might feel like you're Griselda Blanco or some shit right now, but you done fucked up. You done fucked up royally," he replied.

His words enraged me even more, but a pang of fear also flitted through me. "Oh, okay. So you're not going to answer my question?" I pressed the metal into his skin. He didn't say anything.

"Well then, I guess y'all bitch-ass niggas don't wanna live either."

"Fuck y—" the man started.

A point-blank shot to the temple sent blood and brain matter bursting out of the other side of his head. His body fell forward. The smell of the blood almost gagged me. The piss-stained coward to the left of him fell to his knees and began gagging like he was going to throw up.

"Please . . . please don't kill me. I'll tell you where the stash houses is at. I'll tell you where he lives. I'll tell you everything. Just let me go. I got kids. I got a family. I'm just out here trying to eat," the pissy one begged, tears falling from his eyes like a bitch.

"I'm listening," I gritted, the gun dangling at my side. I didn't feel one ounce of sympathy for anyone who worked for my sister's killer. I felt as powerful as King Kong at that moment. I smelled so much fear on the fake goon that I didn't even feel the need to keep my gun pointed at him.

"There's one on . . . on . . ." the man stammered. I nodded toward one of Aisha's men and he grabbed the hotel pad and pen and started writing. We weren't just going to collect the bounty that was on my head, but we were going to hit those fucking stash houses too. With the crew Aisha had put together, the hundred-thousand-dollar bounty from Jay King wasn't going to be enough to pay everybody a decent amount. But knowing we could raid his cash and drugs made it all worth it. Aisha's dudes were all ears. For those petty street corner dudes, finding out a plug's stash houses was like winning the lottery when the jackpot had doubled.

While we were planning this hit on Jay King and his people, Aisha and I had discussed all sorts of things that we would do with the money after we split it with Aisha and her people. She said she would buy a bigger, better house and just lay low for a while. I had told her she was damn crazy to even want to stay in Virginia. I wasn't here for that. The first thing I planned to do was get the fuck out of the United States. There was nothing left here for me. Moving to another state wasn't even going to be enough. I wanted out of the country. Period. I didn't tell Aisha, but I was going to be ghost. I was going to find somewhere to go, change my name and change my entire life. Maybe I'd move to Barbados or the Bahamas. Some place I could disappear onto a beach and never worry about anything again. I had made it up in my mind that I had suffered enough. I had seen enough death and destruction for ten lifetimes. All I wanted was peace. But not until I got rid of my problem . . . Jay King and his people.

"What scares Jay King the most?" I asked the terrified dude who'd just given away all of his boss's locations.

"Lose . . . losing . . . his power and his family. He doesn't like that you crossed his family, and he . . . um . . . he can't stand to lose power and control," the man stammered.

"Losing my family was the same thing that scared me the most, and guess what? Now I don't have any family thanks to him and motherfuckers like you," I said with finality. "I ain't got shit else to lose." The man put his hands up, but it was too late. One last shot and I was done.

With my nerves on edge, Aisha's men and I fled the scene. We had one more stop to make before this nightmare would finally be over and I'd finally be free.

When I arrived at the spot and walked into that room, I felt even more powerful. I smiled and shook my head.

"Damn. Y'all wasn't playing," I said in awe, almost whispering.

Those chicks Aisha had gotten down with us had Jay King drugged and bound to the bed. Even his ankles were tied. Totally vulnerable and helpless. Far from the big, bad gangster Detective Castle made Jay King out to be.

"Isha, you're one bad bitch," I said, complimenting her. "I knew if anyone could help me pull this shit off, it would be you."

"Let's just get this over with. It's not going to be long before the rest of his people start scouring the city for him. Not only that, I already heard you got gun happy, Karlie. That wasn't supposed to happen. We were supposed to tie those niggas up, leave them there, and get the hell out. I ain't want to have to worry about bodies piling up." Aisha was annoyed.

"I couldn't help it. You don't understand what it was like for me to lose my sister," I replied. "It just happened. It wasn't part of the plan, but sometimes shit happens."

Aisha sighed and shook her head. "Let's just do this. He's all yours. I already got the money," she said, pointing to a black leather carryall bag dangling by the handles from her left hand. With that, she walked into the other room of Jay King's suite.

I was alone with my number one enemy. My heart throttled up in my chest. I walked over to the side of the bed and slapped Jay King's face with all of the strength I could muster. It was a few seconds before he came alive from his deep, drug-induced slumber.

"Mmm. Mmmm," he moaned, trying in vain to fight the unknown force holding him down. The bandana that had been shoved between his lips kept him from speaking. But I could see the scrunch of his eyebrows and knew he was angry that he'd gotten caught out there like this—naked and afraid.

"Ahh, payback is a bitch, ain't it," I whispered, with an evil grimace tugging at the corners of my mouth. I snatched off my wig and my shades. No more disguises were needed. I wanted him to know exactly who had him helpless and at her mercy.

"Yup, it's me. The girl you thought you would have coming here in chains so you could kill me once and for all. I guess you were the one who got fooled, huh?"

Jay King's eyes went wide and he flailed against the handcuffs, moaning and grunting. I was amused. It was like something out of a movie when the captured person knew they were going to die and tried in vain to beg for their life.

"Surprised to see me?" I teased.

He grunted.

"Good. You should be. Because you're about to get the surprise of your fucking life," I said.

Jay King was hissing and spitting behind the gag. He was moving his head from side to side and I could see veins popping at the sides of his temples and in his neck. He was straining to get at me. Poor thing. He was as helpless as a newborn baby at the moment. Right where I wanted him to be.

I laughed at him. "You're probably making all kinds of threats behind that gag, huh? Well, your threats don't mean shit to me. I know who you're supposed to be, some dangerous drug kingpin from some dangerous family, but right now, you're a weak-ass murderer about to get it," I said, running my gun down the side of his face.

"Aww, look at you. The powerful Jay King. Stupid ass. You're so bad you let some dirty street pussy from four hood chicks with Brazilian bundles in their heads and fake-ass shot asses get you in a vulnerable position like this. Mmm, mmm, mmm. They always say pussy would take down the most powerful men in the world. I guess it brings life and also is the cause for life to be taken away. I wonder what your big, bad family members, the Kings, will say about this when they get word that you feel for the oldest kind of setup in the world . . . the pussy trap," I said, placing my gun on Jay King's right eye.

"Should I shoot you here?" I said. Then I moved my gun to the center of his forehead. "Or here? Nah, maybe here." I placed the barrel over his crotch. "Naw. I think I'll shoot you in all of the spots that my sister got shot."

He tried to buck his body and was breathing hard against the gag. Sweat was dripping down his face and snot was rimming his nostrils as they opened and closed rapidly like a raging bull's.

"So you're the one who ordered the hit on me and my sister and then put a bounty out on my head, huh?" I asked, knowing the answer to my own questions. Jay King closed his eyes and went completely still. For some reason that infuriated me even more.

"Don't fucking act like you're giving up now. Nah, I want to see you look at me. I want to see the fear in your eyes. I want you to beg for your life like me and my sister did at the hands of your cousin," I gritted. I felt a wave of emotion sweep over me.

He ignored me and lay still. I bit down into my jaw, raised the gun, and cracked it over his head. That woke his ass up. His eye opened with shock and I could see fire flashing in them. He began moving wildly like he wanted to grab me, but his efforts were to no avail. I looked down at him and smiled as I stared right into his eyes. We exchanged evil glares, but I was the first to see a tiny glimpse of fear dancing behind his eyes. And that fueled my wrath even more.

"I love watching your stomach clench and your muscles tense. I love the thought of you thinking, *if I could just get to that bitch, I'd torture her and kill her and make an example out of her*. Is that what you're thinking?" I taunted. I laughed. "I love the message this will send to your cousin, El Jefe. What will he think when word gets back to him that you were found . . . dead."

Jay King began trying to speak through the material of the tie.

"Oh, you want to tell me something?" I asked. I wanted to hear what he had to say . . . his last words. I pulled the gag from his mouth.

"You stupid bitch. You think I was your only problem? You think I was the only one that wanted you and your sister gone? You fucked up a lot of people's money. You stepped into some shit you have no idea about. Oh yeah, it goes deeper than my family. You think it was a coincidence that we knew exactly when you and your sister were getting released? Think about it. You may have me here, but you'll never beat the biggest gang in America. Think about that," Jay King said, his tone raspy and evil.

His words cut through me. The entire place had taken on a red-tinged hue like someone had pulled a red veil over my eyes.

"Fuck you. You killed my sister," I gritted.

"That's what you think. You should check the people you thought had your back," he said.

That was it. He was talking shit to try and save himself.

"Nah, there's nothing else to discuss," I said callously. I stepped back a little bit and aimed at his head. He closed his eyes again, like he had accepted his fate. His words were still swirling in my head.

"My grandmother once told me that only evil could wipe

out evil. So maybe I'm evil," I said in an eerie, crazy-girl voice like a deranged character from a scary movie. With that, I let off two shots that ended his life.

The blood splatter, the smell, the reality, my losses, my life . . . everything came down on me at once like a heavy lead anvil had fallen on my head. My legs gave out and I finally dropped the gun and collapsed to the floor with racking sobs.

"Miley, I did it for you. I got them back. We are free. We are finally free," I cried.

I was finally free. Or so I thought.

CHAPTER 15

THE REAL DEVIL IN SHEEP'S CLOTHING

We laid low at an out-of-town hotel for three days. Aisha's dudes went about their business raiding every single one of the Kings' stash houses. Jay King's people didn't see them coming. They had been caught totally off guard, especially at their super-secret spots. One of Aisha's guys, a dude named Ali, ended up dead behind the stash house robberies. I guess after six or seven hits, King's guys had gotten hip and were waiting for Aisha's peoples to arrive. It was a shame Ali had to die. I thought the crew would've been shaken up, but Aisha didn't seemed fazed by his death at all. In fact, she shrugged her shoulders, poured out a little Hennessy in Ali's honor, and told me it was all part of the life he'd chosen. "Live by it. Die by it," she'd said.

I thought that was some cold-ass shit to say. But I also knew it was true.

On day three, it was finally time to be on my way. I threw the last of my cash into my bag.

"I think that's it," I said, letting out a long, relieved sigh afterward. "We did good, girl. We did good." I hugged Aisha tight and she returned the embrace. "You came through for me big time, Isha. I will never forget all that you did for me. You literally put yourself at risk to help me save my own life and avenge my sister's death. There are not many people out here that would ride for their friend like that. And I really don't have many people who ever cared for me enough to do anything like this for me. You're a rare breed girl, trust me," I said with sincerity as Aisha and I moved out of our embrace.

"Oh please." Aisha waved at me with tears starting to well up in her eyes.

It was rare to see Aisha cry. So I knew I had tugged at her heartstrings with my little speech.

"I been getting your ass out of shit since we were eight years old. Why would anything be different now," Aisha joked. We both busted out laughing.

"You damn right about that," I agreed, still cracking up. "For real though, Isha. From third grade to our thirties. And even through all of our ups and downs you never stopped being a true friend."

"No, but on a serious note, Karlie, it was worth it for me. I've been looking for a quick come up, and it was like God had answered my prayers when you showed up at my door in the middle of the night talking about you needed my help. Our brains together was a dangerous combination on that plan . . . it all paid the hell off lovely," she replied, looking down at the coffee table covered with the stacks of cash that was her portion of the take.

"Lovely," I agreed, picking up my bag of money from the table. "Anyway girl. I got to hit the road. I can't stay around here another day. Just too many memories and too much shit going on. I wish you were leaving too," I said.

"Nah, boo. This gonna be where I live forever," she said.

"A'ight, girl. Then this is see you later, because goodbye seems too final. I don't know where I'll end up, but I know I won't be coming back. I don't have anything left here. I'll keep in touch and maybe you'll come see me on some island somewhere," I said, lowering my eyes.

Aisha gave me another hug. "You know I will. Be safe, Karlie."

I had to turn away before my tears started spilling. For real, leaving Aisha felt too final. The thought of being alone again caused a hard lump to form in my throat. I swallowed hard, got my head together, and walked out of the hotel. As soon as I opened the car door, I dumped my bag on the floor of the rented Chevy Impala she had gotten for me with her friend's credit card. I was still leery, so I didn't want to do anything in my name except use my passport to get the hell out of the country.

I slid behind the steering wheel, clutched it tightly, and let out a windstorm of breath. I looked up into the rearview mirror at my reflection and parted a sly smile. "You did it, Karlie. You fucking did it," I said to my reflection.

I finally put the car in drive and stepped on the gas.

WHAM!

I didn't have time to say another word or to even react. My body bucked forward so hard that my head hit the steering wheel and lurched back against the headrest. The force of the blow sent a searing pain through my skull, and my teeth slammed down on my tongue so hard my mouth immediately filled with blood.

My head felt so heavy, I couldn't keep it up. I was dazed and confused, but I felt the driver's side door swing open. The next thing I knew, I was being dragged from the car. I opened my mouth to scream, but the sound wouldn't come. Suddenly I couldn't breathe. There was a huge, meaty, sweaty hand covering my nose and mouth. I started kicking my legs, but I was no match for whoever had me. I was going to keep fighting until a hard hit in my chest caused me to cease all movement.

I felt like everything around me was spinning. I felt the black bag being placed over my head.

Suddenly I felt myself being thrown down onto something metal. I heard a door slam shut. I could hear feet shuffling next to my head.

"Well, Karlie Houston, you just don't learn, do you?" I heard the muffled sound of a man's voice.

"I tried to warn you. I tried to protect you. I tried to get you out of the fray. No one would've ever found you. But you . . . you just wouldn't fade away. You couldn't stop making waves," the voice said.

My heart began slamming in my chest.

"De—" I started to say. But a blow to my ribs sent my words tumbling back down my throat like I'd tried to swallow a handful of hard marbles.

"Shhh. Don't say another word. You've done and said enough already. I had a good thing going, but you came along and fucked it all up. I was so nice to you. I even saved you the first time to make it all look good. I had people I had to report to and I couldn't risk losing everything. Okay, so you didn't die with the hit at the hospital . . . I moved on to plan B, and you still fucked it up. Then I got your stupid, punk-ass uncle out of jail when you got rid of him. I gave that dumb bastard a clean gun so he could get rid of you, and he was completely incompetent. I kept saying to myself, how does this girl keep getting around all of my plans? At that point, you had pissed me off. You just didn't listen."

"Detective Castle?" I managed to say.

He laughed. "Yeah, that's what you know me as, but really, I'm the leader of the biggest gang in America . . . the crooked cops club," he replied. "I hope you had a good last moment with your friend Aisha. She's now joined your sister in the afterlife."

"Oh my God," I gasped. I couldn't believe my ears. Detective Castle was crooked the whole time? That couldn't be right. There was no way. He had helped me go into hiding. He had helped me bury my sister. He had protected me and saved our lives. I was in shock. My body began trembling fiercely.

"How?"

"There was something about you I liked, so I tried to be official with you. I tried and tried to keep you away. But Karlie Houston is a badass and didn't want to just let bygones be bygones. You fucked up my money. Jay King and I had decided to get rid of his cousin Ashton together, so I busted in and saved you from him and there was enough from that to send him away. Then we figured we'd get rid of you and your sister and Sidney, but you happened to survive the hit. Then we decided to send you away. Just let it ride. It was too risky to keep trying to kill you. But then you started snooping around. Then I tried to use your worthless uncle, but you were smarter than him. Then you joined forces and caught Jay slipping, but I was following you. I decided to let you get him out of the picture so that all of the money would be mine. With him gone, I could make a deal with his family in Jamaica. So you see, Karlie, you kept butting in my business. Now you'll suffer the consequences," Detective Castle said.

"Why? I . . . I . . . was leaving for good," I croaked, my words muffled by the hood.

"You didn't leave fast enough. I guess you can say I'm the real devil in sheep's clothing," he said.

WHO CAN YOU TRUST?

Saundra

CHAPTER 1

Glancing over my left shoulder, I fixed my eyes on the Metal Fusion clock attached to the wall and smiled. It read 2:30 p.m., and I couldn't have been happier.

"Hmmm, I see you watching that clock like a hawk. You glad you don't have to close up tonight, huh?" Judy asks.

"Yes. I swear, three o'clock is not approaching fast enough. It's nice outside and I can't wait to be out in these Oakland streets. Matter of fact, I'm only going to take one more person before I start shutting it down."

"I know, right." Judy smiled, then greeted her next customer as they stepped up to the counter.

"I can help you right over here." I greeted the next lady in line.

"Thank you." She smiled as she approached. "I need to make a deposit."

"Sure, I can help you with that, Mrs. . . ." I trailed off. I wasn't familiar with her, so I used the lead-the-customer strategy.

"Yazz . . . Yazz Armstrong."

"Yazz, hmm that's unique." I notice right away that she had an accent. Not necessarily a country one, but she definitely was not from Oakland.

"I get that a lot since I've been here," she volunteered.

"Where you from?" I pried.

"St. Louis, Missouri, born and raised. I moved here a year ago. And I am not used to it yet." She chuckled; pulling a deposit bag from her Coach purse, she carefully removed a stack of bills.

"Well, you'll get used to it. At least I hope so. The people are somewhat impossible," I joked. "I love that blouse you have on. Where did you get it?" I hoped I was not being too nosy. But I loved clothes.

"From my boutique."

"You own your own boutique?"

"Yeah, see?" She held up her deposit bag. It read *Yazz Couture*.

"That's what's up." I loved to see young black women doing big things. It gave me hope. "So what brings you to Oakland?" The smile on her face faded. I realized that I had gone too far, but it was too late to take it back. "Listen, my bad." I attempted to apologize.

"Aye, it's cool." She passed me the deposit slip. I quickly counted the cash, typed in her information, and handed her a deposit receipt. "Tell you what, why you don't stop by and check out my boutique." She handed me a one of her business cards. I swiftly glanced at the artwork.

"Thanks, Yazz. I'll stop through and bring my best friend Briana."

I wasn't sure if it was something I had just said, but a sadness seem to take over. She quickly tried to replace it with a forced smile, but it was too late, I had seen it. "You do that." And with that she was out.

I watched her exit. She seemed like cool people, but there was something bothering her. Either way, it was none of my business and time for me to get off. Hunching my shoulders I made myself a mental note to check out *Yazz Couture*. For safekeeping I stuck the card in the pocket of my suit jacket.

Grabbing my deposit money bag, I filled it with the cash from my drawer. Next, I grabbed all of my bank slips, then sent my daily report to the printer. Heading toward the cash count office where everyone did their end-of-the-day count, I stopped off at the printer and retrieved my report.

With a huge smile on my face I pushed open the door of Bryers Savings and Loans Bank, where I had worked for the last two years. Recently, I had been promoted from plain old bank teller to lead teller specialist. So instead of me working a full six- to eight-hour shift, most days I worked a ten- to twelve-hour shift opening or closing the bank. Basically, I was given all the responsibility of the branch manager but less pay. However, I did receive a nice raise, which was a plus.

Outside in the heat I all but skipped to my car, jumped inside, and turned up the radio so that *Lemonade* by Beyoncé could blast out of the speakers. Speeding out of the parking lot, I headed toward Lockwood Gardens. That was the public housing addition where my best friend Briana aka Bri resided. East Oakland was where we were both born and raised, for better or for worse. The only difference was I lived in a house.

Leaning on the horn so that Briana would know I had arrived, I reached over to the passenger side, grabbed my purse and pulled out my MAC lip gloss, and applied it to my lips.

"Damn, I was about to call you. Got me window lurking. You ten minutes late," Briana complained as she settled into the front seat.

"Bri, really? I came here as soon as I got off. You have no patience. Get your nerves right, girl," I joked while pushing the gearshift into drive.

"You know a bitch been cooped up in that house all day with Kat." She referred to her mother. Briana and her mother Kat were like night and day—they never agreed on anything.

"You two know you can't live without each other." I laughed.

"I guess. You know she ain't havin' me move out." Briana chuckled. "And what's up with this radio?" Pulling out her iPhone, Briana swiftly connected it to my aux cord and put her Pandora on Future station. Soon Future's "Low Life" was blasting out of the speakers. "Now, that's my shit." Briana threw her hands in the air.

I smiled. I loved my friend; she kept me in good spirits at all times. "I wasn't feelin' it at first, real talk. I'm starting to like it, though. I would like it even better if he would stop beefing with Ciara," I threw in.

"If they got rid of Facebook and Twitter they could squash that shit. Social Media could ruin a wet dream." Briana kept it real.

Pulling into the lot where Hair Plus was located, I searched for a close parking space. The less distance between us and the store, the less panhandling we would have to deal with. Bums hung out in droves in shopping centers and corner stores in East Oakland.

Briana reached over and turned down the music. I knew then something was up. "Speaking of beef, I am so done with your boy Ronnie. He got me so fucked up, I swear," she declared.

"What now?" I sighed as I shut off the ignition. Ronnie was Briana's on-and-off-again boyfriend for the past three years—more off than on because there was always some drama between them, but they always seemed to find their way back to each other. In my eyes he was a straight bum, still running the streets with his boys selling nickel sacks. I was so over him. Hopefully, whatever she was about to say would mean she had finally seen the light. But I wouldn't get my hopes up. That nigga had done some foul shit and she had forgiven him.

Briana twisted her mouth up like she tasted something sour. "This time he got some basic bitch callin' my phone, talking about they have a six-month-old daughter." Briana's neck rolled as if it was on a swivel.

This time my neck snapped. "What?" I wasn't surprised but outdone. Ronnie never seemed to amaze me when it came to bullshit and beyond.

"I told that hood rat good luck and to lose my mother-fucking number. These hoes is crazy. And I'm done smacking bitches over his ass. Then I called him and cursed him out. And just so he wouldn't forget, I reminded him that he was a peon and bag boy. Bitch-ass nigga." she sighed. "I told him to jump in front of a speeding car. And I meant it. I'm done with him. Ugh!" She was pissed. But there were no tears, and something about the calm but pissed look on her face told me she was possibly serious this time. Having a whole baby was a new low even for Ronnie.

Inside the store we headed straight for the hair. "So what did he have to say?" I was curious.

Twisting up the corner of her mouth, Briana looked at me. "Porsha, you already know. That the baby is not his." She shook her head. "And you know that nigga probably lyin'. Either way, I'm done. He has finally gotten on my last nerve. Nigga doing everything possible to pull me down in the gutter wit him."

"Well, I hope you for real this time." I sighed. I was cele-brating inside, but I didn't want to see her hurt. "Real talk, though. Are you okay? Because if you ain't, you will be."

"I promise you, I'm straight, Porsha. Now let's get this hair." Briana was the baddest freestyle do-it-at-home hairstylist in the hood. There was no one in East Oakland that could step to her with hair game. She was the best, hands down. And she didn't take no shit from anyone either. Come out your mouth slick at Briana and her fist was going in your mouth. I, on the other hand, was a bit more reserved. But not to get it twisted, I was no punk. I would get in that ass too. Maybe just not as fast as Briana, though.

After dropping Briana back off at her crib, it was time for me to head home. "Hey, Ma," I said as I entered the front door, which led straight into the living room.

"Hey." She silently shifted her weight to her left elbow and tightened her robe that she appeared to be already snugly wrapped in as she watched *Good Times* on television.

"What'd you do today?" I dropped my purse on the coffee table next to the empty love seat.

"Nothing. I had this awful headache that just would not quit. I took some extra-strength Excedrin."

"So you good now?" I leaned down and kissed her on the forehead.

"Yep," she answered, her eyes never leaving the television.

Thirsty, I headed toward the kitchen, where I was greeted with the smell of no food and darkness. For the past two years this had become the norm. I could remember coming home to sweet potatoes simmering in the pot, fried chicken in piping-hot grease, and Marvin Gaye playing softly in the background. The icing on the cake was my mother, whose name was Jennifer, always had a welcoming smile plastered on her beautiful face. But that had all changed a little over two years ago when my older brother Kenneth had been murdered. I can remember like it was yesterday. It was my first year at community college. We had never had a lot of money, but we did okay. Ma had a job as a LPN, and I had plans of becoming a registered nurse. Kenneth, though, he was on a different path—always had been. Smart as a whip, he declared that school just wasn't for him. Without a male figure in his life, he took to the streets of Oakland dealing like a baby took to a bottle of formula. Making quick money and driving nice cars was how he chose to live his life. And to be honest, he was good at it. He wanted to move us up out of the hood into the suburbs, but Ma would not have it. She refused to have anything to do with the lifestyle his drug money afforded. In spite of how deep he was in the game she still believed she could save him. But then the reality of being the mother of a drug dealer in the dog-eat-dog world of Oakland kicked in, in the form of a phone call. Kenneth was dead. He had been murdered in broad daylight. And no one had seen a thing. Ma's life shut down shortly after the funeral. She refused to leave the house. She stopped working all together. Kenneth had left a safe full of money, but I came home from school to find out she had donated the money, which she referred to as "blood money," to the Salvation Army. I was pissed. But I loved my mother and the last thing I wanted to do was upset her any more than she already was. She had suffered enough. So to pay the bills, I had to quit school. I found a job and went to work full-time. The plan was I'd just work until Ma was better so that she could get back to work.

But here we were two years later, and she was not back working yet. I was not giving up on her, though; I had faith. Back in the living room I smiled as she laughed at James on *Good Times* as he threatened to slap Mad Dog. Like I said, I was not going to give up on her. A year ago you couldn't get her to laugh at anything. Things were moving along, it was just taking time.

"Ma, get dressed and let's go for Japanese?" I was hungry, and Japanese food happened to be one of my favorites.

"Not tonight, Porsha. I don't feel like it. Besides, I had a bowl of Froot Loops not long ago."

"Ma, really? You can't be serious. That's not food."

"I know, Porsha, I'm just not in the mood. Even more I don't feel like putting on clothes." This time she looked at me with puppy dog eyes.

"A'ight." I gave in. I didn't want to force her. "Tell you what. How about I order up some takeout? How about Italian? Some lasagna and garlic bread from Mazzo's?" Just mentioning it made my stomach growl.

"Yeah, that does sound good." She smiled.

"Mazzo's it is, then." Grabbing my cell, I scrolled down my contacts for Mazzo's. I kept them on speed dial. They had some of the best Italian food around. Even better, they still delivered in the hood. East Oakland was no joke. Life was real at all times.

CHAPTER 2

"Thanks, Mrs. Rasrio. Enjoy the rest of your day." I pushed the send button to send her deposit receipt back down the chute. The drive-through was busy. It was the first of the month, which meant nonstop traffic inside and outside. The only difference was the outside people didn't get upset as fast as the people who came inside. Either way, I worked swiftly to keep a steady pace. Taking a breather for a second, one glance at the clock reminded me that lunchtime quickly approached. I signaled Sheila, one of the tellers, to take over for me at the window.

"What's up?" she asked.

"Take over the drive-through while I send Judy to lunch." Being a lead, I had to make sure my team went to lunch before I could even think about going.

"Sure." Sheila stepped over to the drive-through and greeted the next car right away. One of the slower tellers, she would do better on the drive-through; Judy was one of my faster tellers, so I would have to cover her spot while she was at lunch. Sheila would be overwhelmed by the crowd, and I needed at least two strong people on the front end.

"You can close up for lunch." I stepped into the booth next to Judy and asked the next person in line how I could help them. April was standing to the left of me. She was another one of the faster bank tellers. Her only problem was time. She was always late, normally only by a minute or so, but the girl could never seem to make it on time. I was always giving her pep talks, hoping she would get it together. And April was a good worker. The last thing I needed was her getting fired, because there was no way in hell I could work more hours than I already did. I liked working for Bryers Savings and Loans, but they were not quick about the hiring process, not to mention they were all about saving the company money. Now, Judy was dependable and had lead status, but she would check a customer quick if they said or did anything she didn't like or she thought was disrespectful. I had to constantly remind her that the customer was always right.

Sheila, well, she was just slow. Her customer service skills were impeccable, but she could piss a customer off quick taking too long to process their request. Other than that, I loved my team. But most of all, I just wanted back in school.

"Porsha." Sheila said my name just loud enough to get my attention. Turning to face her, I almost stepped on her feet. I had no idea she had closed in on me that quick.

"This guy." She handed me his ID. "He has his own account here, but he wants to cash his check, then put the deposit into his wife's account. I told him that she has to show her ID in order for me to access her account. But he refuses to listen."

I hated when clients chose to be stubborn. Quickly studying the number of people waiting in Judy's line that I was now servicing. I knew I had to be hasty. Speaking into the mic, I explained why we couldn't access his wife's account without her present, but convincing the man proved to be harder than pulling nails out of a block of wood. The guy just wouldn't take no for an answer. In the end he requested his check back, threatened to close his account, and drove off burning rubber. Glad to be rid of him, I sighed with relief as I returned to my waiting customers.

"Sorry about the wai . . ." I stalled. Not only had my line totally cleared out, the customer that had been next in line was no longer there, and I was now standing face-to-face with my past.

"OMG, Porsha." My past was just as surprised to see me as I was to see her.

"Sasha," rolled off my tongue. It was bittersweet.

"Wow, it's been a long time." She smiled. That surprised me too because the last time we had said a word to each other, it didn't end well.

"Yes. How are you?" I wasn't sure how to respond, but I was at work, so being courteous was definitely an option.

"Good. I've been banking with Bryers for a few years, but this is the first time I've ever been in this branch. Now I'm glad I stopped in. What's up?"

"Just living. You know how it is."

"How is Bri? I ain't seen her in forever either."

I couldn't help but smile when she called Briana, Bri. That had been our nickname for her. We were the ones that actually christened her with that nickname. "She's good. Same old Bri."

"She still slaying heads, I'm sure."

"You know it."

"That's what's up." The smile on her face suddenly faded. "Hey, I heard about Kenneth a while back. I'm sorry."

"Yeah, we getting through it." That was absolutely the last thing I wanted to talk about. "So what can I do for you today?" I cut to the chase. This was my job, not the streets.

"Oh yeah, I almost forgot why I was here." Placing her all-white Coach bag on the counter, she unzipped it and pulled out a wad of bills. "I need to make a deposit." She passed me the cash with her left hand. "Here is my deposit slip and ID."

Reaching for the money, I read the deposit slip. It read five thousand dollars. I counted the bills. After typing her account information into the computer, I made the deposit and handed her a receipt.

The smile reappeared as she gripped the receipt I handed her. "I just can't believe we ran into each other. Listen, we got to keep in touch."

"Yeah, we should," I agreed.

Picking up the pen next to her Coach bag, she scribbled numbers down on the back of her deposit receipt. "Here is my number. Call me."

"Cool. And here is my cell." Grabbing one of the bank business cards, I wrote my number down and handed it to her. I wasn't sure if I would call her, but this was my way of extending the invitation.

"I promise to keep in touch. We have a lot of catching up to do."

"Just hit me up." I smiled.

With that, Sasha bounced up out of the bank as if she didn't have a care in the world. Folding up the receipt with her number on it, I pushed it to the side. I chuckled. I couldn't wait to tell Briana who came into the bank.

CHAPTER 3

After a long day at the bank I headed over to Honcho's taco stand to pick up some steak and chicken tacos for dinner. Ma had called me earlier and put in her order, and I grabbed a few for Briana because she was coming over so we could chop it up. It was Monday night, so I had to watch *Love & Hip Hop Atlanta*. That was our show, and we tried hard to never miss it. By the time I hopped out of the shower and got dressed, Briana was ringing the doorbell.

"Man, what time is it?" she asked. "My damn cell phone died on the way over here. Then I had to stop and put some air in Kat's raggedy left tire." She huffed as she stepped around me, headed straight for our mahogany colored sectional. Our living room was set up in a way that some may think of as odd. Although we had a huge sectional, we also had a love seat that Ma refused to get rid of because it had been Kenneth's favorite couch.

"Calm down, you are not late. It's not even on yet."

"Good." She reached for the remote and turned on the television. "What you got to eat? You already know I'm hungry." She flipped the channel to VH1.

"I picked up some tacos from Honcho's."

"That's what I'm talking about. Let me wash my hands." Briana set the remote on the couch and headed for the kitchen.

I was glad to hear she was going to the kitchen. I was tired. "Cool, and grab the food out of the oven. I was trying to keep it warm until you got here." I bounced down on the couch and lay back to recline. I moved around a bit to let the comfortable sectional console me. "Hurry up, Bri. It's comin' on," I yelled as the recap from the last week's show started. I couldn't wait to see what happened with the new girl Tommie and Scrapp's baby mama.

I could hear Briana's footsteps as she scrambled into the living room. "Here." She handed me a plate with three tacos placed on it. I could smell the aroma seeping off the tacos and couldn't wait to devour all three.

"There it is. Smack that bitch." Briana yelled at the television as they started the show with the ending from the previous week.

"Ha." I laughed. "I don't even know why they try, knowing the producers are going to break it up."

An hour later the show was over. *Black Ink Crew* was on, but we didn't care much for it, so we used that time to talk about the foolishness of *Love & Hip Hop Atlanta*.

"Wait. Speaking of crazy-ass Joseline, guess who came into the bank today?"

"Aww hell, just spit it out." Briana sat up on the edge of the couch. She hated when I played the guessing game.

Normally I would make her suffer until she couldn't guess any more, but the suspense of her reaction was killing me. I couldn't wait. "Sasha," I blurted out. I knew this was one she would have never guessed.

Shaking her head, then scratching her scalp, Briana looked down at the floor, then at me. "Sasha who?"

"Bri, how many girls you know named Sasha?" I grinned. "You know exactly who I'm talking about."

She laughed. "That Sasha, huh?" She laughed again.

"Yep, she came into the bank today to make a deposit. Ironically, she ended up in my line." I shrugged my shoulders.

"Hmmm. So did y'all come to blows?"

"Hell no, you know I wouldn't go there at my job anyway. But surprisingly it was cool. She was nice. We even exchanged numbers."

Briana swayed back on the couch in a dramatic motion, making full eye contact with me. "Really? Okay, naturally this is a shock to me . . . I mean, you do remember how she carried on. The bitch went fucking crazy."

I definitely remembered.

Damion was a guy that I started dating in the eleventh grade. He was a new kid at the school who started to hang around us from time to time. Of course we didn't mind because of his good looks, and he always dressed nice. Soon he and I started feeling each other and decided to hook up. Right away I went to share my good news with my girls Briana and Sasha, only to have Sasha flip out, claiming that she had a crush on Damion. To make matters worse, she accused me of knowing how she felt about him, when in fact I honestly had no idea. I was totally caught off guard by her accusations. I couldn't believe that she would think I would deliberately do something like that to hurt her. But she refused to let me explain. Briana and Sasha and I had been friends since we were in elementary school, and one misunderstanding had ruined it all.

"That bitch was insane for a minute, broke into your locker and stole your books. What the fuck was she going to do with them?" We both burst out laughing.

"I remember. That was a mess. I always wondered what she planned to do with them. I'm glad the janitor caught her, though."

"I think she was going to put a hex on you. Shit, I don't

know." Briana continued to laugh. "That bitch was on one. And over some nigga. That whole move made her look weak and desperate."

"I still can't believe how she turned up on me. I would have never expected her to do the things she did. It was bananas." I shook my head in disappointment just thinking about it.

"That's what I'm saying. Now she want to be poppin' up at your job, y'all exchanging numbers and shit. Like none of that never happened. Hmmm." Briana rolled her eyes.

"Don't be like that, Bri. She was our friend for years, and I have always tried not to forget that."

"No, fuck that. She was your friend first in fourth grade, remember? You met her psycho ass, then you introduced her to me."

"Damn, Bri, I knew her five seconds before I introduced her to you." I chuckled.

"That don't mean shit. She still was your friend first." She smacked her lips.

"Shut up. I swear you petty." I grinned. "Oh, and she asked about you."

Briana rolled her eyes again. "I don't know why. Hope you told that bitch that I disappeared."

"Of course not. Why would I say that? She wanted to know if you were still slaying heads."

"Why she need to know that?"

"Why you think? Hell, she probably want you to slay her head for old times. I for one wouldn't blame her."

"Bitch, please. The last time I was in that girl's head, water-fall braids were still in style. And I plan to keep it that way. Trust. I am good." She sucked her teeth. I knew she meant every word. "She won't ever get to accuse me of a nigga she ain't never even flirted with. Crazy ass."

"I swear, you so mean." I continued to grin.

"I'm just sayin'. Besides, that bitch know I always know the business, so she knows not to fuck with me."

CHAPTER 4

"Oh God, I smacked that trick in her face. There was nothing else left for me to do." Stacey chopped our ear off about her latest fight. We were all sitting in the kitchen at Briana's house catching up while Briana put the final touches on Stacey's hair. I was up next and could not wait for my girl to sew in in my bundles of Brazilian hair.

"And she deserved that shit. These hoes be getting too bold these days." Briana put in her two cents.

"I know, right? Just like I told that bitch, Cruz can do whatever he want for her. But at the end of the day, I'm his main chick. Don't ever step to him, in my face, and think I'ma let that shit ride. Bitch must think I went soft." Stacey picked her phone up off the table and started to scroll through it. "But don't worry, I checked his ass too. They both got me fucked up," she was sure to clarify.

"I feel you though, Stacey." I shut the oven door and bit off a piece of the chicken Briana had fried before I came over.

"I'm cool, though. That nigga had to lay ten stacks on me after that. And all still ain't forgiven." Stacey chuckled.

"Damn right. And now you slayed that bitch courtesy of me." Briana stuck her tongue out and laughed.

"Yep, you know how to get a bitch right. Now I'm about to get out in these streets and do me." Stacey stood up, leaned close to Briana, and snapped a selfie of them.

"Yep, you on point." I stood up, ready to take my turn in Briana's magical seat. My girl was a beast with those hands.

After taking a few more pics of herself, Stacey was out.

"Stacey ass crazy." I laughed.

"Hell yeah. That's why she my bitch, though, 'cause she don't be taking no shit. For real, for real. But real talk, she need to be done with that nigga Cruz ass for good. That shit get old, that's why I clipped Ronnie ass. Fucking around with that dead-beat, and I was gon' have to kill one of them ratchet bitches."

I was still keeping my fingers crossed and thanking God she had not drifted back to Ronnie. Hell, this was actually the first time she had even brought up his name since she told me she was officially done with him.

"That's why I'm glad you put that issue to bed." I sucked my teeth. A message from Sheila popped up on my phone. I was reluctant to read it because I was not going in to work. "Sheila hittin' my phone. They already tried to get me to come in earlier and I had turn them down," I shared with Briana.

Briana sighed. "I swear that damn job can't give you a break. Why don't they just make you the head supervisor? 'Cause it seem like they can't function if you ain't there." That was so true.

"Ha." I laughed. "Well, you know what that all comes down to is a bigger title, which means more money. And you know their cheap ass tryin' to keep it in the pocket." I had to be honest.

"See, that's that same bullshit I be talkin' about. This fucking organized pimping. Another reason why I'd rather keep slaying heads at the crib."

I had heard that too many times to count, but to me that was just another excuse for her not to get in school. I wasn't buying it.

"Listen, regardless of how you feel, you need to sign up for cosmetology school and get your license. You are too good a stylist to keep it bottled up in this damn kitchen. With that license you could compete in all the hair shows, national and local."

Briana's sigh reassured me that she was still not convinced. "Porsha, you just don't understand."

"Bri, you my girl so you know I get it, but—" The ringing of my cell phone cut me off. Studying the screen, the number didn't look familiar. I started to ignore it because every now and then an ex tried to hit me up.

"You gon' answer that?" Briana twisted another braid to my scalp.

Thinking what the hell, I answered. "Hello?" The familiar voice surprised me right away. "Oh, what's up, Sasha? I didn't recognize the number, I almost hit ignore," I blurted out.

"You sound surprised to hear from me. I told you we need to keep in touch," she reminded me. Even though we had exchanged numbers, I never really believed she would call. "What's up?"

"Over here at Bri's house. She hookin' me up." Briana stopped doing my hair and came to face me. She twisted up her mouth and gave me a few *don't tell her nothing about me* faces. I almost laughed out loud and waved her away to keep from giggling.

"That's what's up. You know I'm going have to have her slay me soon. Hey, I wanted to invite you and Bri out for dinner at LaBerto's Mexicana tomorrow?" I loved their food, and the offer sounded nice, but I paused for a minute before answering. My eyes went to Briana because I knew for sure she was gon' trip. "Porsha, you still there?" Sasha interrupted my hesitation.

"Yeah, I'm here. I was unhooking my Bluetooth," I lied. Briana was still giving me the evil face. I couldn't bring myself to say no. "But no doubt. We can be there." I accepted for both of us. The word "we" had caused Briana to bulge her eyes at me.

"Cool. Tomorrow around six."

"Bet," I agreed before ending the call.

"Hmmm," Bri mouthed as she resumed working on my head. "What she want? What was that 'we' shit?" She threw questions at me.

"Why she gotta want something. Maybe she just calling." I stalled. I was not ready to hear what she would say next.

"Whatever. Don't be saying my name to that girl. And you said 'we,' which leads me to think you were involving me in some type of bullshit."

"Bri, stop being mean." I sighed and just decided to say it. "She just invited us out tomorrow night at LaBerto's." I smiled. I hoped that alone would encourage her to go, because she loved that place as well. I didn't get my hopes up, though; she could be stubborn.

"When you say 'us,' you mean you and somebody else you know, right?" she asked, her tone full of sarcasm.

"Who else would I be talkin' about? I meant 'us' as in you and me. And why you trippin', you know you love that place," I reminded her.

"True, I love the food, but . . . Nah, not with that girl. I'm good."

"Her name is Sasha, Bri. As in your old friend Sasha. And she offering you a free meal, at one of your favorite places, I might add."

"Stop calling that girl my friend. And old friend or not, I ain't interested in breaking bread with your new bestie."

"Ha, bestie, you tried it." I laughed out. "Wait, are you jealous?" I chuckled.

"Not jealous, just not fuckin' with that bitch."

"Why not? It's just dinner, Bri." I was not ready to give up.

"Mmm-hmmm, I know that . . . But, Porsha." Her grip got tighter on the braids. I was really annoying her. "We ain't talk to this girl since eleventh grade. All of a sudden she pops up after all these years of being angry over some dumb shit. Now she wants to take us out to eat . . . Fuck that."

Everything she was saying was legit, but I wanted to move past it. "On life I get where you comin' from. But that stuff is in the past. We shouldn't be dwelling on it. We were stupid kids. That's all. Hothead females in high school."

"Listen, you might not be dwelling on it. But I ain't fucking wit it. Besides, I'm booked."

I couldn't help but smile because I knew Briana, and she was no easy nut to crack. Which was cool because I didn't give up easy either. I continued, "All that aside, you should just trust me. You know if it was on some bull I would not have accepted."

Still twisting my braids, Briana sighed. She knew at this point I was not trying to let it go. "Damn, I swear you don't give up . . . I'll go." She sighed again. "But on life, if she gets either of us in the wrong, she gettin' her ass beat on sight. And that's a promise."

"Trust I know you will. Everything gon' be cool, though." At least I hoped. The last thing I wanted was Briana to get upset in a restaurant full of people. It could only end with one or both of them behind bars.

CHAPTER 5

Arriving at the restaurant, I pulled into a parking spot and turned down the radio, Drake's voice faded. Briana looked at me like I was crazy. For one, she was still not happy about meeting up with Sasha. Two, she loved Drake, so, me cutting into his music was a problem.

"See, you gotta understand that turning Drake down or off when he rhyming is plain disrespectful."

"Well, when he cut me a check I'll care." I grinned. "Listen, please behave. This a public place full of people. So don't embarrass me. Oh, and I want my free meal. Don't mess that up for me, please," I added.

"Here you go. Ain't nobody gon' embarrass you." Briana unbuckled her seat belt, slid on her Ray-Bans, and opened her door. I followed suit. "Just as long as she don't forget the rules of engagement when dealing with me." She gave a snide grin.

I shook my head in uncertainty. The situation was either going to turn out good or bad. Either way, I was not leaving. "Just come on." I reached out and pulled the door open and made my way inside the restaurant.

I told the hostess who we were meeting and she led us

back. Sasha noticed us and stood up to greet us as we reached the table. With a body similar to Kim Kardashian, Sasha always made sure to show it off, rocking a pair of skintight blue jean cutoff shorts, a black crop top, and a pair of pumps. Her hair was pulled back into a long ponytail that touched the top of her huge butt. The look on her face said "I look good."

"Still a ho," Briana mumbled under her breath. I had to swallow to keep from responding. In high school Sasha had been known for wearing extremely tight and revealing clothing. She had been sent home to change on several occasions only to have her mother bring her back to the school. Then she would curse out the teachers for, according to her, "worrying about something that was none of their damn business." The bottom line was she entertained men for money during the day while Sasha was at school, and the last thing she needed was Sasha coming home interrupting her customers.

"I was beginning to worry you might not show." Sasha reached out and we embraced in a hug.

"You know me, time has not changed. I'm still always late." I chuckled. I noticed Briana quickly hopped a seat. That was her escape from Sasha even attempting to hug her.

"Hey, Bri." Sasha had a huge smile on her face.

Barely opening her mouth, Briana said, "What's up."

Relieved that she had even responded, I grabbed a chair to sit down.

"So I took the liberty of ordering the famous house margaritas. They should be here in a minute." She rubbed her hands together, and I sensed that she was a bit nervous but trying to keep it cool.

"Wait, how you order margaritas, ain't none of us twenty-one?" Briana asked. The sarcasm in her tone was apparent. I tried to keep a smile as I gave her the chill out glance.

Sasha smiled. "Actually, I know the owner. When I arrived he came out to speak with me. He asked me what we would like to drink. I told him, and he put the order in with the bartender."

I could tell by the look on Briana's face that she was not impressed. "Hmm," was all she said before picking up a tortilla chip and dipping it in salsa.

The waitress approached the table with our drinks. Then she patiently took our orders. We all knew what we wanted without looking at the menu. Turned out this was one of Sasha's favorite restaurants as well.

Sasha cleared her throat as the waitress left the table. She rubbed her hands together again. "First off, I would like to thank you both for coming to meet me. I know this is uncomfortable for all of us, being as how our friendship ended." Briana looked up from her chips and salsa. I silently prayed that she would allow Sasha to finish what she had to say. "Second, I want to apologize about the way things went down over Damion . . ." She paused. "The way I behaved was wrong and just way out of hand. Porsha, I know you didn't know that I was into him. I just allowed jealousy to take over. But you both were my true friends and I ruined it . . . I take full responsibility. But today, right here and right now, I want to say I am so sorry. Really, I was completely over it by our senior year, but I didn't know how to approach either of you after the way I clowned." Tears slid down both of her cheeks.

"Hey don't cry. I accept your apology. We were young," I said.

Briana didn't say anything, but I could see the softness fill her face. She was calm and I knew she had let her guard down. She sipped her margarita and smiled. "I'm glad you got the hook up with the boss. This margarita is on point." I knew that was sort of her peace offering. At least, all she was willing to give.

"Yeah, it is good," I agreed.

"I know I get them all the time when I eat here. That's

why I always make sure Nick is going to be here before I come."

"Who is Nick?" Briana asked.

"The owner."

"Y'all be hookin' up or some?" Briana pried.

"Nah, it ain't like that, he just cool people."

I didn't know if I believed her. But really, it was none of my business. I would love getting free drinks from now on. In the future I would be sure to come with Sasha.

For the next two hours we sat and had drinks, talked, and ate. As usual the food was good. We caught up on each other and what we had been up to. But the most interesting part of the night came when Sasha revealed that she had a two-year-old daughter named Rein. Out of the three of us, she would have been the last one that I thought would have a baby. After living with her mother, she always declared she did not want children. Sasha's mother spoiled her—she had everything she wanted—but she never showed her any love. She was always gone or entertaining. Then when Sasha was in the tenth grade, she ran off with some guy and left Sasha alone for good. From that point on all she did was pay the bills so Sasha had a place to stay, and she sent her money for clothes and food. Sasha resented her for it. I mean, who could blame her? And she swore she never wanted to see her again. So to hear she had a daughter was beyond shocking, but I couldn't wait to meet Rein.

CHAPTER 6

It had been a few weeks since Sasha, Briana, and I went to dinner. I had been busy working twelve-hour days with no days off because two of my tellers had been out with the flu. And with Briana being booked doing heads, we hadn't had much time to talk, not to mention we had missed two *Love & Hop Hip Atlanta* nights. But finally things were getting back on track at work and my normal schedule had resumed, so finally I had a day off. The first thing I did was get a much-needed mani and pedi, then I headed home. Briana was on her way over to touch my hair up.

"What's up, stranger?" Briana joked as soon as I opened the door.

"Ready for you to tackle this wig." I played twirling my hair around my fingers.

"Judging by the looks of that head, you need it." Briana stepped past me, then set the keys to Kat's car on the coffee table.

"Whatever, you tried it." I laughed.

"Judging by the fact there is no smoke in the air, I would say Ms. Jennifer here."

"Hell yeah, she up there. But you know I gave that mess up." I had to keep reminding her, and I hated for her to even talk about it. It was hard enough.

"You still on that shit, Porsha. Come on, everybody need to hit the blunt sometimes. It's only natural."

"No, it's natural for you. I'm good." I had to believe that. If not, I would have the blunt up to my mouth daily. But the fact of the matter was I smoked so much of that shit when my brother died I felt like I lost track of time. And that was not good. So here I was challenging myself to see how strong I could be by giving it up.

"All right, stay strong then, but keep in mind your girl keep that fire." She pulled out a bag of weed and ran it across my nose.

It smelled so good I could have snatched it out of her hand, but I had fought too hard to let her break me. "Bri, put that shit back in your purse before Ma come up in here," I said as low as possible.

"Ha ha." She laughed. "Such a square." Then she placed the bag back in her purse. "Guess I should have rolled up and hit it before I got here. Good I didn't, though. You and this weed-free shit would have blown my high."

"Shut up." I had more to say, but the ringing of my cell phone distracted me. Sasha's name lit up. I hadn't heard from her since the dinner and figured she had been busy like us. "What's up, Sasha?" Then I hit the speaker button so that we could all chat.

"Just getting off work. What you up to?"

"Enjoying my day off. Shit been hectic at work. But Bri and I at my crib chillin', she about to touch my hair up."

"Okay, tell Bri I said what's up."

"She can hear you, I got you on speaker."

"What's up, bitch?" Briana said.

"What's good?"

"Over here trying to get your girl to roll up with me. But she trippin'. You still blowin'?"

"Absolutely." Sasha giggled. "Could never give that up. It's my sanity."

"That's what's up. We'll hook up, then."

"Just hit me up," Sasha offered. "Hey, I'm glad I caught you two together. What's up with Saturday night? How would you both like to hit the club up for some fun?"

I looked at Briana, and she was all smiles. With all the working we had been doing lately, the party life for us had all but come to an end. A night out at the club sounded like the type of therapy we needed.

"Yes," Briana and I said at the same time.

"All right, all right. Sounds like a plan, then. Saturday night it is. I'll text you the club information, Porsha. And ladies, I promise we 'bout to turn all the way up."

"Shit, let's do it." Briana was hype. "It's been a minute since I shook my ass."

After we all said bye, I ended the call. Saturday couldn't come fast enough. I was ready. "Sasha coming through," I said.

"No doubt. We need some excitement in our life. I guess having her around ain't such a bad idea."

I was relieved that Briana had accepted her because if she hadn't, I would have had to shut it down with Sasha.

"See, I told you." I smiled. "Hey, Ma," I said. She leaned down and kissed my cheek. I noticed she was still in her robe. I hadn't seen her since early morning when I had left the house. When I came in, I checked on her and she was taking a nap. I really wished she would get out more. I just had to figure out a way to make that happen without upsetting her.

"Hey, Ms. Jen," Briana said.

"Hey, Bri." She headed toward the coffee pot in the kitchen. "So that's Sasha you were just on the phone with. That wouldn't happen to be Sasha that you two were once friends with, is it?"

"Yeah that's her," I confirmed.

"Really . . . Hmmm . . ." All the pausing told me something was up. Briana kept fixing my hair. And I just waited. "When did you start back talking to her?"

Now I remembered why I hadn't mentioned that I had run into Sasha—to avoid this moment. Briana had been enough to deal with when it came to the surprise of Sasha. "Well, actually I ran into her at work. She came into the branch and we started talkin'."

"And just like that you all cool again. She calling you and whatnot?" Ma remembered the confrontation with Sasha.

"Yeah," was my only response. There was nothing else I could say.

"You know I remember when you all were really good friends. And I don't know . . . I always got the feeling that Sasha was selfish. Everything you all did was all about her. If not, she was angry and couldn't do it."

"Yo, I remember that too." Briana wasted no time agreeing. I wished Ma would stop. I had just got Briana to accept Sasha. The last thing I needed was for Briana to start having some kind of negative feedback.

As much as I wanted to defend Sasha, I had to be honest with myself. "I guess she could be a little self-indulged sometimes. But we were kids then. We're all grown up now. And people can change, even Sasha. The least we can do is give her a chance."

"Aye, I'm trying to give her that. But she better not make me regret it." Briana was serious.

"You're right, people can change." Ma tried to sound optimistic. But I knew she too would have her eyes on Sasha. I shook my head. I would have *I told you so* coming from both sides if Sasha started acting crazy. But I was not about to worry about that. Saturday night we were hitting the club for some much-needed turn up action. I could not wait.

CHAPTER 7

Saturday night finally arrived, and it was on. Briana and I had spent all day shopping trying to find something cute that we could flex in. Sasha had texted me Friday and told us to meet her at Club Stylz. Briana and I had never been there. It was a new spot on what is considered to be the upper-class side of Oakland, but from what I had heard in the streets, a lot of Oakland ballers hung out there. According to Sasha, the cover charge at the door was a hundred dollars. I almost screamed "hell no." Briana, on the other hand, convinced me that the price would probably be worth it, since we wouldn't have to duck from any shootings or worry about bottles flying across our heads. That was the type of thing that happened in some of the clubs we frequented. It just seemed people took their hood ways with them everywhere they went. So I was looking forward to enjoying myself without looking over my shoulder. After driving for nearly half an hour, we were finally in view of the club.

"Damn, they got valet," Briana said in awe. That was something we definitely were not used to.

"I see," was my uneasy reply. I slowed down behind the

cars as they turned into valet. "Let's find our own parking space." There was no way I was allowing them into my car. I'm sure they were not used to parking cars that looked like mine. No way. Driving past the entrance, I spotted the parking lot. But again I became uneasy. The lot was filled with Porsches, Maseratis, BMWs, you name it.

Briana and I looked at each other. There was no way I was parking my 2003 Toyota Camry beside those cars. I was not ashamed of my ride, but I did not want to be seen climbing out of it. Briana knew what I was thinking.

"So what are you going to do?"

I continued to look around the lot. "I don't know," I mumbled.

"Just park right here. Fuck it. 'Cause I ain't walkin' far in these heels."

"I was thinking the same thing." I admitted as I scanned the area for the closet open space.

"Let's do it, then. We gon' be the baddest bitches in there anyway."

Briana was right, this Toyota wasn't stopping shit. I found a spot close to the end of the lot. We climbed out and made our way up to the entrance. After paying our cover charge, we were inside. One look at the high ceilings and lounge areas, and we were both impressed. I had only seen clubs that looked like this on television. The club looked like a scene out of the show *Power* times ten. It was nice.

"Look at this badass club," Briana said as we stood still for a second and took in the full view. "And we been wasting time and money over at Club Taj, leaving early just so we can miss the drama."

"For real." I agreed. "But Club Taj only costs ten dollars to get inside," I reminded her.

"True that," she agreed. "But this shit straight bangin'. And the DJ on fire." Briana snapped her fingers. She was ready to hit the dance floor already.

Still sightseeing, we made our way through the club seeking out the bar where Sasha had told us to meet up with her. All eyes were on us. I guess all that time we had spent shopping paid off. Briana, with a body that had been compared to Nicki Minaj, was flexing in her all-black sheer lace short jumpsuit with a pair of pumps. Her caramel-colored skin glistened in the club lighting. Then you had me, a super bad redbone with a set of full lips. I stood every inch of five-six, which I considered to be the perfect height for a woman. Not too tall and not too short. My short red cutout one-shoulder dress fit my butt perfectly. I could feel all those wondering eyes on me, but I was not easy to bait.

"East Oakland in the house," Sasha yelled, stepping out of nowhere.

"In the motherfucking flesh," Briana bellowed over the loud music.

"I see you two came to slay tonight. Y'all killin' in those outfits," Sasha complimented us, observing us from head to toe.

"Well, you know how we do." I grinned. "But you ain't lookin' too bad yourself."

"And this is true," Sasha joked. "Did you have trouble finding the place?"

"Nah, it was not hard at all. The GPS on my phone led us straight here. We arrived down to the minute."

"Yo, Sasha, who is the DJ?"

"DJ Kid Nick. He from the Bay Area. He brings the heat always."

"I see he killin' it." Briana was rocking to his mix of Usher's old love in the club.

"He always on point. I promise you won't catch him slackin' the whole night. From what I hear, he travels between here and New York. He DJs at all the hottest spots," she shared.

"That's what's up." Briana kept rocking her head to the beat.

"Let's grab some drinks. You know I got my fake ID."

"I'm down. Get me a shot of Hennessy." Briana chose that brown right away. I knew she was ready to be on one.

"I'll take a martini, dry, with two olives." I followed. I wanted to keep it light. Home was not right around the corner. The last thing I needed was a DUI. Briana had gotten one a year ago and was just finishing up with all the crap they put her through to get her license back, and the money she spent on license renewal and city fines was ridiculous. I did not need that aggravation.

Once we had our drinks Sasha led us to a table she had reserved for us. It wasn't VIP, but according to Sasha the table was five hundred dollars. Good thing she had taken care of that because I had already dropped a bill to get inside. I would have gladly lounged at the bar or stood all night.

We were all sipping our third drinks and mellowing out. But when the DJ dropped "Set It Off" by Lil Boosie, we all rushed the dance floor. And that's where we stayed for the next three songs. We were all on one and loving it.

"I'm about to have to sit down," I yelled over the music to Sasha and Briana, who both looked like they were just getting started.

"Ah, come on, Porsha. Stop being such a prude," Briana joked.

"Prude, my ass. I need a break." I laughed, then turned and headed toward our table. What I didn't tell them was that I wanted to remove myself from the eyes of this guy who had been watching me all night. He was seated in a VIP booth close to our table, and he had a perfect view of the dance floor.

Back at the table I was relieved to finally sit down. Just as I did, the unknown guy who had been watching me approached my table. My mouth instantly went dry. Why was he at my table? Was he that bold? In that moment I wished I had stayed on the dance floor or that Briana and Sasha had returned to the table with me. But here I was alone, and the brother was fine.

"Hi. I know you probably noticed me watching you all night and were probably starting to feel uncomfortable. So I just thought I'd come over and introduce myself. I'm Reginald Shaw." He extended his hand to me.

Not sure if I should shake it or not, I stalled. Then just as I was prepared to shoot down anything he might attempt to say, one of my jams came on: Usher's "Bedtime." I was weak for that song, so when the question if I would dance with him floated off Reginald's lips, I found myself having absolutely no control as I replied yes. The song and the dance turned out to be everything I could have hoped it to be and not wanted it to be at the same time. Wrapped in the song, I lost myself in his embrace. The song was over way too soon, but that one song and that one dance had loosened me up. Once it was over, we headed back to my table I didn't question the fact that he joined me without being invited. Briana and Sasha still had not returned.

"I'm Porsha," I announced, realizing I had not given him my name for the dance.

He smiled. "That was going to be my next question."

A smile spread over my face without warning. "Yes, first-name basis is always good."

"No doubt. So what brings you to Stylz?"

"I'm hanging out with my girls. I'm sure you seen them."

"Yeah. I noticed you dancing with two other females."

I nodded my head as I started to jam in my seat to the remix of "5 Star Chick."

"Can I get you something to drink?"

"Nah, I'm cool." I said, continuing to bob my head, but keeping it cute. "Do you hang out here all the time?"

"From time to time. I try not to club too often. But occasionally my crew and I come out to VIP and pop a few bottles." He smiled and I wanted to melt. If I had to guess his height, I would say he was about six-three. He possibly weighed about two fifteen, muscular build. His skin tone was milk chocolate, and he had the straightest set of teeth I had ever seen on anyone. The conversation turned out to be good. Before I knew it, time had flown by and it was time go. Before walking away, he had asked for my number. I wanted to say no so bad, and I would have, but he smiled and the numbers slid off my tongue one by one. Briana and Sasha finally reappeared just as he was walking away. We stood outside the club and chatted briefly.

"So who was that cutie all up on you?" Sasha inquired.

"Bruh was fine as hell." Briana chimed in.

"Nobody." I tried to play cool. I didn't want them reading too much into it.

"Don't look like nobody to me." Briana used sarcasm. "That brother was at that table for a long time."

"So you two were watching."

"Hell yeah, why you think it took so long for us to come back? Please tell me you don't think I'd dance eight songs straight for nothing. You know me better than that."

"I should have known you both were up to something."

"Come on, tell us about him." Sasha grinned. "Give us the juice."

I looked at them both and playfully rolled my eyes. They wouldn't leave me alone until I told them something. "His name is Reginald Shaw."

"What?" Briana snapped her neck to look at me. "Reginald . . . sound so preppy. He must be a college boy." She said it as if it was almost a crime. "But his swagg damn sure does not say preppy boy."

"Reginald." Sasha said it as if she was studying it to form her own opinion. "I guess his name is okay."

"Thanks, Sasha. Briana thinks everyone's name should sound like it can catch bullets," I joked.

"Whatever. So what else happened?" Briana kept on being nosy.

"We danced, then talked. That's about it." I shrugged my shoulders.

"And?" Sasha grinned. They both wanted a juicy tell-all.

"That's it. Oh, I did give him my number." I was nonchalant. "But he probably won't use it. You know how guys be out tryin' to see how many numbers they pull in one night. I'm cool with not hearing from him, though. I really don't know why I gave him my number. I don't have time for dating."

"Listen, for that fine-ass dude, I would make the time. Stop being so boring." Briana smacked her lips.

"I am not boring. But you of all people know how busy I always am. That's why I stay single. Guys want and expect too much in a relationship."

"I know what you mean. But I can't front. I wish I had someone. Especially a piece of eye candy like that," Sasha said.

"Shit, that's all I'm saying." Briana cosigned.

I thought for only a brief second about all they said. While it sounded good, I knew what was best for me at the moment, and that was to stay focused on work and getting Ma back out into the world. Then I could get back into school. A relationship would only distract from that. So after thanking Sasha for inviting us out, Briana and I had headed off to my car. Sasha said she had to wait on the valet to bring her car around.

CHAPTER 8

I had been lying around the house all day in my robe. It was my first day off in four days and it had been raining nonstop. So instead of being out enjoying a nice day, I was home lounging on our living room sofa, eating kettle corn, and watching one of my favorite Lifetime movies, *Small Sacrifices*. The movie, which Farrah Fawcett starred in, was so good. Sad but good. No matter how many times I watched it, I just could not figure out how a mother could murder her own kids for a man, and never blink twice. Not once in the movie did she ever seem remorseful. Each time I watched it I cried, and this time was no different. Ma refused to watch it with me. She said it made her angry.

Gripping my Kleenex in my hand, I dabbed my tears for the hundredth time. The ringing of my cell phone annoyed me. I hated when I was indulging in a good movie and someone interrupted me. I cursed under my breath, swearing it had better not be my job. I didn't recognize the number as one of the lines from the bank, but that didn't mean anything—they had tricked me on more than one occasion, calling private or from a different number. Either way, I was prepared to say no.

"Hello," I breathed into the phone, my tone annoyed. I wanted to send a clear message: *Do not bother me on my day off.*

I was wrong. "Hi, Reginald." Hearing his voice on the other end had been a surprise. I really never expected him to call. It had been at least two weeks since we had met, and I hadn't heard a thing.

"I didn't think you'd remember my name."

I recognized the humor in his tone. "Really. And what would make you think that?"

"Just figured you might have better things to do than remember lil old me." He chuckled softly.

"Ha ha," I said playfully.

"So I've been wondering. What is it you like to do for fun?"

That question caught me off guard. I would have expected him to just ask me out on a date. He didn't strike me as the kind of guy to beat around the bush. In that moment I realized no one that I had ever been out with had asked me that before. Normally, it was just a straight invite to dinner. I was puzzled but intrigued. And there was something that I absolutely loved to do. I was no good at it but enjoyed it very much. "I like to bowl," I revealed.

"Bowling." He repeated as if he was surprised.

"What, are you shocked?" I ask.

"Nah . . . Bowling is good. How about you let me take you out for a night of bowling? Then maybe dinner after?"

The offer sounded good, but I hadn't been out on a date in a minute. Since Kenneth's death, my focus really had been Ma and work. Anything else simply was not important. But for some reason, I didn't want to tell him no. "Sure. I'm down."

"Cool. So I'll pick you up." Now that was a no. There was no way I was telling him where I lived. For one, Ma would be asking questions, and for two, I didn't know his ass like that. Niggas be getting too comfortable too quick. "How about I'll meet you at the bowling alley. Then I can follow behind you for dinner."

The few seconds of silence that followed confirmed that he was reluctant to accept my response. "That's cool. When are you free?" I'm glad he decided not to try and convince me otherwise, because I probably would have canceled the whole date.

"Friday. I get off at three and I'm free for the rest of the day."

"One hundred. Text me the time and bowling alley and I'll be there."

Three short weeks later, Reginald and I had been on four dates. It was safe to say that we were inseparable. He turned out to be cool people. And he let me beat him at bowling. That was his first key to my good graces. Hanging out with him, I actually had a good time. I had started to anticipate his phone calls and texts during the day while I was working. Hanging out with him gave me a reason to really say no when they asked me to come in on my days off or stay longer. Tonight had been my night to close up after a full twelve-hour day, but I didn't care. As soon as I got off, I went home, took a shower, jumped in my car, and headed straight to Zeke's Bar & Grill, where I had agreed to meet Reginald for appetizers and drinks. I still had not allowed him to pick me up at home yet. I wasn't ready for that. But I had to admit I was falling for him.

"So how was work?" he asked. We were sharing an order of chili cheese fries.

"Busy." That was the only way I knew to describe it. One customer after the next. But I didn't want to talk about my job, so I switched up the conversation. "What'd you do all day?"

"You know me. All work, no play." He popped a fry in his mouth.

"Here you go with that again," I joked. We hadn't really talked a lot about him and what he did because mainly we were having fun. The only reason he knew I worked at the bank was because they kept blowing me up on one of our dates.

Reginald's smile suddenly faded. Chewing on the fry I had

just put in my mouth, I became concerned. "What's the matter?" I swallowed.

"I'm good." He paused. He said he was good but I wondered if that was the truth, because that solemn look was still all over his face. "Porsha, the last couple of weeks that we been kickin' it been cool. I have enjoyed every moment we were together."

I was really worried now. I guess this was when he was going to tell me that he had children and probably a damn wife. I braced myself because he would get a piece of me that he did not know existed because I was not interested in being no nigga mistress. I guess apprehension was written all over my face as he reached for my hands. I kept it cute and politely moved them out of his reach.

He sat straight up in his seat. "With us getting closer, I wanted to lay it all out for you. Be straight up and tell you who I am."

I was growing impatient. "Reginald, just say it."

"Well, for starters, Game is my street name." He paused. "I'm a hustler, a dealer in the streets. And I ain't no lightweight." He paused again. "I wanted to tell you so that you could hear it from me and not in these streets. A lot of people know who I am even though I try to keep myself low key. But these streets have fame, even when you don't want it. Unfortunately, I have it."

Still I remained quiet. I had to allow everything he had just said to me to soak in. And once it did my heart began to break slowly. I was disappointed. He was living the same life as my brother Kenneth. A life of uncertainty. The streets were dangerous, and no one understood that better than me, now. Losing Kenneth had been the worst eye opener. And a deal breaker for Reginald and me. "I'm glad you told me. Honesty is always key." I gave him a weak smile. "But all I can think about is my brother. His name was Kenneth and he was in the streets. Kenneth . . . was murdered about two years ago. Fast money, you know."

"I'm sorry about that." The look on his face was sincere.

A single tear slid down my left cheek. "No, I'm sorry.

Sorry it has to be like this . . . And I wish you the best." I stood to leave.

"Wait, what you sayin'?" Again he reached for my hands, but I moved them to my sides.

"I gotta go, Reginald . . . Game . . . whatever it is." I walked away without looking back. And just like that, my life was back to its norm.

The days and weeks had slowly crept by since I had walked out of the restaurant and away from Game. All his calls to me had gone unanswered. I had considered blocking him several times but never did. As much as I hated to admit it, I missed him so much. We had only gone out for a few short weeks, but it felt like I had known him for years. In one of my weaker moments I had actually picked up the phone and almost called him. Thank God I quickly came to my senses and hung up. Cutting him off had been the correct choice. I owned that.

Today Sasha was forcing me out of the house to pamper myself. Briana had gone out of town to assist her cousin at a hair show. They had invited me since I was off, but I was just not feeling it. I didn't want to do anything. And when Sasha called me up for a day of pampering, I had immediately said no. All I wanted to do on my two days off was sit in the house, order takeout, and pout. But Sasha wouldn't take no for answer. I had ignored several of her calls. Soon she was at my door.

"Get the door, Ma," I yelled from my room. Reaching on top of my dresser, I grabbed my one and only pair of Guess shades. I loved them so much. I only had the one pair because I couldn't afford to waste my money on designer things. I had to save for school, if and when I ever returned.

"Well, who is this beautiful young lady?" Ma was bent down on one knee when I entered the living room, cooing over Rein. She was a cutie. With curly brown hair and big deep dish eyes, she could break anybody's heart. Smiling back at Ma, Rein showed all of her teeth.

"This is Rein," Sasha announced proudly. Briana and I had already met her weeks ago, but this was Ma's first time. In fact, I had only told her a few days ago that Sasha had a child.

"Hi, Rein." Ma touched one of her natural curls. Rein continued to giggle.

"Ain't she beautiful Ma?" I smiled.

"Adorable," Ma agreed. Then she reached down to pick her up. Rein fell into her arms.

"Wow, you must have the magic touch. She never goes to anyone that she doesn't know," Sasha said.

"Tell me about it. She had a fit when Briana and I tried to hug her the first time we met," I shared.

"Right." Sasha laughed. "And that is usually her response when she first meets anyone."

"Well, Ma does have that magic touch," I add. "A'ight, Ma, give Rein up. We gotta get goin'," I said, looking at the time on my phone. I knew we had a time to keep because Sasha had made appointments.

"Yeah, sorry, Ms. Jennifer." Sasha also checked the time on her phone. "I gotta drop Rein off at her sitter."

"Wait, no. You can leave this sweetie pie right here with me. She'll be fine."

"Ma, she probably won't want to stay." I slid my shades on.

"She'll probably break out screaming when I walk out the door," Sasha added with certainty in her tone.

"Nonsense. She'll love being here." Ma smiled with confidence.

"Maybe next time. We'll come by and hang out soon, then she'll get to know you."

"All right. Bye, my Rein." Ma smiled at Rein. I knew she didn't want to give her up.

Sasha reached for Rein, who started crying. Ma smiled.

"See, I told you. This is my Rein and she wants to stay. You two go ahead and have fun. No rush. Rein and I will be fine."

Sasha grinned. "All right, we out then. Let's go, Porsha." Sasha walked slow, looking behind her, waiting on Rein to cry, but she never did.

"Yo, what's up with you?" Sasha asked while our feet soaked.

"Nothin', I'm good. How many times do I need to say it?" I tried to be convincing.

"Girl, no, you are not. I know we ain't been tight since high school, but we were best friends for years. Point is I still know you, Porsha. And you need to be honest with yourself." I started to protest, but no words came. "Listen, you can't miss out on happiness because you are afraid. Game does what he does, and that's that. It's for him to keep himself safe, and I'm sure he knows what he's doing. Besides, he has workers. It ain't like he out there on the grit, right? You did say he was the man," she reminded me.

I nodded in agreement. All she said was true.

"All right then. Do what makes you happy and follow your heart. Leave the rest of that shit to the wind. I would." I guess that was her terms of endearment. I pushed the whole Game issue to the side, though, so I could enjoy the rest of the day. And I did.

But later that night, lying in bed, praying for sleep to find me, Sasha's words *follow your heart* kept running through my mind. I considered the good and the bad of doing that. Would it be at some horrible cost? Or was I overreacting? My mind was made up.

"Hey, Reginald, or should I call you Game?"

CHAPTER 9

Being back with Game for the past few weeks had been great, and I was excited about all the fun we were having. I told myself I would not think about his lifestyle; that way it wouldn't affect our relationship. I knew that would be difficult, but I was still willing to give it a try. There was something I had to do, though, that was most important, and that was introduce him to Ma. I wouldn't be able to keep it from her much longer that I was dating. So earlier, while on a short, much-needed break, I called him up and invited him over to the house for dinner. I worried that he might come up with an excuse so that he would not have to come, but he made it clear that it was cool.

Originally my plan was to cook myself, but when I called Ma up and told her I had invited someone over for dinner that I wanted her to meet, to my amazement she jumped at the chance to do it. In fact, I was so stunned I didn't ask any questions. I would just allow her to do her thing. Rushing home after work, I jumped in the shower and then got dressed. Picking up my cell phone, I noticed it was time for him to arrive. Tossing my phone onto my bed, I picked up my MAC lip gloss and spread it on. I prayed he wouldn't be late. I didn't want Ma to have any reason to dislike him. Right now she was touchy about anything that involved me. I was all she had left in the world. The knocking on the door sent my heart speed racing. I really wanted this to go well. Putting the lip gloss down, I yelled to Ma that I would get the door.

I wanted to contain the grin that spread across my face as I opened the door, but seeing how fine he looked, I couldn't resist. "Hey," sweetly fell off my lips.

"Hey, sexy." He smiled. Stepping inside, he instantly pulled me into a hug. He felt so good. I laid my head back and allowed him to kiss me.

"Mmmm, I have been waiting on that all day."

I blushed. "Are you ready?" I looked him in the eyes. I needed him to take this seriously.

"Yeah, I can't wait to meet your mom." I started laughing so hard. "Why are you laughing?" He was curious.

"Listen, Jennifer ain't no cakewalk. She don't play when it comes to her kids. And please, if you want to play the son card, call her Ma, not Mom." I gave him a heads-up. She hated being called mom. She said it made her feel old.

"Got it. Ma, not Mom," he repeated. "No worries. I got this." For his sake I hoped that he did. "Food smells good."

"And it will be. Ma can burn in the kitchen," I said just as Ma descended from the kitchen. The look on her face was serious. She gave Game full eye contact. I grabbed his right hand and pulled him alongside me. "Ma, this is Reginald Shaw. Reginald, this is my mother, Jennifer Moore."

Game didn't seem the least bit nervous as he reached out for Ma's hand. "Nice to finally meet you, Ms. Moore." I cringed. Strike one. I'd told him to call her Jennifer. But Ma didn't seem fazed. Maybe she was giving him a pass.

"Likewise. And, Reginald, call me Jennifer." Surprisingly, the serious look had faded from her face. No smile was there either, but a bit of softness appeared. I could breathe now. "I hope you brought your appetite, dinner is ready."

At the dinner table Ma had the food spread out like a feast. Cabbage greens, corn on the cob, lasagna, and Texas toast garlic bread. I couldn't remember the last time she had cooked a meal like this. I wasn't really hungry until I saw all the food. Game's face lit up at the sight of the table. We all sat down.

"Ms. M . . ." Game paused. He had almost called Ma Ms. Moore. I chuckled. "Jennifer, this food looks delicious."

"Thank you. You like sweet tea?" she asked him.

"Yes, one of my favorites."

"Good." Pushing her chair back, Ma disappeared into the kitchen, then returned with a huge container of her delicious sweet tea. It was about to go down. Had I known she was gon' go all out like this, I would have been invited him over long before. Soon all our plates were full of food. Especially Game's—he was not shy about smashing.

"Are you from around here, Reginald?" Ma asked before sipping her tea.

"Yes, born and raised in East Oakland."

"Okay . . . So what are your plans with Porsha?" She jumped right in, not wasting any time. I was so embarrassed I couldn't even look at him. I stuffed my mouth with cabbage.

Game had food in his mouth, so he finished chewing. He glanced at me briefly, then at Ma. She sat with her eyes locked on him, not eating anything. "Well, I want to continue to get to know her like we have been doing since we met. And I want to make and keep her happy."

I could feel his eyes on me again. Slowly I returned the gaze with a smile.

"I guess some of that sounds okay. But . . . I don't know. I don't know if she's told you yet. Porsha has plans. And she needs to stick to them." She looked at me. "For her to do that, she needs to be focused."

"She has told me about her plans for school. And I don't want you to worry. I support her one hundred and ten percent."

"I'm not going to forget my plans, Ma. I told you already, everything is going to work out." The last thing I wanted to do was disappoint her. Losing Kenneth was the last bit of hurt I ever wanted her to experience.

"I'm glad to know that you support her, Reginald. I'll hold you to that." She bit into her corn on the cob, the first bite of food she had taken since we had our plates in front of us. I knew that meant she was satisfied with his answers. The rest of the dinner turned out good. Once we were done, we both offered to help Ma clean the kitchen, but she refused.

And since she refused to allow us to help, we decided to head out to meet up with Briana and Sasha for drinks so that I could officially introduce them. Jumping in Game's black on black Mercedes-Benz SL, we stabbed out. Oh, the luxury of his car; the seats made me feel as if I were floating. I never wanted to leave his car.

Reaching over and softly placing his hand over mine, Game said, "See, I told you not to worry. Your mother adores me." He grinned.

"Adore. That's a mighty conceited word." I laughed. "I mean you a'ight."

"Don't be jealous. She likes you too." He chuckled.

"Whatever, I am the one she adores." I smiled. "But real talk, I think she likes you. And I'm glad." I sighed then rested my head against the headrest.

"Man, she can cook. Everything was bomb! You gon' have to convince her to cook for me again."

I laughed at that as well because what he didn't know was that to get Ma in the kitchen lately, it had to be an occasion or you had to drag her. Tonight we had gotten lucky. "If I were you, I wouldn't count on it. You might want to plan on bringing her takeout when you visit." I giggled but was keeping it all the way one hundred. He would see in time.

We pulled into the bar parking lot. Game found a parking space, then leaned over to me for a kiss. Once inside, we made

our way to the bar to meet up with Briana and Sasha. After I
introduced them all to one another, we had a few laughs and
drinks. Then I decided it was time to go. I wanted some me
time with my man alone. Back in the Mercedes he invited me
to his house, and I happily accepted. It was still early, and I was
not in any hurry to get home. And there was no way I was
going to hang out with him at our house. We drove almost forty
minutes before pulling into a high-security gated community.

At first I wondered why we were there, but after Game
gained access using his credentials, it became clear. Less than a
minute later we were pulling up to this huge house. My
mouth nearly hung wide open. I had never seen anything like
it in real life. On television maybe. The huge home was
attached to a six-car garage. I wondered if he owned a car to fit
in each one. That question was answered quickly. Pulling
inside one of the garage spaces, I was floored when I saw the
remaining five cars parked there. It was like an episode of *Cribs*.
I'm talking Bentley, Porsche, Ferrari, and Cadilliac Escalade.
And I'm talking about all new.

Shutting off the ignition, Game looked at me. "Ready to
retreat inside my humble abode?"

I wanted to say "hell yeah," but I chilled and played it cool.
The last thing I wanted to do was seem too anxious, but damn,
it was hard. "After you," I replied.

Jumping out of the car, he came around to my side and
opened the door. Again I was floored once we were inside. His
home was beautiful. There was this beautiful Tranquil Clear
chandelier in his hallway that was to die for. Of course I didn't
know what kind of chandelier it was until he told me. I asked
him if it was expensive, and he told me it cost twelve thousand
dollars. So I left that conversation alone and quick. In my hood he
could have got that same chandelier for less than five hundred,
minus the crystals. The living room I would describe as majestic.
It was decked out in all white with the plushest white carpet you
could imagine. According to him the furniture had been custom

made. I was excited to see the rest of the downstairs as I asked him to show me every inch. But before we made it to the beautiful circular staircase that sat off in the middle from the foyer, I told him I was thirsty. So we detoured back to the kitchen.

"Who decorated for you?" I asked. We had decided to go back to the den and sit down for a minute after I had my drink. That was much more in my comfort zone, a huge leather sectional with a seventy-inch TV on the wall. I could sit there all day for relaxation.

"Why you ask that? Who says I did not decorate myself?"

I thought about his question for only a brief second, then laughed. "Again, who decorated for you?" I grinned. "It has a female touch all over it."

He gave me that handsome smile that I was growing to adore. "A'ight, you got me. My sister, Keisha. She did all this."

"Wait, you have a sister?" I ask. That was news to me. He had never mentioned a sister before.

"Yes."

"Why didn't you tell me? I assumed you were an only child."

"Nope, I have a sister. Her name is Keisha. She doesn't live here in Oakland. No worries babe." He sipped the Champagne he had poured in his glass.

"Will I get to meet her?"

"Actually, she doesn't come out here much. But if she does, of course."

"Cool. I want to know the people that mean something to you."

"You mean something to me." In one swoop he pulled me into his arms. Before I knew it, we were tongue tied. I really wasn't into kissing with the tongue, but Game's tongue action was so good I was willing to let him suck my tongue dry. My middle was on fire, and the drip that was threatening its way down my thigh confirmed I was ready. Game picked me up, and with his passionate magical kisses all over my body, we ended up in his room. Very gently, he laid me down on the bed. I can't even remember how we ended up naked, but his tongue on my middle was driving me completely insane. I couldn't take it another minute. Reaching for him, I all but begged him to fill me up. And he did just that. My middle was so hot Game moaned as he entered. He was home.

CHAPTER 10

Two months had flown by, and I was the happiest I had ever been. From the first night I spent at Game's house, I never left. He was spoiling me rotten and I welcomed it. There was nothing I could dream of that he wouldn't buy. The first week that I moved in I came home from work to find Game standing outside next to a brand-new, all-black Cadillac Escalade with deep black-tinted windows, all black rims, and a huge bow tied to the front. Excited, I jumped out of my old Toyota and ran straight into his arms. I fell utterly and deeply in love with my new truck. It was the first new vehicle I had ever had. Then there were the unlimited shopping sprees he had taken me on, in places I had only dreamed of going, like Saks Fifth Avenue. We took a trip down to Los Angeles, where he allowed me to shop until I dropped on Rodeo Drive. I was in complete awe.

But clearly that was not the end of the spoiling sessions he had for me because today he had awakened me early with breakfast in bed and yet another surprise. Jumping in his Ferrari, we had taken a ride down to his bank. Outside in the car he told me that he we were going inside so that he could open me a secure bank account. I told him that I already had a bank account at Bryers Savings and Loans where I worked. But he insisted that he wanted me to have one where he banked as well. Inside the bank we sat down with an accountant to set it up. I was stunned when he revealed that he wanted to transfer a hundred thousand dollars into my account from his. My eyes felt as if they would bulge out of my head. The accountant looked at me and smiled. I had to sign a few documents to seal the account. The thought of all that money in my possession made me nervous. Yes, I dealt with that much money at work, but that money didn't belong to me.

"Babe, why didn't you tell me you were putting all that money into that account?" I asked when we were outside the bank.

"That's nothing. I want to you to feel finically secure at all times." The look on his face was sincere. And I didn't want to seem ungrateful, but I wasn't sure about this.

"Listen, I know you're doing this for a good reason. But . . . I just don't know how I feel about taking that much money from you. You've done enough for me already. The truck . . ." I was starting to feel overwhelmed. Tears welled in my eyes. When we reached the car, Game turned me to face him. He wiped at the tears that started to roll down my face.

"Porsha, you are the best thing that has happened to me in a long time. Anything that I do for you is because I want to. Seeing you happy makes me happy. I want to take care of you. You don't have to work if you don't want to. I promise I'll take care of you. That's my duty now. Let me love you." Pulling my face toward his, he kissed me deeply, and I returned every stroke. Gently stroking my face, he asked, "Can you do these things for me?"

Looking in his eyes, I saw nothing but trust and his love for me. "Yes, I'll let you love me. But I'm not ready to leave my job. I have accomplished good things since I've been working there. I'll know when I'm done." I hoped he understood that, because my mind was made up. I was in love with him. Since the loss of my brother I had not felt protected until Game.

It had been over a week since I had seen Ma. Between work and the time I had been spending with Game, I was tied up. But today I was off and made it my mission to spend it with her. Up early, I went downstairs, had a cup of coffee, and talked for a minute with Rosa, Game's housekeeper. She had worked for him for over three years. Rosa was a nice lady, and according to her, she only had two years left to retirement. And she couldn't wait, because she was moving back to Puerto Rico. In only a short time I had grown to like her. She loved to crack jokes and kept me laughing. I would miss her when she retired.

Two hours later I was ready. I jumped in my truck and headed toward East Oakland to Ma's house. I was going to surprise her with lunch and shopping. I also had plans to put some of that money Game had put into my account into hers.

Using my key, I unlocked the door and walked right in. "Ma." I stretched my arms out to her. She had a cup of coffee in her hand and was about sit down when I came in. She quickly set the cup on the table.

"My baby," she said, full of joy, and hugged me so tight I could barely breathe.

"I missed you." I sounded like a kid.

"I missed you too sweetheart." She released me. "I thought you had forgotten about me." She grinned.

"Never. I could never forget my Ma. I told you on my next off day I was coming over." I continued to smile. "How about you get dressed. I got the whole day planned for us." I waited for her to say she couldn't go.

"Give me a minute to get dressed." It came out faster than I would have expected. She wasted no time rushing to the back. I went into the kitchen and made myself another cup of coffee. Ma's coffee was always bomb. Thirty minutes later she was showered and dressed.

I let her choose the spot for lunch, and to my appreciation she chose Red Lobster. We both loved to eat there. My favorite, of course, was the cheesy garlic biscuits. I could eat about ten of those without being full. The hostess seated us. No sooner were we seated than our waiter approached the table and took our order.

"So I see they still keeping you busy over at the bank."

I sighed. Just thinking about it made me tired. "They never stopped." The waitress put the biscuits on the table and I wasted no time reaching for one.

"I remember when I was working all the time like that when you and your brother were little. It was a mess. But what I hated most was being away from both of you."

"You did what you had to do. Kenneth and I understood that."

She nodded in agreement. Her facial expression told me she was proud of me. "I'm glad to see you happy, Porsha."

"I am, Ma. Game is a good guy. He's what I need right now in my life." I was happy to say this. After my brother died, I felt as if nothing would ever make me happy again. I was wrong.

"Don't get me wrong. It's okay for a guy to shower you with nice things. But I feel like Game is moving too fast. Doing way too much too soon." The concern she was feeling was all over her face. I should have known she would worry. The day I pulled up in the truck that he had bought me, she loved it. But she was a little apprehensive of him purchasing something so expensive for me when we had just started dating. Not to mention the fact that I had moved in with him so soon. I thought she would flip, and although it was clear she wanted to, she decided not to. I wondered if she felt like it might push me away like Kenneth. The more she pried with him about his lifestyle, the deeper into it he became.

"I know it seems that way. But he just cares for me, Ma. Right now we just want to be good to each other. Game doesn't want anything from me but to be with me."

"I hear you. But what about his family?"

"His parents are dead, but he does have a sister out in Texas."

"I'm sorry to hear about his parents . . . Listen, all I'm saying is that sometimes people can move too fast when really, there is no rush. I just don't want you to end up with any regrets. I want nothing but the best for you."

"I know you do. And I'm telling you that you have nothing to worry about. Nothing has changed. I still plan to pursue my dreams. School is on the list and comin' soon." I smiled. I wanted to reassure her she could count on me. The last thing I wanted to do was disappoint her.

"All right." She smiled as the waitress sat her spicy Cajun chicken pasta in front of her. And boy, did it look delicious.

I patiently waited for mine. "Now this is what I'm talkin' about." I stirred mine before taking my first bite. "Good," I said with a mouth full of pasta. And there was no shame in my game.

"This food is going to make me fat. I haven't been to the gym in what, two, years?" Ma said, then forked another round of pasta into her mouth. Ma had been an athlete all through high school. She was a top basketball player at her school, even receiving a scholarship to USC, but when she met our dad, her dreams changed. Because of that, she had always been conscious of her body. She kept a membership at the Y, and no matter how hard she worked, she made time for the gym. Even now she still had a slim waist and long legs. At forty-seven, she looked good. When Kenneth died, though, just like everything else, the gym became no more.

"Maybe you should get back into the gym. That would get you off that couch."

"It might." She grinned. It was nice to see her talk and smile all in one motion. My heart chanted.

"I have something I wanted to do for you." I braced myself with this one. She had just finished discussing her concern about Game and how fast he was moving. But I wanted to do this, so I had to step up. "Game put some money into a secure account for me."

"He did, did he?" The concerned look was back. It wasn't harsh, but it made my stomach nervous. I didn't want this to go badly.

"Yeah, just a little something so that I can feel secure." I paused. I didn't know what she would say next. Silence held the air, so I decided it might be okay to move on. "What I wanted to do was put some into your account . . . Just so I don't have to worry. And if you need anything, you can go get it. And if I was at work it wouldn't hold you up." Finally I had it out. I waited.

"Now, Porsha, you know how I feel about drug money. I can't." She shook her head and closed her eyes for a brief moment.

"I know that, Ma." I sighed. I couldn't give up. "But like I told you before, Game ain't into drugs. He is legit. He has his own business." I looked her straight in the eyes and lied. I didn't know what else to do. I felt some comfort in knowing it wasn't a total lie. Game did have his own business, but he was in fact a drug dealer, and no peon at that.

"Porsha, you want me to believe that a few car lots has him living the lifestyle he does? Do you really believe that?"

I swallowed because I was about to lie again. And the one thing I hate to do was lie to my mother. "Yes I do. Ma, you have to trust me. In the past two years, haven't I stepped up? Have I done anything that would give you a reason to doubt me?"

She looked at me for a full minute, then smiled. "No you haven't. You've been the perfect daughter, stepping up and doing everything that I couldn't for this family." A tear slid down her cheek. "I almost feel as if I let you down when you needed me most."

"No, Ma. You have never let me down. You just needed me to be there for you the way you were always there for Kenneth and me. Now it's my turn to make sure you straight. Giving you this money makes me feel that you are secure."

Tears were flowing down her face. I handed her a napkin off the table. She dabbed at the tears. "Okay. You can put the money into the account. I'm so proud of you, Porsha." She sniffed. Tears had already started down my face.

"Now look at us." I laughed. Ma laughed too. We sat and finished our food and chatted some more. After leaving Red Lobster, we drove over to her bank, where I deposited ten thousand dollars into her account. Next, we hit up some stores and did some shopping. Of course Ma's favorite was Bath & Body Works. We both were candle freaks, but she was one times ten. And I let her go all out. Can you believe we spent three hundred dollars in a candle store? It was ridiculous, and I loved it. As long as Ma had a smile on her face, I would go completely broke.

CHAPTER 11

Backing out of the garage, I smiled at the beautiful sun. It went great with my mood. I was on my way to Macy's to meet up with Briana and Sasha to do a little sunglass retail therapy. I couldn't wait. We had been talking about sunglass shopping for the past two weeks, but none of us could find the time. Today we were all free, so it was on. I entered Macy's on the women's side of the store. A few maxi dresses caught my attention, and I couldn't help but browse for a minute. There were at least two of them that had my undivided attention. Vowing to come back once I was done eyewear shopping, I continued on to my destination.

"Oh, I see how it is. Y'all gon' go ahead and start without me?"

Sasha and Briana were busy testing their sunglasses in the mirror with a selfie.

"Our bad, boo." Sasha smiled. "We just got a little caught up."

"Porsha, I swear . . . Could you be on time sometime?" Briana asked while taking off her sunglasses and reaching for another pair.

"So that's your excuse for not waiting on me? It's cool,

though." I pretended to be upset. "Look at these. They're cute." I picked up a pair of Persol that really had my attention. Modeling for the mirror, I was feeling them.

"Bitch, you beat in those," Briana complimented me.

Placing them back on the rack, I reached for a pair of Coach that were screaming my name. "These right here stealing the show, though!" I slid them on.

"Those are sick." Sasha smiled, then held up her phone to take a pic. Briana jumped in wearing a pair of Gucci and we both struck a pose.

"Bitch, we just killed it." Briana was hype. "I'm about to go broke up here."

"Always," I agreed.

"So what's up, Porsha? I see that nigga keepin' you ghost," Briana chimed.

Trying on my next pair of sunglasses, I smiled. "He has not. You know how the bank keep me locked down." I laughed. "That shit ain't changed. But me and bae, we spending some time."

"I hear that. I'm tryin' to be on that too, but ain't nobody passin' the test." Sasha said.

"Shit, that's my problem too. But I ain't even trippin'," Briana threw in.

"Y'all stop. Both of you can have whoever you want." And that was no lie, they both were beautiful.

"I know, but these niggas on the bullshit. And I swear I ain't feelin' it," Briana spat.

"I feel you. And I have Rein to think about. So I can't be pickin' the wrong one."

"Real talk. You have to be careful. Right now I'm still tryin' to get Ma to trust the decision I made to be with Game."

"What's up? Is she trippin?" Briana asked.

"Yeah, she concerned. She just don't want us to move too fast . . . I guess the moving in together was too much too soon for her." I decided to leave out the money and her worries about him selling drugs.

"I wouldn't worry about that much. She'll be fine. It's just basic mother instinct to worry. But I promise she's probably gettin' over it already. I'm sure she ain't thinkin' about you right now anyway. She called me to bring Rein over earlier. And girl, Rein didn't give me one glance when I walked away."

The thought of Ma and Rein ignoring Sasha as she walked away made me smile. "Ma has fallen in love with Rein. I'm sure Rein has her wrapped around her finger."

"And you worried about her concerns for you. Ha, just like Sasha said, she has forgotten about you. She has a new baby," Briana joked. We all laughed.

Looking at the Coach watch on my left arm, I realized it was time for me to get getting. Time had flown by talking with them. Motioning for the salesclerk, I informed her that I wanted the Coach and Persol sunglasses. "It's been fun, ladies, but I have to get going."

"Damn, where you in a rush off to? You just got here." Briana pouted.

"Bri, it's been an hour already. I told you I wouldn't be staying long. Remember?" I reminded her. "I have to get home. Game is cooking dinner for me tonight." I blushed. Saying his name gave me butterflies in the pit of my stomach.

"Hmmm, dinner then bang bang time." Briana smiled with her right eyebrow raised.

"And in that order." Sasha cosigned.

After purchasing the sunglasses, I made a quick stop and purchased the maxi dresses that had caught my eye earlier. With a huge grin spread across my face, I exited the store. I couldn't wait to get home to see what Game had planned for dinner.

The different aromas from the food Game was preparing filled my nostrils as soon as I entered the house. My stomach immediately started to grumble. I was a true foodie and enjoyed eating, although you couldn't tell by looking at me. My body was in top-notch shape. You would think I went to the gym every day. Game looked up at me and smiled as I entered the kitchen. Placing my purse and Macy's bags down on the kitchen counter, I walked straight into his waiting arms. A kiss followed.

"Did you find the sunglasses your heart desired?"

"Something like that. I picked up two pair. And a few dresses."

"Well, I'm glad you made it back. I missed you." He wrapped me tight in his arms again.

"Well, I missed you more," I cooed. Gazing into each other's eyes, we kissed again. "Your food sure smells good."

"And you know this." He grinned. "Top chef in the house tonight, I ain't playing no games."

"Top chef, huh? So what's on the menu, top chef?"

"Wouldn't you like to know?" He slapped my butt and turned back to the stove. Boy, was he serious about his cooking. He even had on a George Foreman apron.

"I like your apron."

"This old thing?" He glanced down at his apron. "I guess you can say it inspires me to do what I do best . . . Everything is ready. Why don't you wash your hands and meet me in the dining room."

"What you tryin' to get me leave the kitchen so your paid chef can exit?" I joked.

"Ha ha, you know this." He laughed.

Grinning, I grabbed my bags and purse off the counter, walked upstairs, and put my things away. Then I washed my hands and raced back downstairs. I was hungry and couldn't wait to see what dinner Game had planned.

The food looked just as delicious spread out on the table as it smelled. Buttermilk biscuits, ribeye steaks with gravy, mashed potatoes, sweet peas with carrots. My mouth watered.

"Bae, did you really cook all of this? It look so good. Wait a minute. You sure you're not hiding my ma in that kitchen?" I laughed.

"Nah, this all me." He rubbed his chest with pride. "Come on, sit down." He pulled out a chair for me.

"Thanks." I smiled. My eyes roamed my plate. I didn't know what I wanted to taste first. I could see the smoke sizzling around the biscuits, proof that they had just come out of the oven. And that was exactly the way I liked them.

"Don't be shy. Dig in." He picked up his knife and cut into his steak. I swear it looked so juicy. I followed his lead. The meat and gravy melted on my tongue. I chewed slowly to savor all the taste.

"Dang, bae. This is good," I commented after I swallowed.

"Did you doubt me?" He forked some potatoes into his mouth.

"Never." I grinned, then bit into my biscuit. I loved bread, and I knew it wouldn't be long before I reached for another one. We finished our food, then retired to the den with a bottle of wine.

"I wanted to talk to you about something important." Game passed me a glass of wine.

"Sure, what's up?" I sat back on the couch facing him.

"I have a new business venture I'm putting together. I'm going to buy some houses in the middle-class areas of Oakland, fix them up, and sell them at a good price."

"Bae, that sounds like a good idea."

"Yeah, this could put some value back into the areas where the houses need fixing up, but also put some good capital into my pockets."

"And with the houses being in middle-class areas, anyone with a steady job and decent debt ratio should be able to get a reasonable homeowner's loan," I added.

"My thoughts exactly." He winked at me, then took a swig from his glass. "But there is just one thing I need." He focused his eyes on mine. "Your help . . . that's the only way to make this work."

That statement confused me. For one, I had no idea how to fix up a house. The only help I could possibly be would be filling out papers for a home loan. Hopefully that's what he meant. "What help could I be to your business venture?"

"Listen, I've been honest with you about my life, so you know my position in the game. Bottom line is I can't risk having all those assets in my name. I have enough of that already. It's just too much of a liability . . . That's where you come in. I gotta have someone who I can trust without a doubt." I waited for him to get to the point. I was becoming anxious. "I need you to purchase all the houses in your name."

My eyes bulged. "Put them in my name?" I was shocked. "You sure?" I couldn't believe he would trust me with something so important.

"Bae you legit. It only makes sense." The concerned look on his face told me he was worried I might say no.

But he had said the one that was true. He could trust me, and this was the best way for me to prove it to him. "You know what, bae, I'm in. I'll do it." I smiled. "Besides, I love the idea and I think it's a huge opportunity for the homebuyers and for you."

Game pulled me into him, then kissed me deeply. Damn, his tongue made miracles. Next his tongue found my breast. And as the saying goes, my panties fell off.

CHAPTER 12

A couple of months had passed, and as usual I was busy. That seemed to be a common factor in my life. But I couldn't complain—in fact, I loved it. I was still putting in work at the bank, and the new business with the houses was going great. In fact, it had been a lot easier than I had originally thought. Game basically put in all the work. He made sure it never interfered with my job at the bank. He respected my job. So he picked the houses and scheduled all the contract work. All I had to do was show up and sign the paperwork for the purchase and sale, and for that I was grateful. So far we had bought and sold ten houses in a very fast turnaround, and the money was looking good. And I, of course, put my cut directly into the bank. School was no longer merely a goal, it was within reach. But between work, Game, and the time I was spending with family and friends, I had not made the time to register. I promised myself I would soon.

Today was another exciting day for me. Game's sister Keisha was coming into town. So I was home getting ready to meet her. I had called Game's personal chef over to prepare a few finger dishes just in case Keisha was hungry when she arrived. I hoped she liked them.

"Babe, hurry up. Keisha just called, she's pullin' in," Game yelled so I could hear him.

I was a bit nervous. Fidgeting with my hands, I made my way into the hallway where he was cradling a shot glass. "Come on." He smiled at me. He knew I was nervous. "You don't have anything to worry about. Keisha gon' love you."

"I know. I'm just being silly." The doorbell rang. Game made his way down the hallway with me on his trail. "Girl, get in here." He hugged his sister.

"Game, I can't breathe," she said in a muffled tone.

"My bad. You shouldn't wait so long to come visit."

"I know. But I got a life too." She looked at me over Game's shoulders. She was about five-eight. I guess tall ran in their family. She was super light skinned like me, with light brown eyes. They didn't look alike at all. Possibly they had different dads. But I couldn't ask that. He'd only told me his parents were dead.

"Hi," I said.

Game released her as if he had almost forgotten he was supposed to be introducing me. "Babe, this is my sister, Keisha. Keisha, this is Porsha."

"Finally I get to meet you. 'Cause I swear he won't shut up about you." Keisha chuckled. I blushed at her mentioning him constantly talking about me.

"I guess he does like me, huh," I joked.

"No doubt." He pulled me close to him.

Keisha looked at us and smiled. For a brief second I thought the smile was one of uncertainty, but I chalked that up to my being nervous. "Game, I know that is not a shot glass? Not at one o'clock in the afternoon."

"Why not? The best decisions I ever make are over a shot. This right here slappin', lil sis." He laughed.

"Porsha, you better handle that. Nah, for real, though, where can I get one of those? That plane ride was mad. First class was sold out, so I had to fly coach. And you know that ain't my style. So I end up riding next to a pervert who smelled like fried chicken and roasted peanuts. Ugh." She twisted up her face. I couldn't help but laugh.

"Well, let us get you that drink. And I had the chef prepare a few snacks, so I hope you're hungry."

"If she ain't, I am." Game rubbed his six-pack.

"You're always hungry." Keisha playfully rolled her eyes. "Porsha, lead me to that drink."

I could tell I would love Keisha. She reminded me of Briana. It was a must I introduce them while she was in town. We all hung out around the pool for hours. Keisha also announced that she was moving back to Oakland for a while. She had some business that she needed to finalize. Game didn't ask any questions. He was just glad to hear she would be close for a while. And so was I. Keisha seemed to be cool people. I was also glad that I would be able to introduce her to Ma. I asked her if she would mind meeting her, and she agreed right away. Ma would be happy to finally meet one of Game's family members.

Saturday rolled around and it was time to party. I had invited Keisha out to Club Stylz. The plan was to introduce her to Briana and Sasha, and what better way to do that than over drinks and loud music? Game had called in a car for us for the night so we didn't have to worry about who was going to drive home, because we both were going to be turnt. 2 Chainz "Fuckin' Problems" was blasting out of the speakers as we made our entrance. Game shook hands with people in the crowd as we made our way through to our reserved VIP section. Everyone seemed to know him—he was like a ghetto superstar. The DJ announced him and he threw up the peace sign with a grin.

And yes, all thots eyes were on him. But I didn't sweat it, I was bad and I knew it. And the wandering eyes from the guys confirmed it. Game must have noticed too; he slowed his stride and wrapped his arm around my waist. I looked at him with approval. In VIP Game once again was greeted like royalty. No sooner did we get inside than I felt a tap on the shoulder. I turned to face Sasha.

"What's up, chica?"

"Heyyy," I sang.

"I love bad bitches, that's my fucking problem." She sang along with 2 Chainz and laughed. "I used to love that damn song."

"Me too." I cosigned while bobbing my head to the beat.

"What's up, though? We gon' turn up tonight."

"Hell yes." I agreed.

"What's up, bitches?" We both turned to Briana's chant.

"Hey, boo." I hugged my friend. I wondered why she was alone. She had been dating this new guy, Rico, for the past month. I hadn't been able to meet him, so she had promised to bring him tonight. Rico was also in the drug game, so I knew he was getting money. And the look at my girl rocking brand-new Louis Vuitton heels confirmed it. "I thought we were supposed to be meeting Rico tonight?" I questioned.

"I know, right." Sasha cosigned. "What, did he punk out about meeting your homegirls?"

"Bitch, don't be ridiculous, you know I don't do punks." Briana playfully rolled her eyes. "Anyhow . . ." She smiled, then turned to face this handsome, tall, dark-skinned guy with long dreads.

Rico was standing over close to the entrance talking to Paco. Paco was one of the guys who worked for Game. When Briana told me about Rico and that he hustled in the Oakland area, the first thing I did was ask Game about him. He confirmed that he knew him from the streets but they hustled different areas.

Sasha had a huge grin on her face as she eyed Rico up and down. "So that's Rico."

Briana smiled and nodded. The look on her face told me that she was into him a lot. I chuckled. I loved seeing my friend happy. Rico, who was done talking to Paco, was walking in our direction. Briana walked away from us and met him halfway. Grabbing him by the hand, she led him over to us.

"What's up, babe?" Game approached and stood between Sasha and me. "Hey, Sasha," he said.

"Hey," Sasha replied, her eyes still on Briana and Rico.

"Bae, Briana about to introduce us to Rico," I announced. "Stay here with us," I let seep through my clenched lips. Rico was closing in on us, and I didn't want him to hear me.

Briana wore a huge smile as she and Rico now stood toe to toe with us. She wasted no time introducing him. "This here is Rico," she announced proudly. "Rico, I think you may already know Game?"

"Yeah, we street," Game clarified. That was slang they sometimes used in the streets to identify hood status.

"No doubt," Rico said.

"And this is his girl, my best friend Porsha that—" Before Briana could finish, Rico reached for Sasha's hand. Sasha looked at me and chuckled.

Briana smile. "No silly, this is Porsha." She pointed directly at me. I smiled.

"My bad. I'm sorry." Rico immediately apologized.

"No worries." I laughed as I reached out my hand. It was an honest mistake. Game had been standing between Sasha and me, a recipe for a mistaken handshake.

"And I'm Sasha." Sasha jumped in and introduced herself. We all laughed.

"Yo, again my bad." Rico grinned, then rubbed his face as if he was embarrassed.

"It's all fam." Game chuckled, then reached out to shake Rico's hand. "You know what it is."

"No doubt," Rico agreed.

"Well, Porsha and Sasha, are y'all happy you finally met my man?" Briana snuggled up close to Rico. He proudly wrapped his arms around her waist.

"Of course. Rico, honestly, I was beginning to believe you were make believe," I joked.

"Me too." Sasha cosigned.

"Ha ha, you bitches stay having jokes. My honey is all real. Ain't that right, boo?"

"Damn right." Rico chuckled, then leaned down and kissed Briana full on the lips.

"A'ight, enough of that. We came out to turn up, not watch you make out," I said.

"I know, right?" Briana said. "It's shot time."

"My thoughts exactly." Sasha agreed.

"You in the right place. Nothing but the best here in VIP," Game reminded us.

"Let's get fucked up, ladies." Briana grabbed my arm, and with Sasha in tow, we headed for the bar in VIP.

From there it went down. Dance floor, back-to-back drinks, and laughs filled the night. By night's end we all were tore up. Good thing Game had his driver bring us out, because we would have been stranded. I had enjoyed my girls, but I could not wait to get home and crawl into bed. Life was good. I was riding a high that I prayed I would never come down from. I mean, what in the world could ruin it?

"I thought you would never make it," I complained as soon as I opened the door for Briana. She had come out to the house so that we could hang out by the pool, chat, and have some drinks. We didn't invite Sasha. While we were still cool with her, Briana and I were best friends, which meant we needed our alone time. "I thought a Porsche was supposed to deliver you anywhere you want to go in this city fast?" Thanks to Briana's new boo Rico, she was now pushing hard through the streets of Oakland in a Porsche. My girl was killing the game.

"While that might be true, a bitch ain't tryin' to get pulled over by Oakland's finest. We all know these fuckin' rookies in Oakland be tryin' to prove a point." She referred to the cops.

"Shit, I guess you right. Hands up, don't shoot," I joked. But these days it really wasn't a joking matter.

Briana hunched her shoulders with a huge grin covering her face. "I'm here, though. And ready to drink. Please tell me you got a bottle of Moscato?"

"You know it. Everything is already set up by the pool. Game made sure the bar was stocked for us with anything we wanted." That's why I loved him. He always made sure I was straight and didn't have to do much when I was off. He wanted me to relax and enjoy myself.

"Game, my motherfuckin' nigga." Briana was hype. The glow on her face didn't go unnoticed either. Ready to turn up with my girl, I wasted no time heading outside. One glance at the pool and I was relaxed. The blue water sent tingles up my spine. Too bad I had no plans on getting wet. Briana had just slayed my hair the day before, and I knew without a doubt she would kill me if I got it wet.

Briana paused as she took in the beautiful pool. "I swear I could sit out here all night. Porsha, I know I have said it before, but this pool is on point. Simply beautiful, girl." The grin on her face was for more than that pool, though.

"Bri, since you been kickin' it with Rico you got a permanent smile on that face of yours. What's up? And please don't give me no bullshit excuse. 'Cause you know I'm gon' call you on it," I teased her.

"Ahhh." Briana playfully rolled her eyes. She pretended to be mad as she sat down on the chaise lounge by the pool. "You stay assuming shit." She gave me a frown. Then she revealed all of her teeth. "Yeah, that nigga is puttin' a smile on my face." She was giddy.

"I knew it. You can never fool me." I praised the fact that I was right.

"Well, you and I both know that I need it." She turned to face me. "Porsha, it's different with him than it was with Ronald's punk ass." The mention of Ronald's name brought back the frown that she used to wear.

"I'm glad to see you happy. He bossin' up too. That Porsche is all that." I didn't even respond to Ronald's name.

"I know. I love it too . . . but, Porsha, he's good for me too. We talk, I'm talkin' about real conversations. He really supports me. He's always positive. And you'll be happy to know that I signed up for a six-month cosmetology course."

"Aggh," I yelped from pure happiness. "It's a about damn time." I was ecstatic. I made my way over to Briana and wrapped my arms around her.

"Yep, your boy Rico already cut the check. So it's a bet."

"That's what's up. See, I told you I'm not gon' give up on you." I smiled as I looked out at the pool. I felt released inside. Things were looking good from all ends. I had never imagined my life being so happy. "Bri, we are blessed. Things seem to be fallin' into place for us, even with Ma. She's been in really good spirts when I visit. And she absolutely loves Rein. She stay taking her to Chuck E. Cheese, just plain spoiling her."

"Yo, that's good. Whatever gets her out of that damn house. I swear I thought she might never leave that house again."

"What you said." I cosigned.

"Aye, but check this out. I really think this is a coincidence, but the other day I was going to Izzy's Steakhouse to meet up with Rico for dinner. As I pulled into the lot, I happened to see Game pulling out. Not even a minute later Sasha comes zooming out past me. She was going so fast I'm sure she didn't even see me. And just for a second I wondered what they were both doing there."

"Wait, you think they were together." I looked at her and laughed. "Nah, it's like you said, that was just a coincidence. Besides, you know Sasha be everywhere eating. I'm sure she was there with some guy. You know she always got a date. And

Game loves a juicy steak." I smiled. I thought of how he was always having the chef prepare steaks or ordering out for one. In fact, once I thought about it, I remembered he had brought one home recently. "Bri, when was this?"

"A couple of days ago."

"Game brought home both of us steaks from Izzy's a couple nights ago. I forgot all about that. Sasha must have just happened to be there at the same time."

"Those were my thoughts exactly. You know the only reason I mentioned it was because it made me think back to last week at the club. Remember, when I introduced you all to Rico? Well, later that night after the club he was sayin' how he basically knew Game from the streets and that he was really sorry for mixing up you and Sasha. But he said Sasha looked really familiar to him and that for some reason he thought they were together. And he knew from our conversations that my best friend Porsha"—she pointed to me—"was Game's girl."

Now I understood why he had been so rushed at judgment when Briana introduced us. "Okay, and with Game standing between Sasha and me, I could see how he could mix that up. And we all know Sasha be everywhere. So ain't no tellin' where he might have seen her."

"That's what I said. Rico agreed too. Yep, all that shit was just a coincidence. 'Cause you know if it wasn't, I would be about to beat Sasha's ass for real." The scowl on her face told me she was not playing. I knew what Briana was capable of. Like I said, she didn't take no mess.

"Bri, stop with the violence." I laughed.

"Damn right. I came over here to relax and get tipsy. Pass me that damn bubbly. Can I get a refill?" She started to sing. I couldn't help but laugh. I refilled my glass, then passed the bottle to her while she continued to repeat the hook of the song. We sat back, got twisted, and took a nap out by the pool.

CHAPTER 13

Life was good. I had hopped a plane with Game to Florida two days ago to accompany him on his business trip. Of course I didn't attend the business, but fun was definitely on my agenda. My job had reluctantly given me the days that I would need while we were away, and I planned to enjoy every minute of them.

We had a house rented on the beach, and it was beautiful. Both mornings I had sat on the deck to watch the sun rise. I had only heard about such foolishness on television, but turned out I loved it. In East Oakland I never got the chance to enjoy God's natural beauty right here on earth. Oakland was concrete streets, fast cars, hustling, and gunshots. I needed some sun, sand, blue water, and pampering, and Game didn't disappoint. In the two days we had been in town, he made sure I got everything I wanted. That everything added up to be twenty thousand dollars.

Since I would be leaving the following morning I had made a special trip to FedEex and shipped my things home. I didn't want to risk the airline losing my precious new clothes, shoes, and bags.

In honor of our last night in town Game had planned us a nice quiet dinner outside on the deck, prepared by one of the top chefs in Florida, Genzaili. And boy, was he expensive, but Game said nothing was ever too good for me. So I smiled, went shopping, and planned to look scrumptious for our dinner. And when I made my appearance on the deck for dinner in my red lace sheath dress by Tadashi Shjoi, which fit my body just right, accompanied by Jimmy Choo satin ankle-wrap heels, I was not surprised by Game's dropped-jaw reaction.

He immediately stood, stepped in close, then wrapped his arm around my small waist. Softly snuggling his face into my neck, then brushing his lips across my ear, he whispered, "You look good enough to eat. And I promise to taste every inch of you later." I blushed. Softly he planted a kiss on my neck. Taking my hand, he led me around to my side of the table and pulled out my chair.

"Thank you." I sat down carefully. Game always made me feel like a lady. His swagg was always on ten. At the present moment I couldn't have cared less about dinner. What I really wanted to do was take him back to our room, rip his clothes off, and ride him like the true stallion I knew him to be. But like he said, later. "Bae, I swear it's so beautiful out here at night. It gives me that feeling that I could stay here forever." I breathed in the sand and blue water. The breeze coming off the ocean was just right.

"You like it that much out here, huh?"

"Yes. I never imagined it would be so beautiful. I know we have our own beaches out in California. But . . ." I shrugged my shoulders.

"Well, if you like it that much, how about I invest in some property out here? Maybe a beach house or something. That way you could come out here whenever you felt like it. You and your girls could do like a Florida takeover or something."

Just another reason why I loved him so much. There seemed to be nothing he would not do to put a smile on my

face. Everything about him was solid. "Bae I would love that."
A beam spread across my face.

"Done." He smiled. Our personal waiter approached the
table. He filled both our glasses with Champagne, but it didn't
go unnoticed by me that Game had his favorite bottle on the
table. Hennessy. He would be taking shots.

Next the chef introduced our first course. First up was
shrimp cocktail, followed by a spinach salad, which Game knew
I loved. Then we were served the main course: filet mignon,
asparagus, and chopped squash, another one of my favorites.
Vanilla ice cream and peach cobbler was the dessert. I nearly
melted. The meal was plain, but everything that I loved, so I
knew Game had requested it.

"Did you enjoy everything?"

"Every bite. Clearly you're learning your way to my heart."
I giggled.

Game chortled, then saluted. "My honor. Real talk, though,
I want you to know that I will give you the world. Like I say all
the time, all I ever want is for you to be happy."

The look on his face was so full of love it made me want to
cry. "I am happy. Every moment that I'm with you, I'm happy."
I gave him a smile that only my heart could carry.

Game stood and walked over to my side. I knew what was
coming next, and I could hardly contain myself. He had gotten
up to put his soft lips on mine. I waited. Reaching my side, he
stood, towering over me. I wanted to kiss him so bad I almost
jumped out of my seat into his arms. But I waited. Then my
heart skipped a beat. Instead of leaning down to kiss me, he
planted himself on his right knee. I became a bit nervous as I
looked into his eyes.

"Porsha, will you marry me?" I couldn't believe my ears.
My head swooned. "Babe, are you okay?"

I was fine but at a loss for words. I wondered if he was
serious, but the big diamond ring that blinded me from the
box had me convinced that he was. Tears burned my eyes.

Game's left hand traveled to my face, and he softly rested it on my cheek. "Porsha, I love you. Possibly from the very first moment we met."

God I loved this man. He didn't need to say any more. "Yes." The tears that had been threatening to fall, fell. Game glided the new diamond onto my finger. I couldn't help but stare at it. Game planted a million kisses all over my face before finding my lips. After a long, passionate kiss he stood and pulled a chair up close to me.

"Are you still in shock?" he asked. I couldn't take my eyes off the diamond, or *rock*, as some might call it.

"Pretty much." I gave a shy smile, then my eyes wandered back to my ring. "But on life you did good, bae."

"I aim to please." He laughed. "No really, I was worried you might not like it."

"Bae, there is no way any woman wouldn't be in awe of this rock." I showcased it to him as if it was his first time seeing it.

Suddenly his face turned serious. "There is also something I need to talk to you about."

"What is it, bae? What's up?" I wasn't concerned. With this ring on my finger, it couldn't be anything too serious.

"I have to go away for a while . . . and I would like it if you could go with me."

"Wait, what do you mean you have to go away? What for, why?" Now I was confused. He had asked me to marry him not even ten minutes prior, now he had to leave? "Go where?"

Whatever it was, it was serious, and I knew that once he dropped his head. I sat on the edge of my seat. My stomach churned.

"It's beyond my control, a'ight?" He sighed. "The feds have been building a case against me for some time now. Ever since my last lockdown, they just won't seem to let it go. So my lawyer needs me to vamp so that he can straighten things out. He want my presence to be ghost." I soaked up everything he had just said to me. "Feds" and "leave town" were rolling through my mind in a ball of confusion. "I know this is a lot, but it's what I have to do. But I didn't want to leave town without us being married. And that's regardless if you decide to go with me or not. I also want us to be set up for life, financially, in case something were to go wrong and we have to be gone longer than expected."

"Is everything okay with your finances?" I asked.

"No my finances are good." He paused. "As you know, I have a great deal of money and I have worked hard for it. But I also came from nothing, so I always think with the mind-set that there can never be enough money. That is why I want us to make a big-time score before we leave."

Now the words "score" and "us" had my undivided attention. Again I was confused. It must have been written all over my face. He looked down again, so whatever was brewing was serious. He reached for my hand. "I need you to set it up so that I can make a clean hit at your bank."

There was no doubt in my mind I was being punked. I turned around and looked at my surroundings to see if there were people watching with cameras. I didn't see anything. The beach was clear. I faced Game again and laughed. But he did not laugh back.

"Porsha, I know this may come as a surprise, but I'm not kidding. This is real. I need you to do this for us."

At that moment I become stunned. Did he realize what he was asking me to do? "Game, you have enough money already. We will be fine."

"I explained that to you already."

"Well then, there has to be some other way to get the money besides my work." I loved him and wanted to help, but we had to think rationally.

"Babe, I have thought this through long and hard. There is no other way."

I didn't agree with that. "There is." I was adamant. "We could double our house sales," I suggested. "That has made good money for us already. We have two houses that we can have gone in two months. Less."

"Babe, that ain't gon' work. Two months ain't fast enough." He shot that idea right out of the air. "And quite frankly, not enough dough." He shrugged. "Not to mention I don't have a lot of time to blow. Like I said, the Feds, they on my ass. I gotta make a move and it has to be a fast smart one."

"But . . ." I tried to speak, but he stopped me.

"Listen, I know I'm asking a lot from you. But I need you to trust me. This is what we need. It's quick, clean, and damn near perfect. The score from the bank is the only way," he stressed.

This time I dropped my head. He had his mind made up. So here I was, backed into a corner. The man I loved just put a huge rock on my finger—I'm sure it cost him no less than forty thousand dollars—asked me to marry him, and was also asking me to run away with him, but only after we robbed the bank where I worked. What the fuck?

CHAPTER 14

It had been a couple of days since I returned home from Florida, and truth be told, I felt as if I was walking between clouds of two different worlds. Elated because the man that I loved had asked me to be his wife, but also inside a ball of confusion that the man I loved had asked me to jeopardize it all for a quick come up. So for the two days I had been home, the only thing I had done was lie around the house, mostly in bed, trying to figure things out. I didn't want to see anyone. I had told Ma, Briana, and Sasha that the trip had exhausted me and that I had to work. I hated to lie to them, but it was partly true.

Hours before our flight was to leave Florida, Game had received word that a few things still needed to be handled, so he stayed behind. As much as I would have loved to have him home, I thanked God for the time alone to think. Over several bottles of wine I searched for answers to my questions. Had Game really considered the risk of what he was asking me to do? How could he say he loved me but ask me to do such a thing? I was confused yet angry at the same time, and I still had no reasonable answer to these questions. The worst part was I could not discuss it with anyone. Briana and I told each other everything—we had no secrets between us—but Game had warned me about the seriousness of anyone even knowing we had that conversation. And even though I knew I could trust Briana with anything, the last thing I wanted to do was disrespect Game or put Briana at risk, so I kept quiet.

The alarm going off on my cell phone interrupted my thoughts. I turned it off. I had set the alarm so that I would not forget about the shopping I had reluctantly committed myself to with Briana and Sasha. They'd allowed me to rest for two days, but they refused to take any more of my excuses. I told them that Game had spent 20k on me in Florida and I was good. But truth be told, my motto was a girl could never shop enough. Pushing back my Donna Karan sheets, I threw my legs over the side of the bed, sat up, and stretched. The shower was my destination. The hot water did my body good. My mood was comfortable, so I threw on a pair of blue jean boyfriend shorts, a white wifebeater with pink lettering that read *Oakland Chic*, and my pink and white Jordan Retro 12s. After sizing myself up in the mirror, I concluded I was ready.

"We missed you," Briana and Sasha sang and hugged me at the same time.

"Really? Did you two practice that?" I teased them.

"See, Sasha, I told you she would be suspicious."

"I knew it was fake." I gave a fake pout.

"Just kidding. We missed your big head butt." Briana laughed.

"How was the beach?" Sasha's eyes lit up.

"Beautiful. I loved it." I really didn't feel like talking about the trip. It brought back the decision I had to make. But I knew they would have questions. I was happy when the saleslady brought us out a glass of wine. The wine would calm my nerves so that I could get through the questions without breaking down.

"Now, this is what I've been waiting for." Sasha referred to the wine. She took a sip right away.

"Yeah, me too. We should have told her to go ahead and bring out round two." Briana added. I felt the same way but kept it to myself and sipped instead.

"Ladies, let's toast to heels and bags, because I plan to buy both before we leave up outta here." Sasha raised her glass. "This retail therapy is two weeks overdue," she added, then sipped her wine as if her life depended on it.

For the next hour we shopped, chatted, and drank wine. Although I hadn't done much talking, I was glad I had come out. Being with the girls kinda cleared my mind, and I needed that. I wanted to tell them about the engagement so bad, but Game had warned against that too. According to him, we didn't need to bring any extra attention to ourselves. He said we would announce it at the perfect time. So when I returned to Florida I had taken my diamond off and put it in the safe at home. I looked at my ring finger as I sipped my wine, and a tear almost fell.

"So I've been thinking about something long and hard," Sasha said, then paused.

"Well, is you gon' tell us? Or we gon' have to play charades?" Briana joked.

"I swear you have no patience, Bri." Sasha grinned.

"Shit, you already know. Plus these drinks got me anxious." We all laughed. "So please, spit that shit out before I grow old here and now."

"Well, I think I'm going to leave Oakland," Sasha announced with a hint of uncertainty in her tone.

"Really." I was shocked.

"Leave Oakland . . . bitch, and go where?" Briana probed.

"That I ain't sure about yet. But somewhere. It's time I try something different. I been here my whole life. Shit just not working out for me no more. I want a change."

"Yo, in that case, I feel you," Briana said.

"Me too. Hey, seeing Florida gave me this different feeling

also," I admitted. Suddenly I noticed both of them staring at me. Was it something I said?

"Aye, what's up with you, Porsha? You been kinda quiet." Briana had cold busted me. With all the shopping and laughing we had been doing, I thought they wouldn't notice I had not said much.

"You have been quiet." Sasha gave me this accusing stare.

"I ain't been quiet." I tried to deny it, but I knew Briana was not trying to hear that. I had to come up with something better. I shrugged my shoulder. "I did work a twelve-hour shift the day after I returned from Florida." I continued that lie. "Not to mention I never had a moment's rest in Florida," I added. Hopefully this would be enough to satisfy their curiosity.

Briana gave me a suspicious look, and I knew she wasn't sold.

Sasha finished off her drink. "All I have to say is perk up, honey, because from all those pictures you sent us of the clothes, shoes, and bags Game bought you in Florida, I would have to say it was worth all the sleep you missed. What you think, Bri?"

Briana sized me up, then a grin spread across her face. But I could still see a hint of concern. "Yeah, that shit was worth it. Hell, I wish I was there shopping with you. I done already made Rico promise to take me out there soon." She winked at me. I knew Briana cared about me, and I knew shopping sprees and money didn't change that. She couldn't have cared less about the glitz and glamor—she wanted to be sure I was okay.

"I promise you gon' enjoy it. I'm going to give you the names of all the stores I hit."

"No doubt." Briana reached for another drink when the saleslady returned. We were all on drink number four, but our shopping bill between all three of us would be no less than seven thousand, so I knew she was not trippin'.

"See, you bitches got it made." Sasha seemed sad.

"What?" Briana asked.

"You got a man to take you shoppin' and on trips. Look at me. Can't find a man for shit. I wish I had someone to take me out. Hell, anywhere." She chuckled. "That's why I'm getting out of Oakland."

"Sasha, you can have anyone you want. You're beautiful," I pointed out.

"Yeah, but all the niggas I meet be selfish and whores. And I ain't havin' it. All they want is an arm piece. Fuck that."

"I know, right." Briana agreed. "That's the same shit I was going through before I met Rico. The shit is exhausting."

I had to nod and agree. Dudes stayed trying to have me on their arm for how I looked in the past. But I always squashed that as soon as I figured that out. Game was different. I was lucky.

"I swear in the whole city of Oakland ain't one good dude. 'Cause if I could find him, I would gladly settle down," Sasha shared.

Briana started giggling. "Sasha, please be real, bitch. All you want is money. Since when did you want to settle down?" Briana laughed but was being real.

Sasha smiled. "Bri, I know, get them dollars. Hell, it's pay up or shut up. But I'm a girl, so trust. I want love too."

"Yeah, love with a sack full of gold." We all cracked up laughing.

"Or at least a sack of rubber band stacks." Sasha continued the joke. Even in high school Sasha wouldn't date a dude who didn't at least have a part-time job, and he had to be willing to give her money. The lifestyle she was living now, it was apparent she had someone taking care of her. Although she didn't admit it, we knew her, so there was no need to pry. She was her mother's daughter.

"But are you good, Porsha?" Briana slipped the conversation back to me.

"I'm great. I'll be even better if you drop those stacks on these fits."

"No doubt. You know I got you." Bri flexed two stacks of hundred dollar bills up out of her all-white Burberry bag. Rico had her on point, and I was not mad. My girl was getting paper out of her man, and I for one didn't see anything wrong with that.

Shopping with the girls had turned out to be a much-needed outing. I felt up beat after all that shopping and drinks. With Yo Gotti "Law" blasting out the speakers of my truck, I hit the interstate headed to Ma's house.

"Hey, Ma." I hugged her tight as soon as she opened the door.

"I thought I was gon' have to make a trip out there to suburb territory to see you," she joked. She was excited to see me.

"Oh, Ma. You knew I was coming. I missed you lady."

"I'm sure you did." She grinned. "Tell me all about Florida. Did you enjoy it?"

I smiled but almost teared up at the same time, I wanted to tell her about the engagement so bad. "Yes, it was beautiful. And you know I couldn't come back without bringing you something." I reached down and grabbed the bag I had set down next to my leg. Opening the wrapped boxes she discovered a pair of red bottoms and a pair of Jimmy Choo topped with two outfits, both evening wear. A bad pantsuit and a dress. Ma didn't go out anymore, but the glow in her eyes told me that she loved everything I had picked. I had her eye for fashion.

"Good news," she announced. "I will be returning to work. I took a job."

For a brief second I thought I had heard her wrong, but the excitement on her face was clear. I couldn't believe it. I thought about how lately she had been in good spirits. I was so excited we sat down and talked for a while, and she gave me more details about the job.

On the ride home I realized that everything I had prayed for was happening. Ma was back to her old self, which for the longest I was almost sure wouldn't happen. I had worried so much over it and cried myself to sleep, praying, many nights. But now everything was coming full circle. And I had found true love with Game. Life was perfect. A warm sensation like relief came over me.

Walking inside the house, my heart nearly leaped out of my chest from excitement when I saw Game standing in the hallway.

"Bae, you came back early," I cried and laughed as I fell into his waiting arms. Never had I felt so safe.

"I had to get back to you. So I worked my ass off, wrapped things up, and jumped on the first available flight. I wanted to surprise you. You miss me?" He gave me his usual captivating smile.

"Of course." I wanted to scream, "Hell yeah with your fine ass!" But I chilled.

"What I needed to hear." He held my chin up facing him then kissed me deep. I all but melted in his arms.

"Bae, I know that everything we discussed in Florida initially took me by surprise. I wanted to be sure it was the best thing. But I want you to know that we are a team and that I have your back in all things you do. We do life together. So I'm down for the score," I revealed.

Game wrapped his arms around me with so much love that I moaned. I wasn't sure exactly when I had made up my mind, somewhere on the ride home, or the moment I laid eyes on my man. There was a lot to be learned about love, respect, and loyalty, but there really wasn't much lying in between the three. A woman knew when it was time to stand up for her man. I wanted to be true to Game. Hold him down, trust his judgment. That would be my true meaning of being his woman. And I owned that. A one-time heist would be nothing compared to the lifetime we would have together.

CHAPTER 15

My time in Oakland was winding down and day by day I felt it. Although it was a must move, I wasn't 100 percent sure how I felt about it, only because I would be leaving behind loved ones. I knew it wouldn't be forever. But how long would it be? Even Game didn't have the answer to that. Now I just had to come up with a way to tell Ma. She was doing really well, but I worried my leaving might trigger her to shut down again. Hopefully, the news of me getting married would smooth that over. Somehow I doubted it. I knew Briana would be happy for me either way.

Not being able to tell anyone about the engagement was nerve wracking. The suspense of everyone's reaction was unnerving. With each passing day I became more anxious. But today I decided to shelve all of this, and I had just the thing. The other day when I picked up a few of my work suits from the cleaners, they handed me a card that had been in one of my jacket pockets. The card belonged to Yazz, the owner of Yazz Couture. She had invited me to visit her store nearly a year ago, but I had lost the card and for some reason couldn't remember her name or the name of the store. So today I decided to meet up with my girls and Keisha there. This was another chance for me to try and introduce the trio. Keisha hadn't showed up that night at the club. She claimed something came up at the last minute. Hopefully this time she would come through.

Pulling into Yazz Couture, a quick glass in my rearview mirror revealed Briana was right behind me. Grabbing my Michael Kors bag off the seat, I hopped out. The Oakland sun was beaming, but the breezy wind blended, and it felt good.

"Heyyy," Briana sang with a huge grin spread across her lips.

I had to smile. Rico was still bringing out the happy in her. "I swear you better be with Rico's ass forever. That nigga done put a permanent smile on your face."

"Damn right." She adjusted her Cynthia Bailey shades. "A bitch on cloud nine," she joked.

"That's what's up."

"So where your girl? Or should I say sister-in-law. That bitch betta not be standing you up again today because this time it's gone be a problem." Briana looked around as if she was scoping for Keisha.

"Don't start, Bri. Be nice. I told you something came up that night."

"A'ight, whatever you say. Shit, I'm ready to spend either way."

"Where Sasha at, though?" I asked just as a Maybach pulled up. The driver stepped out and opened the back door. Keisha got out.

"She's here," I announced as a feeling of relief came over me. I didn't want Briana and Sasha to think that Keisha was standing us up on purpose.

"Who?"

"That's Keisha." I pointed.

Briana glared at the Maybach. "Guess you can be late when you bossin' up." She smiled.

"What you said." I cosigned.

"Aye, what's up, Porsha?" Keisha said as she approached.

"Hey, I'm glad you could make it today."

"Absolutely. Again, I'm sorry about that night at the club. Shit happens, you know." She apologized again.

"It's cool, Keisha. Aye, this my best friend Briana. Bri, Keisha." I introduced the two.

"Hey." They spoke in unison. I prayed Briana behaved. Anything big or small could set her off.

"So finally we meet Game's sister. We thought he was an orphan," She chuckled. I gave her a *shut up* look, but with a quick smile.

"Briana, that's not funny." I tried to smooth over her comment.

Keisha laughed. "It's cool. Everybody always think that. Sometimes I think my own brother is ashamed of me."

"Real talk, though, I'm just kidding. Aye, but I love that Maybach."

"Yeah, that's my driver while I'm in town."

"A'ight. Sasha's not here yet, so why don't we go inside," I said.

"Whose boutique is this again?" Briana inquired as we made our way inside.

"Her name is Yazz. See?" I pointed to the sign that read in all red *Yazz Couture.*

"Oh, I never heard of this place before."

"Me either. But I met her some months back and she was rockin' this cute shirt. Anyway, she gave me her card and invited me out, but I lost the card for a while." Pushing on the door handle, we made our way inside. The boutique was real nice. Very classy. Reminded me of Kandi's store on *Real Housewives of Atlanta.*

"Welcome to Yazz Couture." A tall, dark-skinned model-type chick greeted us. "I'm Raquel, can I help you with anything?"

"We're just going to browse for now," I informed her.

"I take it that's not Yazz." Briana chimed in.

"No, that's Raquel." I playfully rolled my eyes at Briana. I knew she was trying to be funny.

"She got some cute stuff in here." Keisha observed a blouse.

"Yeah, and it ain't cheap." Briana held up a tag on another blouse.

"Shut up. You pay top dollar for that crap down at the swap meet," I joked.

"Word up. Gotta support Pookie and nem." We all laughed.

I looked up, noticed a familiar face, and realized it was Yazz.

"I see you finally came in." She smiled as she approached me, her hand extended.

"Yes. I misplaced the card," I admitted.

"It's Porsha, right?"

"Yep."

"It's been a minute, but I'm pretty good with names. Well, I'm glad you stopped in today."

"No doubt. I wanted to check out your boutique. Like I said, I love clothes . . . Oh, and this is my best friend Briana that I was telling you about." It was brief, but I could have sworn I saw sadness in her eyes again when I mentioned my best friend.

"Hi." She extended her hand to Briana.

"And this is Keisha, my sister-in-law."

"Hi." She also extended her hand to Keisha.

"I'm supposed to have another friend coming, but she's late."

"You have some nice pieces in here," Keisha shared with her.

"I'm here, ladies." Sasha strutted in like she was America's next top model.

Briana sighed with an attitude. "We can see that, and you late, so keep the grand entrance." Briana was on her feelings today.

"Well, I'm glad you made it."

"Sasha, this is Keisha, Game's sister." I wasted no time introducing them.

Sasha seemed to pause before speaking. Keisha did the same. Sasha cleared her throat. I'm sure she had been talking to Briana, who was clearly offended that Keisha didn't show up at the club the other night. "Hi." She gave this little princess wave. Until then I had almost forgotten how stuck up Sasha could be at times.

"Hey." Keisha's response, in my opinion, was dry as well. I looked at them both but decided to dismiss it. Sometimes I could read too much into things.

"And Sasha, this is Yazz. This is her boutique."

"Yes, and welcome." Yazz smiled and extended her hand. Sasha shook her hand, then looked around as if she was not satisfied with what had been presented to her. "Well, I'm going to let you ladies browse. And as my guests today, you can have twenty percent off anything you decide to purchase."

"Sweet. I love a deal." Keisha turned back to the blouse she had been looking at only moments earlier.

It didn't take long before I found several things I wanted to purchase. I had a few designer pants, red bottoms, and a bag. And I wasn't through. So far everything was cool with the girls, except for Sasha. She couldn't seem to find anything that, as she put it, she "cared for."

"Keisha, do you miss living in Oakland?" Briana asked, making conversation.

"Hmm, you know, I don't think about it much. But I guess not. Damn sure don't miss the panhandlers." She chuckled.

"I feel you. They ass be bugging. Just the other day I damn near had to smack one. Bitch refused to stop hounding me about two dollars after I had already given her ten." Briana sighed with aggravation. "I mean, I always give, but that shit gets out of hand sometimes."

"You just gotta be quick about it. Give and move on fast," I added.

"Hmm" was Sasha's only reply.

"I guess the only thing I miss is Game. Thinking about my

bro is the only thing that makes me homesick. The rest of my family far and wide . . . humph. And they never gave a damn."

"Family should always be close. Mine is small too, but we make it work. And I don't give two fucks about the ones that ain't thinkin' about me 'cause I'ma gets mine," Briana said matter-of-factly.

"Most of all, you got to be about your hustle. Shit, that got me where I am today. Moms was on her thing. Shit, I'm on mine. And I don't care much about much else. I got my mind on money and money on my motherfuckin' mind. I'm running up checks with these sucka-ass niggas." Sasha was not holding back. Sounded just like something her mother would have said.

"Damn, bitch, I got them coins on my mind too. But that shit sounded a little dangerous." Briana chuckled.

"Hey, I got my hustle and my brother. So I only need a nigga for what I need him for." Keisha was confident. "Don't matter day or night, Oakland or Texas. I'm a motherfucking boss."

"Dig that." Briana smiled. "Bitch, that's bars." Briana high fived Keisha.

Yazz came over a couple times to check on us. She was really cool people. It was getting late, so we all decided to check out. I was the last one to check out, so I told the girls I would catch them outside, while Yazz finished up my order.

"I'm so glad you invited me out. I really love your boutique, and I promise I'll be coming by more often. You got yourself a customer."

"That's what's up. I try to keep it quality and quantity."

"And that's what I need. Keep the Louis comin'." I laughed.

"No worries, I got you." Yazz bagged up my last item. "So those are your friends?" We watched as the girls exited the store.

"Yep. Well, Keisha is my sister-in-law, like I said earlier. We haven't known each other long." I wasn't sure why I said all that, but I did.

"Hmmm. I remember hanging out with my best friend all the time . . ." She seemed to stare off into space, but very briefly.

"I know you can go home to visit, then, so y'all can turn up."

"That would be nice . . . She passed away, though."

I instantly felt bad. Then it dawned on me. That was the reason for the sadness. It all made perfect since now. "I'm sorry. I didn't mean—"

She cut me off. "No, it's not your fault. Things happen. Just cherish your true friends because you may never have another."

"I know," I agreed.

Yazz seemed to stare at the girls while they packed their things into their vehicles. All but Sasha, of course. She had only purchased a pair of Prada earrings. According to her, she couldn't find anything else. So after dropping three fifty on her earrings, she was ready to bounce. "You know having friends is cool. Especially hangers on. But sometimes you have to be careful of the company you keep. There is something to be understood about people and true intentions. Especially people who desire being in your shadow. Most important, you should know they come with a smile, a handshake, a tear, and a hug, and honestly more." She laughed, her eyes still focused on the girls in the distance. "Sometimes people we keep close are simply poison soaked into the ground. They'll never be your friends."

Now I was looking crazy. I think Yazz knew she had lost me. It must have been written all over my face. She chuckled. "I guess you are wondering what the moral is to my story. Well, it's simple. Be careful of people and smiling faces."

Yazz really seemed to be wise. I wasn't sure of her age, but I concluded she was at least a year younger than me. But she owned her own business and seemed so mature. I wondered what she had really been through. Either way, she inspired me.

CHAPTER 16

After a few weeks of constant plotting and planning, the official day that the heist would be going down had finally arrived. Unable to get any sleep during the night, I was feeling completely exhausted in the morning. To make matters worse, Game had been out all night handling business, so I had suffered alone. However, he arrived an hour before I was to walk out of the door. He brought me lunch—my favorite tacos. Unfortunately for me, my stomach was not in the mood for eating. But instead of saying that to Game, I lied and told him I had eaten a big turkey sandwich for breakfast. There was no way I could tell him how nervous I was. I didn't want him to worry that I would mess it all up.

Before going inside for work I said a prayer, but the funny thing was by the time I made it inside, I couldn't remember what I had prayed for. The first line of business for me was to use the bathroom. My nervousness was lying heavy on my bladder. I had to get it together. Thankfully, my work was demanding, and before I knew it the day had passed me by. I looked at the clock, and the fluttering instantly took over my stomach again. I was nervous as shit. For a brief second, I thought I might hurl my insides up. I started to go to the bathroom, but I didn't want to do anything out of the ordinary. The goal was not to do anything that someone could remember as odd or out of my character. If anyone looked at me, on the outside I was cool as a fan. Inwardly, I was sweating bullets.

Finally, the big bosses started packing up to leave for the day, which left me in charge of the evening shift. I was the closer. Then it was time for the tellers and me to start shutting down for the evening. Everyone was busy counting their deposits when Sheila decided she needed to bother me at the wrong damn time.

"Porsha." Sheila hung over my shoulder.

"What's up?" I continued my count. I didn't want to look at her because my facial expression would probably read *get the fuck out of my face.* Whatever she wanted, now was not the time.

"I hope you didn't forget about my upcoming birthday party?" She had to be kidding me. What? Were we twelve? Ugh, I was annoyed. But I stayed cool.

"I haven't forgotten." But to be honest I had no intention of attending. Sheila was a'ight, but I really didn't want to be that tight with anyone I worked with. "I'll let you know, though. I need to check and be sure it's not the same weekend as my friend's bridal shower." I lied. It was the best I could come up with to wiggle my way out of it.

"I hope you can make it. It's gon' be ignorant off the hook. Turn up, turn up." Sheila was hype. From what I knew about how she got down outside of work. Sheila was the type of chick that drank forties right out of the bottle. So when she said turn up, she meant it.

"A'ight. Bet." I popped my gum. I prayed she left me alone. Seconds later she had disappeared.

Minutes later tellers started to leave the building—all except Sheila, who had wasted two minutes of her time talking about her party to another teller. Finally, I was walking Sheila to the door. She was the last to leave. I bid her a good night before locking the door. I stood still for a brief second. What I was about to take part in flashed before my eyes.

I could hear Game's voice as he spilled his plan that would keep me from being a suspect in the heist. He had hired one of his goons to come after we were done. He would set the bank on fire to make it look like a heist. I would hang around the bank for about a month, then leave under the pretense of attending school full-time. No one would be surprised. I had made it clear when I was hired that I would not be staying long because school was my goal. I had just started to shed some of my nervousness when I heard a boom on the door that almost made me shit myself. I turned around all unnerved to find Sheila back at the door. She was on my last damn nerve.

I sighed as I attempted to unlock the door. She was really becoming a thorn in my ass. The lock wouldn't turn. Finally it opened. "I'm sorry, I didn't mean to scare you, but I left my car keys, and you know I can't go anywhere without them." Her breathing was labored. It was clear she had run all the way back. I couldn't have cared less. I wanted to scream for her to hurry up, but instead I kept my cool. "Here they are." She grabbed her keys and started doing a happy dance.

Wasting no time I gave Sheila a fake smile and said, "Getting late, Sheila, gotta lock up."

"I know, girl," she responded. Without saying another word I headed straight for the door, opened it, and waited seemingly patiently for Sheila to exit. As soon as she did, I locked it and walked away.

I had no more time to waste. Game was waiting. I made my way to the back, making an exit from the camera, then to the back door. And with no camera watching, I carefully unlocked the back door, and Game stepped inside.

"You damn near a minute and a half late!" Game's tone of voice was annoyed. It kinda caught me off guard. I wasn't used to him being angry. But I brushed it off because I understood why. "Every minute counts," he reminded me.

"I kn-know," I stuttered. "It was Sheila, she wouldn't shut up. Then she left her keys," I explained. "What could I do?" I hunched my shoulders.

"Time is wastin', let's get to it." He pushed one of the three Louis Vuitton suitcases that he had wheeled in over to me. I gave Game one quick glance before turning on my heels with him following close behind. Soon we were standing in front of the stash. So much money was at our disposal.

Game stood before the money, and I saw what I was sure was a gleam in his eye. He didn't utter one word to me. He didn't even look at me. Laying both suitcases flat, he wasted no time filling them with stacks upon stacks of hundred dollar bills. I could feel my palms sweating profusely. I looked down at my hand that was gripping the suitcase. Suddenly I realized Game would need that suitcase as well. Slowly bending down on one knee, I laid the suitcase flat and waited. I knew I should have been helping out, but I couldn't bring myself to do it. And Game never asked me to. It was possible that he had even forgotten that I was in the room.

Soon all three suitcases were full. I watched as Game slowly stood up and admired the money. Without notice, he turned to me and swept me up in his arms. I wrapped my arms around him, easing my nerves as they bounced around in every inch of my body.

"I love you," Game whispered in my right ear. I blushed. Bending down to put us face-to-face, he parted my lips with his. The warmth of his tongue as he slid it inside and outside my mouth made me want to scream out from pleasure. I matched his tongue stroke for stroke. For a minute I thought we were going to rip each other's clothes off.

Suddenly we both froze as we heard what sounded like the clearing of someone's throat. During our passionate kiss my eyes had been closed; I slowly and reluctantly opened mine. The pupils in my eyes filled as if they would bulge out of my head. Over Game's shoulder I saw Sasha. Then I felt relief that it was only Sasha. But that quickly changed. Why would she be here?

Game was still holding me tight, his back to Sasha. He slowly turned around and made eye contact with Sasha. He seemed to hesitate when he turned back to face me. Without a word he looked me in the eye, then dropped his head. Now I was even more confused. I started to voice my confusion, but Sasha beat me to it.

"Game, you are taking too damn long," She got straight to the point. "Why?" Her tone was demanding.

I couldn't have been more confused. I looked to Sasha, then back to Game. Again I opened my mouth to speak but quickly closed it as I watched Game. While glaring at Sasha, he started shaking his head with a look of disappointment spread over his face.

I had to clarify something. "Sasha, what are you here for? What's going on?"

A smirk gradually formed on Sasha's face. She sucked her teeth. "I'm here to get my man, that's what's going on," was her strange and shocking answer.

For some reason I came to the conclusion that she was only kidding. I chuckled at her humor, then looked back at Game, who had serious written all over his face. His eyes were burning a hole through Sasha. The grim look on his face wiped Sasha's smirk away. He didn't make any eye contact with me. With his teeth tightly clenched, he asked, "Sasha, why did you come? This isn't what we discussed."

My stomach twisted in tight knots as I looked at him, then slowly back to Sasha.

The smirk slightly appeared back on Sasha's face. "I changed the plan." Her voice was full of confidence, as if she was the one in control. "I had to bring a little insurance, Game. You didn't think about that." She took a few steps back toward the wall that led down the hall, reached her left hand out, and pulled in yet another surprise.

"Ma," I screamed. Her hands were tied up behind her back, her mouth duct-taped. I swiftly took a few steps toward her.

Sasha pulled a gun from under her shirt and pointed it directly in my face. "Stay put, Porsha. I'm pretty good with this thing," she bragged.

"Are you going to shoot me?" I yelled. I was so pissed I was sure smoke was flaming out of both of my ears.

Sasha let out a hearty laugh. "Shoot you . . . Girl, no." She laughed again. When she was done laughing, she hunched up her shoulders. "If I did that, then who would be left to go to prison for your highly schemed bank heist and all those sheisty house sales?"

The room suddenly grew larger. My mouth dropped wide open and I turned to Game. "Game, how could you do this to me? How could you set me up?"

"Hey don't blame me for none of this shit." He boldly demanded, "If you need to place some blame, why don't you talk to your friend right there?" He pointed at Sasha. "She the mastermind who set everything up. All I had to do was play along." He said it as if it was no more than something he did for sport.

Sasha laughed out loud. Looking at her, I recognized that she was exactly who Briana had warned me about. "I should have never dealt with you again . . . Briana warned me about your scheming ass. Fucking bitch!" I screamed.

Sasha started to speak but shut up. All our eyes went to Keisha, who had suddenly appeared in the room. I looked to Game and once again saw the same gleam in his eyes that I had witnessed earlier when he first laid eyes on the money. He seemed to be genuinely happy as I witnessed his lips curve into a stupid smile.

Sasha's eyes rolled like flying saucers in her head. Her neck bobbed from Keisha, to me, then to Game. "What is she doing here?" she asked him, then twisted her neck and body back in Keisha's direction.

Keisha's eyes focused on Sasha as a slow scowl became king player on her face. Her lips moved slowly and her words seeped venom. "I never liked you . . . you talk too damn much." She spat the words out.

Sasha seemed stunned but jumped straight into action. "Bitch, well, I can assure you, the feeling is mutual. The only reason I was ever nice to you was because of Game and the fact you were Rein's auntie." Wait, these bitches knew each other all along? And what was this about Keisha being Rein's auntie? My head was spinning.

Keisha didn't seem fazed one bit by Sasha's comment, but the hearty laugh from Game turned all of our attention to him. The laugh was full of sarcasm. I couldn't find any words for any of them, so I waited. Game's eyes again fell on Sasha as his laugh slowly came to a halt.

"Sasha, really, when are you going to stop telling that lie?"

Sasha gave the most perplexed look she could muster. "What lie?" She challenged him.

Game twisted his lips up as if to say she knew what he was speaking of. "Bitch, Rein don't belong to me." His voice boomed. "You and I both know she just ain't mine. Shit . . . I knew that a year ago," he revealed. The look in his eyes was distant. I couldn't tell if he was hurt or just upset. I was again dumbfounded. What the fuck was going on? I had to be dreaming. She been knowing this nigga and they got a whole baby together? Damn, I had been played. But my voice still would not show up. I watched as if I was in an unbelievable dream.

"Nigga, you must be smoking that killa because that's the biggest damn lie you ever told. Rein is yours," she protested. "Don't be no deadbeat-ass dad, listenin' to this miserable bitch." Her eyes were glued to Keisha.

Game waved his hand in dismissal. "Bitch, just stop lying. You should be tired of doing that anyway. Hell, I swabbed her mouth for a DNA test."

Sasha's chest sank in like all the air had been sucked out of it. She was in disbelief. Her face turned dark red as if the blood was rushing from her head. "You a crazy motherfucker. And so fucking disrespectful. But I don't give a fuck what you say. Nobody want to hear this shit anyway. Ugh." She sighed.

"Shut the fuck up, Sasha. You're not about to lie your way out of this." Keisha barked. Sasha's focus had been on Game, which gave Keisha the upper hand. Keisha was in Sasha's space in no time flat. We all paused when we heard the pistol's slide being pulled back. Within seconds the gun was pointed at Sasha's head. "Baby" was the most disturbing word I had ever heard, spilling from Keisha's full lips, her eyes fixed directly on Game. He gave her this look that made me want to vomit. Sexual and full of love. I almost choked on my own saliva. "Are you ready for me to finish the plan to blow Sasha's brain out?" A vicious smirk took complete control over Keisha's face.

Beads of sweat were forming on my forehead. My lips started to quiver as I attempted to speak. But just as before, nothing came out. And Game had yet to answer Keisha's question before she continued. "Oh yeah," she chuckled and waved her gun. "I'm not Game's sister . . . I'm his wife."

I felt as if someone had punched me directly in the stomach. There seemed to be no air in my lungs. I opened my mouth wide and sucked in a gulp of air. Sasha bent over a bit and vomit spewed out of her mouth. "What?" she managed to say, with her hand right hand on her abdomen.

"Now that was some repugnant shit, Sasha. You could have done that shit outside." Game spat at Sasha, then laughed. "But yeah, that's the one small detail I forgot to tell y'all."

The grin on his face was evil.

"Motherfucker, that ain't all you forgot to tell us," Sasha screamed. "I can't fuckin' believe you been tryin' to play me." Her entire face was on fire red. "You introduced me to this bitch three years ago as your sister. What the fuck was that all about?"

I shook my head. "So you been lying to me all this time. Playing me you like you been playing this slut." I snap my neck in Sasha's direction. The words finally came to form off my lips. "All that talk about marriage, the ring, and everything. All lies?" Tears ran down my face. "All you ever wanted was to use me?" I threw my hands up in the air with disgust. "And for this donkey bitch." I pointed at Keisha.

"Bitch, shut the fuck up. Ain't my fault you stupid," Keisha replied.

"No, bitch, you shut the fuck up." Briana entered the room with a gun already cocked and put it straight to Keisha's head.

Keisha was legit scared, and her eyes start to dart around in her head. "Listen, y'all want to put the blame on Game and me, but this shit is all about Sasha's bitch ass. She's the one who wanted to set Porsha up. Over some dumb-ass grudge since high school about a dude. She said she hated that bitch, and the deal she brought to the table just happened to be profitable. Hell, we already had her bitch ass in our pocket. Game was pimping her since day one. She just got it in her head that she could be his wifey."

One look at Briana and I could see her face was full of tears. She made eye contact with Sasha, then Game. Game threw up both his hands like Briana was the cops. Briana's entrance had stunned him. "Aye, Bri. Hold up . . . Put the gun down," he pleaded. "All of this is just one big misunderstanding. Shit, like she just said. Shoot that bitch Sasha."

Sasha rolled her eyes at him.

"Nigga, shut your bitch ass up," Briana popped off. "Ain't no misunderstanding. I know all about you sick-ass motherfuckers tryin' to set my friend up. All of you is to blame. But I'ma put an end to this shit tonight. Believe that shit like you believe in Jesus."

"Listen." Game tried again.

"Nigga, I told you don't speak to me," she screamed. "It ain't shit you can tell me. I know everything. Rico told me all about your plan a few hours ago, before your wack-ass girlfriend right here killed him." She pushed Keisha's head with the tip of her gun. "Yep, bitch, I know that you killed him, and for that you'll be sorry." Keisha dropped her head. "I swear, all of you are a bunch of sick, heartless bastards with no morals. And you, Sasha, bitch, you trifling. I knew from the moment you stepped back into our lives you was on some bullshit. I just knew it. You ain't never been shit but a selfish bitch. Yeah, and Rico told me that Rein belongs to Kenneth."

I stumbled backward with disbelief. I wasn't sure how many more surprises I could take. But in that moment I realized the resemblance. It had been there all along, I just hadn't paid enough attention. Reluctantly I looked at Ma, her face drenched in tears as she cried, nodding in agreement. She had known all along. Reaching over to her, Briana used her left hand to pull the duct tape off Ma's mouth. Guns were pointing in all directions at different people. I dared not move.

"I knew from the very first time I laid eyes on Rein in my living room. She was the living image of Kenneth. Plus I remember Kenneth telling me vaguely that he spoke with Sasha from time to time. That meant they were fooling around. But he didn't know how to tell you, Porsha." Ma looked at me, then at Sasha. Now I understood why she had taken to Rein so much. And I knew it was Rein who had breathed life back into her. "I just wanted to see how long you would wait before you said anything, Sasha."

Sasha chuckled with sarcasm. Just to look at her made me want to pull her eyes and hair out. "Dream on. I would have never have told you about Rein. She is mine, she belongs to me," she spat.

I had had enough of her. I felt nothing but contempt and hate. "Bitch, I swear you are low down and trifling," I barked. "I don't know how my brother ever messed around with you. Such a bum bitch!" I seethed.

"Girl, sit yo stupid ass down. That's why you got fucked."

"That's okay, bitch. You about to get fucked next. Ho!" I yelled back. "All this for some shit that happened in high school."

"Bitch—" Sasha started back in.

In that moment Game took advantage of our distraction. He reached for his gun but not fast enough. Briana shot him directly in the head. Standing next to him, I screamed as I saw his brains spill out the back of his head. He fell backward.

Sasha went for Keisha, who was distracted as she watched Game's body make contact with the carpet. Sasha's gun fired as it hit the floor, hitting Keisha in the neck and abdomen. Sasha paused and watched Keisha's body hit the floor.

Briana attacked Sasha. Carefully stepping past Game and over Keisha, I picked Briana's gun up off the floor. "Move, Bri," I ordered her with the gun pointed at Sasha. Briana stopped punching Sasha in the face.

Out of breath, Sasha laughed with blood dripping from her top lip. "Bitch, you ain't gon' do shit. You too weak. That's why Game was able to use you so easy. Gullible." She gave another hearty laugh. "You even got that same dumb look your brother had on his face when he realized I had set his as up. Nigga tried to play me, but I set that shit straight." I couldn't believe she had just admitted to having my brother killed.

"Bitch, and for that you gon' burn in hell." *Pop, pop.* I pumped two bullets into her head, straight between the eyes, then watched as the blood dripped down both sides of her mouth and the life drained from her body. Never again would I have to see her face.

CHAPTER 17

Two short weeks had passed since everything went down, and I must say I was truly over it. I didn't feel any remorse for anyone who was bodied that night. All three had deserved everything they got. And thankfully, we were able to explain away all that had happened inside that bank. After everything went down Ma, Briana, and I had concocted a quick story that we would use for the cops. With all the bodies, we concluded that there was no way we could all make it up outta there without being noticed.

So instead we sent Ma home and Briana and I stayed behind. The story for the cops went like this. Game was my boyfriend. He had come to pick me up after work. I had let him inside without knowing he had left the door ajar for his sister Keisha to come in. Keisha had come in with Briana and Sasha, who they had kidnapped. Holding them all at gunpoint, Keisha and Game had threatened to kill them if I didn't let him get the money. Afraid for my own life and for those of my friends, I complied.

Then while Game packed up the money and Keisha ran her mouth, Sasha tried to make a break for it but fell. Game then stood over her and shot her in the head. Meanwhile, Briana attacked Keisha and they fought over her gun, it went off, and the bullets hit Keisha. Game was distracted trying to check on Keisha, and I grabbed Keisha's gun and shot him. Fortunately for us, the cops believed our story with no doubt. Game and Keisha had rap sheets a mile long. The cops also broke some news to us that we already knew: Game and Keisha were married. In some ways I got the feeling the DA was glad Game and Keisha were dead. They'd been a part of Oakland's problem, and now they were no longer. Case closed.

The bank was also happy that we were able to fight back and save their money. They couldn't stop thanking us. They deemed us heroes and cut us checks for fifty thousand each. But of course I expressed emotional distress from the incident which, combined with my desire to go back to school, meant I could no longer work there. With a going-away party and warm goodbyes, they wished me well.

But that was far from the end. After cleaning out Game's safe and doing a quick sale on his home for half of what it was worth, I cashed out in his name. Talk about greedy—that nigga was it. The two safes in his house had over three million dollars in them. It wasn't enough for him, but I would gladly take it. Ma and I decided we wanted to leave Oakland. Subsequently, after receiving the DNA test results for Rein, we filed for full custody, packed our bags, and headed for Florida. I begged Briana and her mother to come along, but they wouldn't have it. Briana had graduated from hair school and wanted to stay in Oakland. So after buying Briana and her mother a house and giving her money to open up a salon, I was out. Twisted Deception had changed my life in more ways than one. But payback was a motherfucker.

DON'T MISS

Pearl Tongue
by Tyrone Bentley

The first book in the Dallas Diamonds series

With a drug addict mother and a drug lord father Aphtan
learns how to fend for herself at an early age. Being the
princess of an empire has its perks—until her father gets
arrested. From stealing clothes and food to committing fraud,
Aphtan does what she has to do to take care of her mother
and herself. But when her schemes prove problematic, she
turns to a new hustle: dancing at Pearl Tongue, the most
notorious strip club in Texas . . .

Enjoy the following excerpt from *Pearl Tongue* . . .

PROLOGUE

"Up next to the stage is your all-time favorite performer here at Pearl Tongue. After a hiatus, she's back, and as fine as ever. Get the big faces out because anything else will not do. Please welcome the beautiful, talented pole professional Lotus."

Aphtan's heart beat ferociously in her chest as her lungs desperately begged for air. Her fingertips went numb as the long, black trench coat she wore swept the marble floor underneath her now-sweaty feet. Her butter-colored skin sparkled under the lights as her stomach thumped uncontrollably with mixed feelings.

"Fuck." She took a triple shot of Cîroc to help clear her nerves. "You got this," she told herself. "It's like riding a bike. You got this."

Aphtan slowly transformed into Lotus the closer she got to the door that led to the stage. The bass from the music boomed through her ears as a feeling of nostalgia took over her. She looked down at her red-bottomed heels as she leaned against the pale blue door that separated her from her past.

She couldn't believe that she was about to strip again. It had been six long years since she had been inside Pearl Tongue, which had been her only home at one time. It had been all she knew when she was seventeen, and although she hated to admit it, it felt good to be back.

Aphtan leaned her back against the door as the crowd's roars intensified in anticipation. Her straight, red-hair wig hung gorgeously over her shoulders as she signaled for the DJ to play her signature song. She smiled as the familiar tune filled the building and brought back into her mind bittersweet memories that she had tried to forget.

All she could think about was Scooter as she opened the door and walked through it, strobe lights flashing in her eyes. The crowd went crazy once they saw her. The love in the room made her feel good, but making enough money stained her brain like bleach mixing with colored clothes in a washing machine.

She put her finger in the air, telling the DJ to run it back and start the song over. The scratching of the turntable flushed away her thoughts as she focused on only the pole. She removed the trench coat, letting it fall to the ground, revealing her two-piece custom-made gear that she hadn't worn in years and which complemented her small, well-built frame.

Money covered the stage seconds later. She knew she would give the crowd exactly what they came for. Aphtan grabbed the pole, swaying her body up and down against it as she made her ass cheeks clap to the beat. She released one hand's grip, spun around slowly to build up speed with the other, and climbed the pole with ease until her head was at the very top, almost touching the ceiling.

She posed on the pole, using her upper body strength to change positions. Money kept flying onto the stage as the crowd's cheers and praise competed with the volume of the music. Aphtan continued to make her ass cheeks clap as the door at the entrance of the club swung open wildly. A hint of worry stole over her face. Her eyes grew to the size of golf balls as Scooter and his crew walked in.

"Oh shit," the DJ spat into the microphone. "Y'all get ready. Here's Lotus's signature move."

Aphtan watched them slowly. Her eyes met Scooter's. Fear immediately came over her. She could see the hate in his eyes; the desire to take her life. She positioned her hands, then her legs as they split in the air. She never stopped looking at Scooter as she slid all the way to the ground into a split on the floor.

Scooter stared at her from across the room. He just stared; nothing else. Aphtan could feel his pulse beating in her ears from across the room, blocking out all other sounds except the breath that was raggedly moving in and out of her mouth at regular, gasping intervals. If she could hear it from all the way across the room, she imagined it was deafening in his ears. Their eyes locked, so now it was apparent that she too was staring.

Aphtan could not take her eyes away from the other set of eyes across the room that were staring her down. Nothing else mattered. The connection had to be held. If it broke, she would die. He would die. Maybe both of them would. Aphtan had never felt so certain of anything else in her life. Aphtan discerned that Scooter could no longer control his hands; they were shaking in an odd trembling rhythm as the color drained from his face. Yet still he stared. He looked as if he was willing himself not to run, willing the connection to hold.

"There it goes." The DJ spun around, tangling himself in his headset. "That's the move that has been imitated by many, but only Lotus does it right. She is the one and only Lotus."

Aphtan eased herself off the ground. Scooter and his crew were now in the front of the crowd. All she wanted to do was get away. She put two fingers in the air to let the DJ know to end the song. She ignored the crowd's disappointment as they yelled for their money back while she gathered the bills from the ground.

Grabbing her trench coat, she put it on and walked quickly

off the stage. She could feel Scooter's eyes follow her every move. She opened the door and rushed through it and into the dressing room. Her feet sped up with each second that passed. She ran to her locker while shock consumed her body. Her heart beat inside her throat as she gathered all of her belongings. All of the strippers looked on with wonder as beads of sweat formed all over her face.

Aphtan hadn't thought Scooter would come for her that quickly. It had only been a few hours since he'd accused her of something she had not done. She thought for sure that she could make a quick few grand and be on her way, but as the door closed behind her in the locker room, she knew that wasn't going to happen. She was caught, and there was nothing that she could say to save her life.

She turned around; the smell of his cologne confirmed that it was him before her eyes ever could. A loud ringing formed in her ears as he smiled at her. He winked at her, antagonizing her. A scarce stream of pee rushed out of Aphtan as Scooter removed the gun from his waist and pointed it at her.

"Ladies," he yelled, getting attention of the other dancers in the room. "May we have a moment?"

The dancers screamed as they ran like a herd of bulls at the raising of a red flag. The sight of Scooter meant something bad was about to go down, and they didn't want any part of it. He walked over to Aphtan. Tears rushed down her face without a sound exiting her mouth. He rubbed the small dimple on her cheek while they glared into each other's eyes. He pressed the gun into her chest as she closed her eyes, inviting her end.

"Why?" He pressed the gun as hard as he could into her bare flesh. "Why would you betray me? I gave you everything, Aphtan. I upgraded you. I took you out of this place." He pointed around the room. "Still you betrayed me. I guess a bitch will always be a bitch."

"I didn't steal from you." Aphtan shook her head.

"You don't have to lie, my love." He leaned over and kissed her.

"What do you want from me?" she screamed as she opened her eyes. "Stop playing with me. Kill me if you're going to kill me."

"Can I have a moment to remember you as you were?" He kissed her lips. "I do love you, despite this moment."

"Then let me go," she cried. "I'll leave and I won't come back."

"You know this game." Scooter pulled the trigger and released a bullet into her chest. "I just can't do that."

As the sweat dripped down her forehead, she pleaded for her life. She pleaded, but her cries weren't good enough. Before she'd even had a chance to pray, she heard the bullet scream out of the gun. The connection of metal and her skin was quick.

As the hard, cold, evil lump of metal penetrated her chest, she sighed. She sighed out of anger, anguish, and agony. She could feel the life being sucked out of her, and her eyes began to shut. Shut for good. Her life was over. And it didn't even flash before her eyes. It was just gone. Finished. She was about to die.

Scooter caught her body as it was falling and went to the ground with her. He let her rest in his arms as blood gushed from her wound onto his freshly ironed button-up. She looked around the room, her eyes wide with fright; no, not fright, but wonder. Was she in the light? Could she see the light at the end of the tunnel?

Her skin turned a pale, opalescent color. Her hair stuck to her forehead. As he laid her head down slowly, she looked above her, at the dull roof. And before she closed her eyes, she smiled and took her last breath in the arms of the man she once loved.

ALSO AVAILABLE

Cold Flash
By Carrie H. Johnson

In this explosive series, forensic firearms specialist Muriel
Mabley takes a one-way plunge that's outside the law . . .

Enjoy the following excerpt from *Cold Flash* . . .

CHAPTER 1

Lord only knows the things we'll do or how far we'll go for the people we love.

Flailing around in the pool at the Salvation Army Kroc Center this Friday morning was my "thing" I was doing for my girl Dulcey. She has breast cancer. I committed to doing a triathlon, as in a quarter-mile swim, twelve-mile bike ride, and three-mile run. Mind you, I am scared to death of the water, have not been on a bike since childhood . . . that would be forty-plus years . . . and have not run with any speed since the police academy more than twenty years ago.

The SheRox Triathlon Series raises funds for breast cancer research. I admit the whole triathlon thing is a smoke screen for coping with the fear of losing Dulcey. Somehow my crossing the finish line will turn the nightmare into a fairy tale, with a happily-ever-after ending.

So here I am, three months into my training. It's not like I never work out. At five foot three and 140 pounds, it is necessary to keep all my parts in check. I work out on a semi-regular basis, three or four times a week for a month or two, then I'm distracted by any good reason. Not this time. At least not for another month until after the July event.

I learned to swim five weeks ago and have since mastered a slow, steady stroke. Grab the water, push it away in an S motion with flat hands. Turn my head, suck in air, put my face in the water, blow out air. Each time I turned my head to gulp air, I saw this guy whipping the lifeguard, Pam, with his pointer finger. White guy, six feet, 250 pounds maybe. He was wearing a green, black, and silver sweat suit and a black Eagles cap pulled low on his brow. At first I thought maybe he was a disgruntled parent of an eel, pollywog, or fish—names that indicated a child's level of swim achievement.

Children's squeals bounced off the pool's dome, signaling the end of adult swim time. The sounds were muffled each time I put my face back in the water. I dug deep to squeak out the last lap, which totaled sixteen, a half mile. I got to the deep end and flipped to retrace my path for the final length.

When I reached the shallow end and walked up the stairs, the guy had Pam's arm pinned behind her back. He pressed against her body, talking into her ear, red-faced like a heavy drinker or druggie. His other hand was stuffed in his pocket, which bulged with what I suspected was a gun.

A quick check had the children on the opposite side of the pool with their instructors, making enough noise to part the waters.

Pam wriggled under his hold. Her wide eyes darted in every direction until they set on me. She watched me walk past them and sit on the bench. I dried my feet, my arms, and my head, the whole time pleading with the good Lord to move this guy along or grow me large enough to pound him.

He yanked Pam's arm backward. Pam yelped like a hurt puppy. Damn. I approached from his blind side, aware of my inadequate clothing and dwarfed size in comparison to him.

"Is everything all right here?" I asked, my voice steady, my nerves shivering.

"Mind your damn business, lady," the guy said, twisting Pam's arm harder.

"You're hurting me, Bunchy," Pam whimpered.

"Shut up. Do what I'm telling you or I really will hurt you."

Pam pulled away from the guy and screamed. I pushed her to the side and stepped in front of her.

"Easy, mister. I'm Philadelphia Police. Take your hand out of your pocket, slow."

He pulled his hand out, holding a Beretta. I rushed in with one shoulder down and grabbed his arm. He got off a shot. Loud screaming. I knocked the gun from his hand, spun around, grabbed his wrist, spun around again and twisted his wrist, bringing him to the floor. I jammed my foot into his neck. He squirmed, trying to get loose.

"I'll break it if you don't keep still," I said.

"You stupid bitch. I'ma kick your ass. I'ma kill you." Spit sprayed from his mouth with each word.

I twisted his wrist a little harder and stepped into his neck a little deeper. "Not today," I said.

Pam came up the stairs from the pool with the gun in hand. She walked over to us and pointed it at Bunchy.

"Put the gun down, Pam. He's not going to hurt you or anyone else. Believe me, you do not want to kill him. He's not worth it, Pam."

"He'll just come back. I tried to get the police to do something. A restraining order doesn't do any good. He'll just come back."

"Not this time. This time he'll go to jail. Put it down, Pam. Think about your little girl."

She kept pointing it.

"Don't shoot me, Pam. I'm sorry. I love you," Bunchy pleaded, relaxing his pull on my hold. I dug my foot deeper into his neck.

She lowered the gun as police stormed into the dome. An

officer took the gun from Pam and pulled her arms behind her back for cuffing.

"She's good," I said. He released her.

Three officers gathered to relieve me of my charge. "You sure you need our help with this guy?" one of the officers joked.

I stepped off Bunchy's neck. Bunchy growled as he rose up and lunged forward headfirst, pushing me backwards. I went down.

"Welcome back."

Fran Riley, my partner, put his hand out to stop me from trying to sit up. "You should stay put a few." I brushed his hand away. He sighed a helpless verse and pulled me forward to a sitting position.

I tried to speak, but the words stuck in my throat. I looked around at the uniforms helping the parents and children to calm down. Other uniforms were snapping pictures and asking questions. A little girl lay out on the deck, an EMT bent over her. I stretched my neck to locate Pam. A police officer restrained her, blocking her path to her daughter. I rubbed my eyelids but failed to clear my blurred vision.

"Muriel? You all right? You with me? Muriel?" Fran asked, as he waved his hand in front of my face. I brushed his hand away and nodded. I tried to stand with his help. Halfway up, another EMT interfered and I was back on my butt.

"That might not be a good idea yet." The EMT motioned Fran to move, then knelt and flashed a light in my face.

I could see he was talking to me. The sounds were muffled, as though I was still under water. My ears popped. I covered them with my hands, a buffer against the sudden loudness of the hollow voices. ". . . a bump on your head. You'll be fine. You're lucky he didn't break your neck." The EMT turned to Fran and said, "Keep an eye on her for a few hours. Precautionary."

Detective Mosher, who I knew from the fifth district, stood in front of me. "What happened here, Mabley?"

I took a deep breath. "Is the little girl . . ."

"She's alive. Now, what happened?"

I settled down. "The guy . . . he was having words with the lifeguard, with Pam." I closed my eyes and put my head down to ward off a rush of dizziness.

"You good, Mabley?"

I looked up and continued. "I was in the water doing my last lap. He was cursing her out. I noticed a bulge in his jacket pocket that appeared to be a gun. I got out the water, dried off . . ." Dizziness blurred my vision again. I bowed my head and closed my eyes against the desire to puke.

"Big guy," Mosher said.

I took a deep breath. "Yeah, but he went for his gun." I nodded toward the little girl. "What happened? Where's the guy?"

"After you went down, he pulled an officer's weapon and tried to shoot the lifeguard but hit the little girl instead. Grazed her head. She'll survive. She's their daughter. Took six officers to bring him down." He shook his head. "You had him on your own. I need to invest in some of that kung fu stuff." Mosher moved his arms in a chopping motion.

My fuzzy thoughts repelled the humor. "Where is he?"

Mosher put his arms down and got serious again. "He had some kind of seizure. Hopped up on drugs, didn't make it. I would bet some junk—heroin, fentanyl, cocaine, a mix. You know. Mother said the guy is her ex-husband. He's an army vet. Suffered from PTSD, spazzing over custody of the daughter. She's seven. She could have been killed." Mosher walked away, barking orders.

Fran helped me up. "Nice suit." He half-ass smiled, trying to rile me. I had on one of those triathlon suits that cover everything, including thighs. I had no room for his humor either. I cut my eyes and sucked my teeth as loud as I could.

Fran wrapped a towel around my shoulders. "C'mon, I'll help you outta here," he mumbled.

I let him lead me out holding my arm, like I was an invalid unable to do or say anything but what I was told.

"Can you handle dressing yourself? I can come in and help."

I pulled away from him and gave him a sideways F-U glance and leaned on the door to the locker room. "Don't get your brain in a knot about it."

The locker room was quiet. Clothes, towels, flip-flops strewn in the aisles between the lockers. I sat on the bench and closed my eyes. The uneven quiet seeped in and calmed the tension that squeezed my temples.

I was startled when Fran yelled in, "Hey, Muriel, you about done?"

"Yeah. Out in five."

When I finished dressing, I met Fran back in the pool area. Parents were gathering their children and moving toward the locker room, police were leaving. Fran insisted on driving me home and picking up my car later. I conceded.

"Why were you at the Kroc anyway?" he asked, on the way.

"I'd rather not say, you know."

"No, I don't know."

Fran had been my partner for three months; blond-haired, blue-eyed, Mark Wahlberg–faced Fran. Before him I had the same partner for seventeen years. Laughton McNair. Suffice it to say that Fran is at the opposite end of the spectrum of cool, color, and charisma from Laughton. Laughton and I were partners, friends, and for a time, lovers. I shake off the longing I feel every time he invades my thoughts, like now.

We are firearms examiners in the Philadelphia Police Department. We examine, study, test, and catalog firearms confiscated from criminals and crime scenes, and testify in court about the findings.

"My best friend, Dulcey, I think you know her; she has breast cancer. I'm doing a triathlon in her honor."

The few moments of uncomfortable silence made my insides boil. Really, it wasn't the silence that had sweat dripping off the tip of my nose. While the silence was indeed uncomfortable, the heat was a part of the aging process that came on now and again and made me want to jump out of my clothes; that or punch something or someone. I glanced over at Fran with balled fists.

"Yeah, I met her at your house. We'd just finished our first tour together, remember? Damn. I'm sorry to hear that." He hesitated. "You got a call from a Detective Burgan after you left last night. Said she had some information for you."

"She could have called my cell. Thanks. I'll call her when I get home."

"What's it about, Miss M?"

"It's a personal matter."

That is, unless Hamp got his butt thrown in jail, I thought. Hampton Dangervil—Dulcey's husband, aka Hamp or Danger. You think you know a person and then you are slapped upside the head for thinking. I got slapped when Hampton confessed his transgressions to me like I was his priest and could offer him divine mercy. He said he lost some money gambling. He said he was trying to make enough money to keep Dulcey living in style. Silly man. Dulcey loves his dirty drawers no matter rich or poor, right or wrong. I asked Burgan, who runs the Mobile Street Crimes Unit, to do some checking on two characters Hamp said he owed money to. He only knew their street names—Bandit and Muddy—laughable if it weren't for the gurgling in my gut pushing out sharp pangs, which always meant something messed up was ahead.

"I'm not going to push, but if you need me you know I'm right here."

I shifted in my seat and rolled the window down.

"I can turn on the air if it will help."

"Damn it, Fran. Stop trying so hard. We're partners and that doesn't mean you need to be patronizing about everything or try to be inside my head. I'm over everything that happened. I'm over it, despite what you heard before you decided being my partner was right for you."

I cringed at my outburst. I guess you could label me still in recovery. It had not been quite a year since I shot Jesse Boone. Boone was a psychopath responsible for twenty-plus murders dating back twenty years. He almost took my life and my sister's. His death still sparked much discussion among police officers, with a positive vibe. For me it sparked emotional torment.

Fran kept face forward and did not respond. When we pulled up to the house, Fran opened his car door to get out.

I said, "I can make it on my own."

"Yes, boss," he said in a playful subservient tone.

"Sorry, didn't mean to sound so righteous." I moved to get out and he pressed my arm, stopping me. I turned to match his stare.

"I took this job because it is exactly where I wanted to be. I wanted to learn from the best, which I understood to be Laughton McNair, if he was still around, and you. If there's an issue with me, either embrace it or request another partner."

I wanted to exit the car and slam the door. I wanted to tell him to go to hell, not because I was angry but because a rookie had put me in my place. I felt like I was moving fast down a slope that meant I had no good nerves for police work anymore. Instead all I could muster was "I'm good" as I pushed the door open.

"I'll pick you up in an hour. We can pick up your car on the way to the lab. You have court at one o'clock."

"Yeah, yeah," I said before I closed the door. I turned back and bent down to peer at him through the window. "Thank you."

"No problem," he said, flashing me a cheeky grin.

I waited until he pulled away from the curb before I limped

up the walkway to the door. It opened before I got to it. My nine-year-old twin nieces, Rose and Helen, jumped out. The twins are my sister Nareece's children.

Only nine months earlier, the twins lived in a million-dollar home in Milton, Massachusetts, with their mother and father. Now their father was dead, murdered, and their mother was in a semi-unresponsive state at Penn Center, a long-term care facility, the result of being raped and tortured by Jesse Boone, before I killed him.

"Hi, Auntie," they said in unison. The twins are best described as striking. Their father was Vietnamese. Their dark skin, almond-shaped gray eyes and jet-black, crinkly hair, turns heads.

Rose took over. "Travis left us here with Bethany cuz he said he had to go do an errand and he'd be right back, but he didn't come back."

Fifteen-year-old Bethany is our neighbor and the backup sitter. The twins begin attending camp next week. Until then, Travis, my twenty-year-old son, is the designated babysitter. Travis is a sophomore at Lincoln University, home for the summer.

"What do you mean he didn't come back? How long has he been gone?"

"He left at seven. He didn't even fix us breakfast. He should have taken us with him. He left you a note on the kitchen counter," Rose said.

"Calm down. Nothing happened, right?"

In unison they chimed, "Yeah. We're big enough to care for ourselves. We are on the case to find out where he went and why."

My nieces took on more of me than I sometimes could handle. They started the Twofer Detective Agency in my honor. As investigators, they question, research, and detect everything, and I do mean everything. I liked that they wanted to be "like me" in that way.

Rose said, "We know he got a phone call from Uncle Hamp. After he talked on the phone to Uncle Hamp, he left. From what we heard, we speculate that Uncle Hamp has troubles."

"You speculate, huh. Enough of the speculation."

"Yes, ma'am," they said in unison, standing at attention and saluting.

"Hi, Miss Mabley," Bethany said, emerging from the den. "It wasn't nothing for me to come over," she said, sashaying her way to the front door. Bethany's round baby face—big wide eyes and dab of a nose—made her appear younger than fifteen. She was another version of striking, having a German father and Haitian mother, both musicians. "I'm usually available anytime, so just call when you need me."

Bethany agreed to come back in an hour if Travis had not returned. After she left, the twins sang, "Bethany likes Travis, Bethany likes Travis, and Kenyetta's going to be pissed."

Kenyetta is Travis's girlfriend since freshman year in high school. She ran away from her foster home and was living on the street when Travis brought her home and asked for my help. We found her a better living situation. Their friendship blossomed, not surprising since Kenyetta is a beauty—dark skin, long, thick coiled hair, and curvaceous frame. They have been bound together since.

"Enough. Besides, how do you know Bethany likes Travis?"

"We've been watching them talk to each other and inter-rogatin' her and Travis, separately of course, about their associations."

I was sorry I asked as soon as the words escaped my lips. "C'mon. I'll fix you breakfast," I said, moving toward the kitchen while checking my phone. There were four missed calls from Travis. I tapped his name in my phone and waited. No answer.

"We already ate. Bethany made us pancakes. We're watchin' *Transformers*," they said, running back to the den. Their voices and footsteps echoed through the large newly remodeled five-bedroom Colonial that we had just moved into a week ago, which was still mostly decorated with unpacked boxes. Nareece and I had grown up in the house. I rented it out after my parents died, until the last tenants moved out a year ago. After everything that happened with Jesse Boone, I decided to remodel it so we could all live here together.

I went to the kitchen and found Travis's note on the floor. Bending to pick it up made me dizzy. I grabbed ahold of the counter and inched my way to an upright position.

Moms, I'm sorry I had to leave the kids with Bethany. Uncle Hamp called and said he couldn't reach you and he needed help. I had no choice. Travis.

Considering Hampton's earlier call to me, for help with his gambling debt, my feelings of relief at having arrived home curdled into worry.

Connect with  U s

Visit us online at
KensingtonBooks.com
to read more from your favorite authors, see books
by series, view reading group guides, and more.

for sneak peeks, chances to win books and prize packs,
and to share your thoughts with other readers.

facebook.com/kensingtonpublishing
twitter.com/kensingtonbooks

Tell us what you think!

To share your thoughts, submit a review,
or sign up for our eNewsletters, please visit:
KensingtonBooks.com/TellUs.